THE
SECOND
STRANGER

THE
SECOND
STRANGER

A NOVEL

MARTIN GRIFFIN

PEGASUS CRIME

NEW YORK LONDON

THE SECOND STRANGER

Pegasus Crime is an imprint of
Pegasus Books, Ltd.
148 West 37th Street, 13th Floor
New York, NY 10018

First Pegasus Books cloth edition November 2023

ISBN: 978-1-63936-487-9

10 9 8 7 6 5 4 3 2 1

Printed in the United States of America
Distributed by Simon & Schuster
www.pegasusbooks.com

1

Since the night was going to be a milestone for me, I poured a plastic cup of wine and took a moment to watch the storm.

It was a quarter to seven, I'd handed my notice in twenty-eight days before and I was about to begin my final ever night shift. Leaning against the snow-covered balustrade of my balcony, I was dreaming of the following morning; of packing my meagre belongings, driving my Nissan into Aberdeen, and dropping it off with its eBay buyer. Car sold and cash in my purse, I'd be at the airport for my 11 a.m. flight. A hop to Heathrow, on to Madrid for my connection, and then heading out to Santiago, Chile, by tomorrow evening. *Tomorrow evening.*

The wild possibility of this unburdening, an escape I'd dreamt about for fifteen years, made me dizzy. I sipped the wine. Thinking like this felt something close to lunacy. *My final night at the Mackinnon.* It was a chance to say goodbye to my old self; to escape abroad a new person. I might not have box-ticked the other expectations associated with one's early thirties – I had no career any more, no permanent home, no children and, after tonight, no job – but my final shift felt like it was the start of something. Live-in staff all got attic rooms with balconies, but the remainder of my colleagues had started their leave so I was the third floor's only occupant. It seemed somehow appropriate, given the course of my life so far, that I was marking this special occasion alone, a woman in a winter jacket and beanie hugging herself against the snow.

The wine was the cheap stuff that came in minibar bottles, but it tasted good enough as I cast my eyes across the Mackinnon's grounds for what might be the final time. On summer days my quarters had a beautiful view, but early February was different. Loch Alder was frozen over the colour of Lakeland slate, a silent presence between our two mountains: Bray Crag on its far shore, snow-covered and wild, and, rising above the hotel on this side of the water, the peak of Farigaig. Tonight it was nothing but a silhouette on tracing paper, though the tangle of its steeply forested flanks came all the way down to the hotel's perimeter fence. The sight of the loch, the mountains and the distant prison had become my life this last eighteen months. Most of HMP Porterfell was hidden by the pine plantations of Farigaig's foothills, but the lights of the exercise yard were bright points haloed by driven snow, and the north watchtower was visible. I raised my cup in its direction in a final silent toast to Cameron and sipped, relishing the warmth of the alcohol.

I was still staring at the place when I heard the klaxon's wail.

　　　　　　　　　　　　　　　MARTIN GRIFFIN

The sound was a familiar one. When trouble flared at Porterfell, as it often did, overcrowded and outmoded as it was, the first signs were always barking sirens and strobing lights. I felt a sudden rush of memory. I had to set my cup down and steady my pulse with big, deep breaths. A year ago, a Porterfell riot had killed my brother. The same wail of sirens had marked its beginning. Back then there'd been the flicker of fire against distant brickwork, a windborne roar of crowd noise and a night punctuated by the droning engines of security vehicles going back and forth along the mountain road. I hadn't known Cameron was dead at first. Next of kin weren't informed until later. In a fifty-five-inmate brawl, it's apparently impossible to finger the murderer of a particular individual and, because unlawful killing was hard to prove, Cameron's passing was recorded as misadventure. So now my brother was gone, his death remained unpunished and I'd been stranded here, a thirty-three-year-old woman working night shift at a highland hotel, studying the place that had penned him in.

I watched the distant buildings, listening to the moan of the siren. Through curtains of snowfall across the loch, I could see the intermittent flicker of lights. The prison gates were open now. Three distant vehicles were pulling out; a car either side of a van that looked like a high-security transport. That might explain the disturbance. An inmate leaving, violence erupting as desperate scores were settled. The siren continued its looping moan and I watched the convoy turn left towards us, setting off along the mountain road in our direction. I thought about the drivers, thought about my two-hour drive tomorrow. I'd have the advantage of daylight, but we'd had plenty of snow in the last week and plunging temperatures had hardened the drifts into sculptured pack. The wind had changed direction, polar air from Siberia triggering red weather warnings, and Storm Ezra had arrived, bringing new snow and turning the old into ice. Driving on a night like this was surely an act of desperation.

By morning it would be clearer, though. It would be. Everything ended in twelve hours. At 7 a.m., Mitchell, my colleague on the day shift, would park his Fiat 500 outside reception and trot across the tarmac in his brogues and hotel livery. In the course of a fifteen-minute handover I'd bring him up to date for the last time, put my bags in the boot of my car and go.

I retreated back into my room, shutting the noise out and warming myself at the electric heater before shucking off my coat and dressing for work. I tugged a vest on beneath my blouse for extra warmth, pulled on my trouser-suit and buttoned my jacket before removing my badge. *Remie Yorke*, it said. Underneath, the gold plastic was embossed with, *How can I help?* The Mackinnon's last two guests knew me by name so I left the badge on my bedside table next to the few items I hadn't yet packed: my pro-turf hockey ball, my Eyewitness guide to Chile and Easter Island, my Spanish phrasebook. Locking my door behind me, I followed the third-floor corridor past empty rooms to the old service stairs. The prison sirens must have stopped; the only sound as I descended was the old hotel creaking in the rising wind.

The Mackinnon is sixteen guest rooms in a grand Victorian lodge tucked into a dell at the bottom of Farigaig, steep-roofed, with turret windows and two spires rising above squat chimneys. Guests adore the conical clocktower, the formal gardens and the wisteria across the entrance. When I'd arrived to take up the post of night manager eighteen months ago, all I'd needed was somewhere to work that was driving-distance from my brother Cameron's prison cell. To find instead this loch-side curio had been a sliver of good news in a world of bad. At first, I'd cherished the hope I might actually fall in love with the place – my flat in Leith had always felt temporary and, even though I didn't visit often, I'd felt cast adrift when Mum and Dad split up and the Northumberland family home was sold – and those first few months at the Mackinnon really had seemed like they might be a fresh start. I'd almost allowed myself to relax. Once or twice, I'd even woken in the morning refreshed. Then there'd been the violence at the prison and Cameron's death. After that, I'd been forced to return to my previous existence of permanent, exhausted vigilance. But those days were nearly over now. In sixteen hours, I'd be on a plane.

Downstairs I checked reception then took the main corridor towards the bar. The grandfather clock stood sentry outside the garden room. The kitchens still smelt of roast game and garlic even though the catering staff had spent the afternoon buffing worktops and freezing leftovers in preparation for the winter break. Across from the kitchens, at the Mackinnon's loch-facing side, was the bar. As the night manager I was responsible for its running until last orders. It was a task I relished; the fire banked high, the logs stacked and drying, the leather chairs warm.

I tended to get the place to myself, our only February customers being prison staff taking a dram on the way home, and I was looking forward to some solitude. I was to be disappointed. There was a figure at the taps. Jaival Parik – Jai – one of our two remaining guests; late thirties, wearing a blazer over a cashmere sweater. He'd brushed his hair back into a bun and sported a pair of thick-rimmed glasses and a single AirPod. He'd been in the bar last night too, and we'd introduced ourselves. Jai had sat with his back to the near-empty lounge, eyes on his screen while he scrolled emails and worked his way through a large glass of Malbec. He was particular about his wine, it turned out; we'd covered South American reds briefly – I knew nothing but I'd told him about Santiago and he'd recommended a vineyard tour. We'd talked walking routes up Farigaig, and mountain biking. And of course we'd discussed the topic on everyone's lips: Storm Ezra.

'One night left!' he beamed at me as I entered. 'I was going to buy you a drink to celebrate but I guess you're on duty.' I rounded the bar, smiling, and he ordered another Malbec, thumbing his phone.

'Had a good day?' I asked as I poured his drink.

He nodded towards the French windows at the far side of the bar, locked up against the weather. 'It's been kind of restricted,' he said, grinning. 'I'm starting to regret my timing.'

I knew exactly what he meant. I thought of the airport and nearly screamed at the cruelty of it. Instead I took a breath and said, 'I'm sure you'll be able to get some walking in.'

He sipped his wine and swirled his glass. 'Let's hope so,' he said. 'So, what brings you out to the middle of nowhere? Got family up here?'

I thought about Cameron, about Porterfell. 'Guess I just grew sick of the city.' I said.

'Know what you mean. Cairngorms are majestic. When you can see them through the snow.' We laughed. I tidied the bar and he resumed. 'Do you find the place a little remote, though? No shops, no internet.'

I wasn't one for sharing. I shrugged. 'It's beautiful. And the net's only down because of the weather.'

He indicated his phone. 'Could do with some connectivity,' he said. 'Few things I need to deal with. Seen a recent forecast?'

Not since earlier in the day, when talk of possible snow slips had sent the site manager scurrying to the maps on the Scottish Avalanche Information Service. The space between Montrose and Inverness bristled with pins every year and the Mackinnon was right in the heart of red-pin country. Each night I'd been checking the five-day forecast. The latest had Storm Ezra easing by midnight. The main roads east of here had apparently been well gritted. I kept telling myself there was a good chance tomorrow's drive to the airport would be safe.

'News 24 will have one,' I said.

'If the TV still works,' Jai quipped. As he pushed himself up to cross the lounge and turn the TV on, he brushed his phone with the heel of his palm. It glowed alive, though he was oblivious to the fact as he left his seat. Its pale light drew my eye and I felt a slow tremor of alarm. The red line of the voice memo function was unspooling as the timer ticked forward.

He was recording our conversation.

I stared, holding my breath. Normal men didn't tape women in hotel bars. I put together what I could recall of Jai. As my shift had ended early this morning, I'd seen him sipping coffee in the breakfast room with a backpack at his feet, a New York Yankees cap and his Culloden OS map folded into a weatherproof pocket. He'd looked a younger, hipper version of the standard hiker-birdwatcher; nothing unusual. I swallowed, my throat dry. He must have hit record in error. A mistake, that's all. I moved away to polish tumblers as he wandered back from the TV, and I watched him turn his phone screen-down on the bar when he returned.

'Not looking good for tomorrow,' he said, twisting his beard between thumb and forefinger. 'Red weather warnings. Further heavy snowfall, strong winds for at least another five hours.'

I smiled, trying to keep my voice light. 'You'll be able to stretch your legs by morning,' I said. 'There's a route along the shoreline of the loch that'll be beautiful once the storm clears.'

'Yeah, I was checking the map.' He gave a whistle. 'So remote. There's pretty much nothing out there until Braemar. Except the prison.'

And there it was. The mention of Porterfell. I felt my anxiety thicken, thinking, *this is about Cameron.*

My brother was born when I was seven. When he was little, the four of us were happy; a proper family. But after Cam's troubles at school, and then his first arrest at fourteen – possession with intent to supply – my father's strategy was simple: disown him. Cameron responded by doubling-down. He became the family's bringer of shame and breaker of reputations; a troubled teen on a mission to turn career criminal. Dad gave up, Mum broke down. Which meant after Cam's eventual imprisonment, I was the one to sacrifice my career and move up from Edinburgh, the one who'd worked with the lawyer on the appeal, the one who'd visited three times a month.

Then my brother had been killed. Prison violence was normal enough not to be national news but in the aftermath of his death there'd been some media attention; a local journalist had made her way up here to interview me and I'd turned her away. The staff on reception had a script in case they got calls about me, and they'd had to use it on a couple of occasions. All that had been a year ago now, and since then it had been quiet.

Except a man at the bar was recording me as he steered the conversation towards Porterfell. I was steeling myself against further questions when the oddest thing happened.

The reception buzzer sounded.

It was unexpected. The sign at the top of the hotel drive told passers-by we were closed and the website made it clear we weren't accepting guests until we re-opened for the spring. I was the hotel's sole staff member until the morning. Whoever was out there, I'd be turning them away. I excused myself and left Jai cradling his drink.

I wasn't frightened as I walked to reception, past the trolley of dust sheets and paint pots left out for the decorators during close-season, and down to the front desk. I can't admit to any premonitions of danger. What I actually felt was a temporary relief at having avoided a conversation with Jai, a feeling still strong as I settled myself at the reception desk.

My lack of concern seems ludicrous now.

2

'The Mackinnon,' I said into the intercom. 'I'm afraid we're in close-season and not taking guests. Is there anything I can help you with?'

There was no answer, just dead air. It had been dark for hours and the hotel's interior lights were reflected in the floor-to-ceiling windows of the modern lobby-extension. The glass was as black as a polished loch. I could detect, just beneath the surface, a flash of swirling snow but whoever was out there could see me clearly, and I was light-blind. Thankfully I'd locked the revolving doors.

I pressed the intercom button and tried again. 'Hello. The Mackinnon. I'm afraid we're in our close-season now and aren't taking bookings. How can I help?'

Again nothing. Something about that black absence made me nervous. I tried to ignore it as I crossed to the doors. From ten paces the glass looked opaque but at arm's-length I could make out shapes in the night. The turning circle and fountain flitted intermittently through the dark. I could see the squat outline of the old larch; over two centuries old, they said. The tree's base was a wizened knot and the trunk a vast map of creases and clefts. It had been tall in its heyday, over two hundred feet, but its highest sections had been badly damaged in a storm a couple of years ago and, after a spat with the council over a preservation order, surgeons had removed them so the old thing was barely the height of the hotel now. I squinted further out. Up the drive, huddled amongst black woods, I could just discern the guest garages, empty for the winter. Beyond more shrouded darkness; sentinel silhouettes of Scots Pine.

I took a few steps to the left and right, aware of how I must look to the visitor; a woman in a suit with tied-back hair and an uneasy expression. I didn't much like this exposed perspective of myself so I returned to the desk. It occurred to me the appearance of a phone call might be helpful. Picking up the receiver, I cradled it between shoulder and cheek and pretended to stab a number in. It took me a second to notice the outside line was dead. The inside line, wired-up in the fifties after they took the bell-pulls out, was a weatherproof closed circuit but Mitchell had warned me about outside lines coming down in bad weather. The mute emptiness at the end of the phone caught a thread of fear in me and pulled. For the first time, I preferred the prospect of bartending, defending my secrets from Jai.

The reception buzzer came again, making me jump. I replaced the phone, pressed the flashing intercom button and picked up. 'The Mackinnon. How can I help?'

A breathy voice said, 'Police officer.' Local accent. 'I need to come in.'

I looked into the reflective pools of glass. There was a male shape there now, one shoulder against the frame of the rotating doors, leaning in. He was standing in the dark but I could see a heavy ski jacket, collar upturned against the wind.

'I had an accident up on the mountain road,' the figure said. He paused, breathing hard like he might be in pain. 'My radio's down. I need access to your phone.'

My mind slipped its gears and raced free. 'I'll have to ask for ID,' I said. 'Hotel policy.' I thought about phone lines. It was possible to get a mobile signal from some of the upper rooms if the booster was still operational but chances were the officer would be out of luck.

'Gaines,' said the voice. The figure pressed a card up against the glass. 'PC 4256 Gaines, Police Scotland. Open the door please, miss.' The man's silhouette was slewed and I realised he was putting his weight on one leg, raising the other. He was injured.

'Give me a minute.'

I crossed the lobby and unlocked. He was a black bulk in the revolving doors like a penned animal in a slaughterhouse turnstile. Once inside, he became a man again; six feet tall, broad-shouldered and bulked out by a stab vest beneath his police-issue snow jacket. A ripped flap swung from the trouser at his right knee, exposing damaged skin. He had a weathered, forty-something face.

'Thanks,' he said, limping past me, rounding the reception desk. He smelt of petrol.

I followed. 'You're hurt,' I said, feeling a stab of alarm. 'Can I get you bandages? Antiseptic?'

He ignored me, checking the phones and grimacing at the silence at the end of the line before looking across the lobby. A quarter-circle of snow, driven in as he entered, was melting on the rug. 'You need to lock up.' I nodded and returned to reception's revolving doors, fixing them shut.

'Your phone is dead,' he said as I crossed back.

'Lines are down,' I told him. 'You can sometimes get a mobile signal from the third floor. What's going on exactly?'

The officer was scanning the expanse of the lobby, giving the space a narrow-eyed assessment of risk and safety, lines of sight, points of entry. 'Can we shut these lights off?'

'I guess,' I said. 'Why?'

'How many guests are staying here?'

'Just two. And me.'

'And you are?'

I remembered I'd chosen tonight to leave my badge upstairs. 'Remie Yorke.'

'No other visitors tonight, Miss Yorke?' I shook my head, perplexed by his brusque urgency. 'Can you kill the lights please? Along the whole front of the building. You look like a Christmas market from out there.'

'That's the point,' I said, aiming for levity. He furrowed his brow, wearing the kind of expression I knew from bitter experience police officers used when delivering bad news. 'I can switch the lights off,' I reassured him. 'What's happening?'

'I have reason to believe we may have an escapee.'

I thought of the Porterfell siren's wail and felt a tug of concern in my stomach. 'A what?'

The police officer – Gaines, he'd called himself – straightened, hands on hips. I took him in anew; the stiff-collared grubby white shirt, polyester tie. Blond beard, grey along the jawline. A heavy leather belt across a paunch. His holster was empty and the pockets of his stab vest – I'd seen officers carry pepper spray, radio or torch in them – were empty too, except for a phone. 'There was an RTA,' he said. 'Road traffic accident.' What he said next drew the breath from me. 'I was assisting in the transportation of a suspect. I lost control of my vehicle in the snow. If he's out there, I don't want him paying us a visit. For your safety, I'd like to lock the doors and switch off all lights.'

The procession of vehicles I'd seen leave the prison. I felt suddenly hot. 'You came from Porterfell?'

'Correct.' He began hunting for switches, limping along the rear of the lobby towards the main corridor, the one that passed the lifts before reaching the garden room, the restaurant and bar where Jai was still sitting waiting for a top-up. 'Any other points of entry?' he said as he hobbled. 'I passed an outbuilding.'

'The garages,' I said, helping him extinguish the lights. 'They're not connected with the rest of the hotel. We're all locked up. Who's missing?'

The wind thumped at the glass and upstairs a window shuddered in its frame. Gaines huffed hard, likely exhausted by the steep walk. The mountain road was a mile further up at the end of the drive, which climbed at a hard thirty degrees. He'd have had to thrash down through thigh-deep drifts; not easy territory for anybody. 'What about these?' Gaines tapped the LEDs that lined the base of the desk with the toe of his boot. They looked like small blue landing lights.

'I don't know. They're always on.' They were low and cold, enough light to render us insubstantial silhouettes to any outside viewer. I wished I hadn't pulled a vest on; my hotel uniform felt sticky and uncomfortable.

The officer switched tack. 'Who are your guests?'

'We've someone in sixteen,' I said, circling the desk and bringing up the details. 'Alex Coben. With us until tomorrow. And Jaival Parik in thirteen.' The mention of Jai's name triggered another flush of anxiety. 'He's checking out tomorrow too. After that, we're closed.'

He rolled his jaw as he thought. 'I'd like to see them both. I'll be encouraging them to stay in their rooms for a short while.'

'OK, this sounds serious,' I said. I'd visited Cameron regularly and he'd told me about his fellow prisoners. They weren't in there for tax evasion. This escapee could be desperate, dangerous. I exhaled slowly and swallowed. When I spoke, my tongue felt thick. 'Should I be worried?'

His eyes were on the dark windows. Beneath the petrol I could smell fast food and supermarket aftershave. 'Let's get this handled,' he said, returning his gaze to me. 'I'd like a good look at the place, just to be on the safe side. We can shut off the lights as we go. Do you have torches?'

'In the office.'

The office lay immediately behind reception; part stud partition, part glass wall. Inside was the desk I shared with Mitchell on the day shift, a terrible coffee machine, two filing cabinets, a cork display board with a calendar plus schedule, handover notes and reminders.

Gaines assessed it quickly. 'Whose desk is this?'

'Mine,' I said. 'It's just me on duty until seven tomorrow morning.'

'And the rest of the hotel staff?'

'Left this afternoon. Hunting season's over. No more guests.'

'What's this?'

An old desktop screen and keyboard, tucked away in a corner. 'CCTV,' I said. 'But it needs an upgrade. We rarely use it.'

'I didn't see any cameras coming down.'

'There's a couple along the perimeter fence where the deer sometimes get trapped. One at the top of the drive. One in the rear courtyard, one at the boathouse.'

'Boathouse?'

'We have a little cruiser moored up at the loch's edge for guests,' I told him.

'Any interior cameras?'

'Outside the lifts just beyond us here.'

'Show me.'

I nodded, clicking the screen on, shuffling the mouse until the thing woke up. The screen had a six-way split of grainy footage, pictures struggling through the fuzz as if they'd been beamed back from another planet. The outside cameras were fogged with snow.

'Jesus Christ,' he snapped. 'I can't get any sense of the site from this.' He ran a hand across his mouth and briefly closed his eyes. I realised he was trying to calm himself.

'Sorry,' I said, pointing him to the cork board. 'There's a map here.'

Gaines leaned in close and studied the fire assembly points. I found my eyes drawn to the reception's revolving doors. My imagination populated the dark with sinuous shapes. I dragged my attention away, rifling the desk drawers and coming up with a couple of rubber-coated torches. I checked them both, then busied myself locating the first aid kit.

'Sit down,' I told him once I had it. 'Let me look at that knee.' I rooted through plasters and painkillers, and Gaines lowered himself, wincing, into a desk chair. 'These swabs will sting, but we need to clean the wound.' Something jagged had ripped through the flesh above the officer's knee and the blood had stuck his trousers to his skin. He grimaced as I peeled the material back and dabbed at it with the alcohol. Once clean, I pressed cotton pads hard against the wound, trying to hide the tremble in my fingers.

It must have worked because the officer, on a sharp intake of breath, said, 'You look like you've done this sort of thing before.'

I wiped the blood clear and prepared a bandage. 'Used to have a delinquent brother,' I told him. 'He got into so many scrapes, convinced he was bulletproof. And he was scared of hospitals, so I ended up doing a lot of this work for him. Fights, falls, that sort of thing.'

I didn't want to mention the two-inch knife wound I'd once had to deal with. I could still remember Cameron, fifteen years old, pointing out stars while I stitched him up, naming constellations for me. Swan and Vulture, Fox and Goose.

3

'It's just the soft tissue,' Cam whispered, his pale skin sweat-streaked, a scarlet hand pressed against his right hip, his t-shirt a sticky black mess.

By fifteen Cam was a lean, muscular hawk-eyed boy with a shaved head. He had spiralled badly in the two years since the trouble at school had started everything. Where I'd breezed through high school, safe in the cosy, conscientious top sets, Cam had developed more slowly and wound up in the lower streams. The classes down there were wilder places; regularly disrupted and peopled with coarse kids from local gangs. One day a knife was discovered on campus and Cam was implicated. Though he said he wasn't responsible, he received a temporary suspension. Seven years his senior, I was at university when this happened, but the way Mum told it that spell away from the classroom was a turning point. He fell in with a group from the local pupil referral unit and when he returned to class, his school-yard standing had changed. Teachers had given up on him. His reputation grew and, by fifteen, there was no way back. He stopped attending. Each evening he was out working.

The night he named the constellations he'd called me to pick him up. I had this dilapidated Volvo I'd bought from a friend on the hockey team, and I'd driven down from university in Edinburgh. Cam didn't usually phone me. When I picked up, his desperate voice suggested our parents weren't an option. And as he'd emerged from the scrub at a road's edge, checking the night with quick glances and pressing his t-shirt against his side, I saw why.

'Soft tissue? What the hell do you know about knife wounds, Cam?' I hissed as I accelerated away.

'Just calm down a minute.' He managed a watery grin of reassurance. 'I swear, get me out of here and I'm gonna quit all this.'

All this meant the dodgy courier work he'd got caught up in over the course of that year. He rode shotgun in an uninsured van while an older kid called Danny Franks drove. Packages got delivered, money changed hands, fights broke out. That's all I knew.

My hands gripped the wheel, knuckles bone-white under streetlight. The place was all waste ground, litter-choked scrub. We passed a rusting shipping container converted into a truck-stop caff. Driving was difficult because I needed as much attention in my rear view as I had on the traffic ahead. There was a black Range Rover a street-length behind us, ominous. I climbed the hill up through Newburn and it followed. Pebble-dashed fifties houses, redbrick terraces backing onto bin-filled alleys. Soon, fields on the left and an estate of council houses.

'There's a car following,' I told Cam. We were in open

countryside now, the night sky coming alive with stars, the streetlights fading.

He craned his neck. 'I don't fucking believe this.'

His fear charged the air. This was before everyone had a decent satnav on their phone; I knew the city centre pretty well, but out here was another world. Terraces huddled against each other at crossroads, their windows dark. A shut-down petrol station, its forecourt backed by thick-canopied trees.

'If they catch me we're both dead,' Cam hissed.

Back then, aged twenty-two, I wasn't a sibling so much as an extra parent, driving home each weekend to make sure Cameron behaved, which, given Dad's lack of interest, was lucky. Surrogate parents learn fear quickly. The feeling teemed through me for most of my twenties; fear of what he might do, or what someone might do to him, but that night was the first time I'd heard him actually admit he could die. My heart hammered so hard I saw stars. I blinked back tears. 'Cam, I don't know where I'm going.'

'Turn right as soon as you can. We have to hit a main road soon.' I scanned desperately but the road was cut deep into the fields. Still the headlights followed. 'They're big guys, Rem,' Cameron whispered. 'I wasn't going to get out alive if I didn't call someone. They've got a dog.'

I still remember that stomach-flooding feeling as I searched for a turning, the white heat of panic as I pressed the accelerator, climbing at speed into country darkness. 'This is the last time,' I told him, my voice rising. 'If we get out of this, you stop. You stop whatever

MARTIN GRIFFIN

it is you're doing and you get a job. They'll make it hard for you, Cam. But you have to be strong because I'm never doing this again, you hear me?'

He watched the following lights, one hand pressed hard against the soft flesh of his side. I could see it glisten, smell it. There was a lot. 'Just get us away.'

The dash beeped at me. Fuel warning. A wave of nausea, almost paralysing. 'We've got maybe ten miles left. This right-hand turn better appear soon because if it doesn't—'

'There,' Cam pointed.

'Just a gate into a field.' We passed it.

Cam swore weakly. 'Another,' he said, eyes ahead. 'Is it a drive?'

'I don't know!' I was going pretty quickly, and we'd opened up a gap between us and the car behind. I braked hard and we swung right. Just a track. Too late, we were committed. Rattling down it, I saw a gap in a hedge and swung the car through. We stalled in a field next to a silage truck. I switched the lights off and the two of us ducked low, unclipping our seatbelts and waiting hunched in the darkness, ready to run. Horse shit, fear and the coppery smell of blood in the air. Cam's knife wound opening as he crouched forward. I could hear his shallow breathing. I reached out a hand and touched his shoulder. That night was the first in five years he hadn't shrugged me off. We waited there for what felt like hours, in terrified silence, hyper-aware of every night noise, knowing that if we were discovered we were both dead.

But the car that was following us never came past. When I crept back to check, my body jagging with pent-up fear, the road was empty. I was certain they were waiting for us, hard guys with rabid dogs somewhere just beyond my sight, so back in the car we waited side by side with the lights out, Cameron wincing and pressing pale hands against his t-shirt.

'Keep pressing it. How's the bleeding?'

He lifted a red palm to examine the cut. 'Slower,' he said. Some minutes later, he leaned forward and pointed. 'Look. Vulpecula, the Fox.'

'Which one?'

When Cameron was eight he'd got a huge box of glow-in-the-dark stars for his birthday and a map of the constellations. He worked hour after hour sticking them to the ceiling above his bed. He wanted them exact, so the project had been punctuated by tantrums and tears of frustration before it was finally done. I can still recall opening the door to his bedroom, seeing him lying in the dark on his solar system duvet, panning a torch across his private universe. At fifteen, his encyclopaedic knowledge remained.

'The band of stars under Cygnus. Used to be called Fox and Goose,' he said, his voice trembling as he pointed. 'Now it's just the Fox.'

'I could do with the Fox and Goose right now,' I joked. 'The kind that served wine.'

He drew breath and I heard him whimper with pain. 'At night in the Atacama Desert in Chile,' he croaked, eyes on the sky, 'you can't see your hand in front of your face. Just the stars, billions of them. Best place in the world to stargaze. No radio interference, no light pollution, no cloud cover.'

'Imagine.'

'I'm going there one day, Rem,' he said, wincing. 'Got it all planned. Has to be in February, when night-time temperatures are good. You just need a tent and a few quid for food. San Pedro – biggest public telescope park in South America.' His grimace became a sneer and he added, 'Seven thousand miles away from this shithole.'

'You could study Astronomy, you know,' I said. That was me back then; worrying about the blood, trying to keep my brother's spirits up, and somehow managing to be both dumb and insensitive.

'Fuck *that*,' Cam had said vehemently, both hands on his wound. 'More years behind a desk in some crappy college? I've wasted enough of my life on that. I'm going to be there in person seeing it all for myself, not trapped in a classroom.'

I didn't know what to say. It was the first time I'd heard this perspective on school life from Cam, or anyone. Over the next couple of years, though, that would change. I started volunteering with young offenders and found myself hearing this story over and over again, told in different voices using different images and analogies but at its heart the same.

I'd like to think if I'd been a little older and wiser I might have been a better sister to him. That in moments like that one, hiding in a starlit field together studying the Fox and Goose, I might have found some nugget of insight to share. Something that might have changed the course of his life.

~

'Here,' I said, passing Gaines some painkillers. 'Take a couple of these. I'm nearly done.'

I unrolled a wad of bandage and pulled it as tight as I dared around the wound. 'This will need stitches,' I said as I threaded a safety pin through the frayed edge of the material. 'You'll need to get to Raigmore when the roads clear.' Gaines moved his leg experimentally, tested his weight on it. Satisfied, he clicked the lamp off. For a second I was in a darkened office, just me and the uneasy shape of a stranger. Then his torch clicked on, washing the grey pallor of his skin, illuminating his uniform.

'If you could show me around,' he said.

'Absolutely,' I said. 'Anything I can do to help, just ask.'

We locked the office behind us and set off, me thinking about this strange and unnerving start to my shift. I reassured myself. *Santiago tomorrow.*

MARTIN GRIFFIN

4

I narrated as we made our way up the main corridor. 'Lifts here,' I said. 'Basement access through here . . .'

'What's this about?' He'd paused by the trolley of paint cans and brushes, and was lifting dust sheets.

'We close for a fortnight tomorrow,' I said. 'Got decorators coming in. Some guys are going to hang new wallpaper. There's a team sorting an unsafe bridge along the shoreline, roofers here to re-tile, gardeners, that sort of thing.' He nodded and I resumed my tour. 'Further up here we have the kitchens, the bar, and here on the right, the garden room.'

Gaines waited while I unlocked the door and flicked the lights on. The Garden Room was our conference space: tables dressed with white linen, carafes, bowls of boiled sweets, complimentary pens and notepads. French windows looked out over the terraced lawns, though tonight the view was nothing but a grandstand vista of Ezra's interior. I listened to the storm's hollow howl as Gaines checked the latches and assessed the fire door. Satisfied, he gave me a nod and we left the place in darkness.

'Kitchen's here on the left,' I said as we reached a pair of steel swing doors. 'I can fix you some food if you're hungry.'

Gaines didn't answer. I wondered what had caught his attention. Then I saw it; the left-hand door sucked in slightly on its hinges, the fur of its brushes hissing as air played through. Another door or window was open somewhere inside. There was a service entrance in there, opening onto the rear courtyard. Back in the autumn I'd watched butcher's vans unloading carcasses for Christmas; pigs halved down their spines, turkeys like plucked rucksacks. The kitchen door exhaled again. Maybe the service door was open. If it was, someone could get in.

'That normal?' PC Gaines asked. Without waiting for an answer, he nudged the doors open with his shoulder.

The glow of metal surfaces in the brittle dark. Outlines of worktop shapes, cooker-hoods and storage cupboards. The kitchen staff had mopped up before leaving and the floor still gleamed in the light of Gaines's torch. The darkness was cooler than the warmth of the corridor and I waited by the doors as Gaines made his way inside, portioning the space with the blade of his torch, illuminating worktops, the flat-top grill, sinks and taps. 'Where's this lead?' Gaines said over his shoulder.

'Walk-in freezer,' I said. It was all swinging carcasses and boulders of conjoined potatoes peeled for roasting. Gaines ignored it and checked the service doors at the rear — securely locked — then traced the source of the air current to the rattling grille of an air-conditioning

MARTIN GRIFFIN

unit. 'False alarm,' he said, and limped back. 'Story of my life,' he added as he passed me back into the corridor.

I flushed with relief. 'The bar's next.'

Jaival Parik turned as we entered, eyes refocusing from his phone. He blinked in surprise as he assessed Gaines but recovered quickly. I introduced the officer and they shook hands. 'Looks like you've been in the wars,' Jai said.

'There's been an RTA on the mountain road,' Gaines said. 'As I've explained to Miss Yorke here, I need to focus on the security of the hotel site. My first priority is the safety of the guests so I'll be asking you to keep to your room for the foreseeable future while I deal with a situation.'

'A situation?' Jai swapped his open gaze from me to the officer, then back. 'What's going on?'

'There's nothing to be alarmed about, sir. I'm just asking all unnecessary lights are switched off during the storm. For safety.'

'Surprised we haven't had a power cut already in this weather,' Jai observed. 'I brought a signal booster – fancy one, dish-shaped thing, cost a fortune – but I can't get anything. It was fine the day before yesterday but when Ezra came in . . .' He inflated his cheeks.

'Are you here working, sir?' Gaines asked.

Jai grinned. 'No. I'm here for the hiking. Bad timing, though. The weather's driven me back to my inbox.' He held up his phone in demonstration. He had an expansive smile that took us both in: bright teeth. 'Can't see why us hiding in the dark might help,' he said.

'If you just let me do my job,' Gaines said, examining the fireplace, 'we can get this situation resolved quickly.' He moved to the far end of the room, drew the curtains carefully back and began checking the latches of the windows.

Jai leant in and whispered, 'What's he up to?'

I didn't like his conspiratorial posture and had no intention of sharing anything more than I already had to with a man who recorded conversations. On the other hand, neither did I want to be responsible for holding back information unnecessarily. 'He's concerned there may be an escapee,' I said. I flexed my fingers, trying to shake off an uneasy chill. Sharing the situation had made it somehow worse. If the prisoner was indeed out there, he'd need to escape the storm. It was up to me to ensure the safety of the guests.

'A what?'

'Some sort of crash on the mountain road,' I said, watching as Gaines checked the fire door was securely locked. 'Someone escaped.'

'From the prison?'

'I guess so. The officer's not exactly eager to answer questions.' As I spoke I checked off entrances mentally; reception, the kitchens, the cellars, the outhouses. Was it possible our visitor was already inside?

Jai whistled. 'Hell of a last night for you, isn't it? Bet that flight can't come soon enough.' He rubbed his hands together. 'Any danger of another Malbec?'

I poured him one. He swirled and sniffed, momentarily transported. Gaines had satisfied himself that the bi-fold terrace doors were securely locked, and was now cupping his hands to the glass, scanning the darkness beyond. Window-checks complete, the officer crossed the room towards us, swiping at his phone to confirm Jai's assessment of the signal availability. He tucked it back into a Velcro pocket of his stab vest, eyeing the wine as he rejoined us. 'Does the hotel have an internal phone system?'

'We can contact guests in their rooms if that's what you mean.'

The officer nodded. 'And if I wanted to contact colleagues at the station? Have you got a satellite telephone? Hand-held radios?'

'The site team have walkie-talkies,' I offered. 'They've an office in the basement.'

'I need to check it. Miss Yorke, do you mind?' Gaines indicated my key chain. I had close to thirty keys and I leafed through them, pinching the correct one between thumb and forefinger. As I held it up, my hands trembled. Gaines turned to Jai. 'Sir, why don't you take your drink and return to your room, keep your doors and windows shut.'

Jai pulled a face. 'But this is the most interesting thing that's happened in days.'

'For your own safety, sir, I'd rather you did as I said.'

'Officer—' Jai smiled '—I can take care of myself.' He pushed aside his drink. 'I'd like to come along. I'm in communication technology as it happens. Broadcasting technician. Good with gadgets – any problem with those radios, I'm your man.' Gaines studied him in silence for a moment. 'And if the radios work,' Jai compromised, 'I'll stay out of your hair.'

'Right,' the officer said eventually. 'Miss Yorke, if you could lead the way please.'

We descended the steep concrete steps from the cellar door. The basement corridors were low-ceilinged, lit by cobwebbed strip lights. The brickwork was white, the floors concreted and the walls lined with pipes, arteries wrapped in a reflective silver sponge. Somewhere nearby the boiler rumbled. The place was stuffy, unusually damp. I led us part-way down, swung a side door open and clicked a light on.

Gaines ignored the room and examined the corridor. 'What's further up here?'

I didn't spend much time below ground. 'The boiler, lost property, old storage . . .'

'I'm going to give it a check through.'

'I don't think there are any windows. And no external doors. You're not going to find anyone hiding,' I told him. But even as I said it, I felt doubt gnaw. If someone had gained access – maybe using the old coal chute or the ground-floor fire door – where would they hide? Well, fourteen empty guest rooms for a start. My pulse quickened.

Either side of us, low archways opened into storage rooms for tarp-wrapped furniture and filing cabinets. Gaines flashed a torch into them and stiffened. I followed his gaze. The uneven floor of the dark space was gathering water.

Back in the corridor Gaines ran a gloved finger along the white walls. Wet. 'This is either meltwater,' he said, 'which doesn't seem likely, or you've got burst pipes.' Thin rills were gathering in the cracks of the concrete floor. Dust was dampening to a grey ooze. The site team hadn't mentioned anything as they'd packed up this afternoon.

'Is this normal?' Jai asked.

'No.' I led them further down to another hot, damp space. The heating system hissed in an ankle-deep pool. I felt a distinct sinking in my belly as I thought of the accident log and the accompanying paperwork. Maybe if I got it started tonight, Mitchell could finish it tomorrow. 'I've never seen it like this,' I told Gaines.

We checked the end of the basement corridor – no doors, no windows, no leaking pipes – and returned to the site team's office. 'One problem at a time,' Gaines said. 'Let's have a look at these radios.'

I led them in. The site team had prettified the place. The walls might have been exposed brick, but there was a rug, a desk, a sofa and an easy chair with a Cally Thistle cushion. The walls looked dry; lined with industrial metal shelves. Most held books and files, one an ancient radio-CD player, and others archived shelves of CCTV footage in labelled boxes. An ashtray with two hand-rolled cigarette butts. A clock on the wall reading 8.10 p.m.

On the desk were two hand-held transceivers lying next to an empty five-slot charging dock. Gaines looked the radios over, rotated a knob, clicked a few buttons.

'No charge,' he said, slotting the two of them into their spaces on the dock and turning to Jai. 'You familiar with this model?'

'Not this one exactly but a lot like them. They're standard site security radios. My uncle had a whole shop full of stuff like this when I was a kid; mobile phones the size of bricks, second-hand desktop computers. Bubble-jet printers, CB radios.' He grinned at Gaines and plucked the handsets from the charging dock to examine them. 'You'll have something similar in your squad car, I bet.'

The officer shrugged. 'I keep it to the same channel and press the button to talk. No idea how it actually works.'

'I can have a play with these, figure them out,' Jai said, placing the radios back in the dock and rubbing his palms together as he took a seat.

'You stay here, Mr Parik, for your own safety. I'll come back shortly, see how you're getting on. Don't move, OK?' Gaines turned to me. 'While Mr Parik works on the radios, I want to check in on our other guest.'

'Alex Coben, room sixteen,' I reminded him.

'And where is Mr Coben now?'

'Ms,' I said. 'I haven't seen her since my shift ended this morning.'

A grunt from Gaines. 'Well, I need to speak to her. Could you lead the way please?'

I found myself hesitating. 'Is it safe, do you think?'

Gaines gave a nod of understanding. 'Miss Yorke, we'll stick together and do this thoroughly, OK? There'll be no need to worry once we've secured the site.'

'Sure,' I said, trying to sound convinced.

We left Jai leaning back in his chair, absorbed in an examination of the two handsets. I closed the door behind us.

5

I took PC Gaines along the main corridor, listening to the officer wince with each unsteady step as I led him to the lift. The second floor was William Morris wallpaper, framed hunting scenes and etched-glass wall lights. The shadows made me jumpy.

'Looked from the outside like there are three floors,' the officer observed as we emerged.

I nodded. 'Live-in staff on the top floor.'

'So your room's up there?' He indicated the ceiling.

'That's right. The top floor will be your only chance of a phone signal if Jai can't get the radios working.'

'I'll deal with that shortly,' he said. 'First, let's ensure we're all safe and well.'

We walked the corridor, reaching the window seat and coffee table at the end. Fanned copies of *Horse and Hound*, the *Shooting Times*, *Conde Nast Traveller*; a cream vase of roses, their scent cloying and their petals browning at the edges. Gaines took a moment to look at the bookcase of leather-bound hardbacks whilst I leant out across the seat and peered through the window panes. The storm pushed cold fingers between the sashes, making the hairs rise on the backs of my hands. *Whump* went the night, currents of icy air kneading against the roof tiles. Beyond, unyielding darkness.

Room sixteen was to our left. The officer knocked. 'Hello?'

He gave me an expectant look after a few moments of silence. I shrugged. Gaines rapped the door again. 'Ms Coben?' I expected her voice in reply, irritated, maybe from the bath, but there was nothing. Perhaps she was asleep. Gaines tried the door handle. Locked. 'Taking a nap?' he asked me. I shrugged again. 'Ms Coben?' We waited. 'She must be out,' he said. 'Seems unlikely, though. When did you last see her?'

The breakfast room that morning; the bright clatter of cutlery as the kitchen staff laid out for the last time before close-season. The smell of Lorne sausage, black pudding, potato scones. Classical music for the guests, commercial radio in the kitchens beyond the serving hatches; Chef singing as he plated poached eggs with a slotted spoon. Jai had been up early examining his maps and sipping black coffee; Alex Coben had arrived later and seated herself at the far end of the room at the window table overlooking the terraced gardens running down to the loch's edge. She'd read the *Herald*, ordered an omelette, and had then made calls while her food went cold. I'd left her there, clocked off and climbed the stairs to bed.

I'd been on shift the night before, when she'd first checked in, so I tried examining her arrival with fresh eyes, but couldn't come up with anything out of the ordinary. She'd pulled up in a hire car, crossed reception, pulling a big suitcase, and we'd exchanged a few words as she'd signed the forms, but if Gaines had asked for a description I'm not sure I'd have done her justice. At five eleven I'm taller than a lot of men so I'm used to a small height advantage as I stand to greet guests; Alex Coben was a few inches shorter and dressed in sports gear – a black top, leggings and running shoes. She was slim and agile, with the kind of build that suggested fell running. And her hands, small and strong, were those of a rock climber. We got a lot of physically athletic folk up here – mountain biking was a big part of Fort William's outdoor scene – and she had the kind of aesthetic that suggested that crew: cropped black hair, a stud in her lip, more in her ears up at the top, some sort of tattoo on the side of her neck above the line of her sweatshirt. She was around my age. I told Gaines what I could remember.

He rolled his lower lip between his teeth and stared out into the night. 'A tourist?'

I shrugged. 'Hardly spoken to her. She came night before last, booked a two-night stay. Spoke a lot on the phone this morning so maybe she's working.'

'What visitor details do you keep at reception?'

'Name, address. Contact number.'

Gaines nodded, his expression troubled. 'Let's get this door open.'

I swiped the card. Room sixteen was dark and the air was cold. I called her name, got nothing, so slipped the key card into its power slot and clicked the lights on. A fireplace and scarlet rug, a claw-footed bath and thick curtains drawn across a bay window overlooking Loch Alder. Beside the bedhead was a second, smaller, window. Its curtains were drawn but they were wet and billowing. The sash window beyond was open, humming in its runners like a wasp in a jar.

It looked for a moment as if Alex Coben had thrown herself out of her room.

Gaines crossed the carpet, lifting his boots gingerly to check he wasn't leaving prints. 'Switch the lights off please, Miss Yorke,' he said, waiting by the curtains. I could see his breath.

I removed the key card, returning us to darkness, and found myself leaning against the wall, my body rigid. *Where was she?* Gaines parted the curtains and looked out into the storm, examining the dark pines. Next, he studied the snow that had settled on the windowsill – carefully checking for any signs of disturbance – before brushing it out with a gloved hand, lowering the window and shutting the wet curtains again.

He cleared his throat like a man who'd been holding his breath and said, 'No sign of anything out there.'

In the gloom I could see the rest of the room was neat. Our staff had remade the bed and refreshed the bathroom towels before heading off, leaving Mitchell to take care of any further cleaning when he clocked on tomorrow. A light above the mirror had been left on. The sink-shelf had a zip-bag for make-up and toiletries. I watched as Gaines checked the wardrobe. Empty hangers chattered. There was the shell-suitcase I'd seen her arrive with, its zip-grin wide. Gaines lifted the lid with the tip of his boot. I expected a change of clothes but the case was empty, her stuff gone.

Only the tripod telescope standing in the bay window suggested anything. It was nothing to do with the hotel; she must have brought it with her. Gaines seemed struck by it, though it was standard-issue birdwatching kit. He opened the bay-window curtains and rounded the telescope, stooping to look through it, adjusting the viewfinder with wet gloves. 'What's over there?' he said, beckoning me.

The bay faced northwards across the loch to the lower slopes of Bray Crag. I didn't need to look through the lens to know what it was pointed at. There was nothing but frozen water and hillside to see. I struggled my mind into motion. 'Golden eagles?' I tried.

Gaines stooped, grunting, and looked again. 'Possibly. White-tailed eagles just as likely near a body of water like this. The central section isn't frozen over yet. Or geese? Isn't Alder famous for geese?'

It was. Each winter, barnacle geese come over from Svalbard in vast numbers. They're not like the brents I used to know back on Northumberland's mud flats; barnacles holler and honk like jammed cars, particularly when they gather on the water or fly in long lines. Loch Alder is no Lomond, but it has deep ravines along its edges cut by water coming off the side of Farigaig, and the geese liked nesting away from predators up among the cliffs. It was possible Alex had been watching them.

Gaines was opening desk drawers. 'Well,' he said when he was finished, 'no phone here. Empty luggage, no sign of outdoor clothes or walking boots. Which suggests she went out, probably on foot and, if the telescope is any guide, probably to explore the loch edge. So, she left sometime earlier today?'

I tried to draw some sense from the situation but it didn't yield to logic. *Alex Coben had been gone all day?* I felt a fist close around my stomach. If she was out there in Ezra, she might not be the only one. 'I'm not ... I can't help you with specifics,' I managed. 'I was off duty.'

Gaines ran a gloved hand across his mouth. The sound of stubble against leather as he stared at the empty room. 'Have you got a gunroom?'

I felt my strength evaporate.

The Mackinnon had originally been built as a private hunting lodge and our guests seemed to be split pretty evenly between those who wanted to watch the wildlife and those who wanted to kill it. We still had our fair share of shooting parties and we hired out firearms. In my eighteen months at the hotel, one particular space had become indelibly associated with misdemeanour. It was my fault the gunroom retained an uncomfortable power to disturb.

What I'd done there over a year ago still kept me awake at night.

'We do,' I confirmed, fingering the keys in my pocket. Housed above the garages in an outbuilding at the foot of the drive across the car park, the gunroom was only supposed to be visited by staff licensed to use the stock of rifles. I wasn't one of those staff.

'I need you to give me access.'

'Look, Officer Gaines,' I said, 'do you mind telling me what exactly is going on?'

He gave a smile that struck me as over-rehearsed. 'Just a precaution.'

'I can't allow access to shooting rifles,' I said. 'I'm not licensed to use them. And doesn't prisoner-transport mean a firearm?' Even as I said it, I remembered the officer's holster was empty. Like the pockets on his stab vest. There was a silence. 'What happened to your gun?'

'I lost it in the accident.' Gaines took a breath and squared his shoulders, reading my face. We left sixteen and hovered in the corridor. 'OK, you want to know what's going on.' He sighed, assembling an appropriate response. 'I was part of a three-vehicle convoy. We were transporting a prisoner to another facility after a prolonged stand-off at Porterfell.'

'The trouble I saw earlier?'

Gaines nodded. 'The weather was treacherous and the prisoner transport I was following slid off the road. I lost control of my vehicle. Once I came around, I established that the transport was open and the prisoner was gone. I knew of the hotel and I made my way straight here. It was hard to see clearly in the storm but I don't recall any tracks. The recent snow is still fresh so unless he took a totally different route, it's unlikely our runner is somewhere down here. Nevertheless, it is a possibility. My first concern is contacting colleagues and asking for a team to be dispatched before our escapee gets too far. In the meantime, we all have to stay safe so I need access to the gunroom. I take full responsibility.'

I tried moistening my lips, and asked the question I'd been thinking since Gaines first told his story. 'So exactly how dangerous is this man?'

The officer rubbed an eye with the heel of a hand. 'In these circumstances he poses a threat,' he said. 'But we've established he's not inside the building. So my next priority is to ensure we're well protected.'

Ezra reminded us of its presence with a petulant slam against the bay windows. 'The gunroom is above the garages,' I told him. A cold feeling thickened beneath my ribs, like I was sinking. 'I'll show you.'

I liked the idea of going to the gunroom even less than I did the prospect of meeting the prisoner.

6

The garages were at the first switchback of the steep drive towards the mountain road, only ten minutes' walk in the snow. I felt a ridiculous need to justify the hotel's security arrangements, as if I had any personal stake in them. 'The garages are a converted stable building,' I said, 'locked on the ground floor.' We took the lift back down to reception. 'There's CCTV. And the room itself is protected with an electronic keypad.'

'Right.' Gaines zipped his coat as he limped for the reception office. 'Miss Yorke, I'll need to look at the layout of the grounds again. Entrances and exits.'

In the office I reached for a staff coat, quilted with hotel livery, and pulled it on as Gaines studied the site plan once more.

'It's best we don't go out by the revolving doors,' he said. 'We should use a service entrance. I saw one at the back of the kitchens.'

I hadn't been out in a storm like this one. The dark air was a punishing slab, a mass of noise. In moments, blown snow was under my shirt, beading along the back of my neck, and I was hounded by its twists and turns as I re-locked the kitchens' rear entrance. Keys pocketed, I indicated the direction and we worked our way through calf-deep snow towards the drive. The car park's edges were nothing more than raised ridges now. My feet numbed fast. Around us, low ragged cloud blew in swift strips. Bellowing trees loomed under a sky the colour of pack ice.

Gaines slogged uphill, head down, leaning into the wind. The driveway lights were off so the garages, out to the right of the drive in a pocket of pines, were nothing but a low dark shape, their margin uncertain. I thought about the desperate man who might be out here in the night, freezing to death, seeking the shelter of the hotel. Ahead a light blazed and I had to raise an arm to block my eyes. The hotel's big garage doors had a movement-activated spotlight above them, next to the CCTV. We gathered in the lee beneath the camera, backs against the stone of the old building. Shelter made it possible to hear Gaines's ragged breathing. Illuminated clouds of breath billowed. Looking back the way we'd come, the Mackinnon, usually a blazing beacon, wore a dark mask, its face an empty-eyed shell. Over by the reception doors the old larch shuddered, its stunted top dipping.

The officer jerked a thumb at the two big garage doors. 'What's in here?'

'SUVs,' I said. It was a relief not to have to shout. 'They're for the site team mostly. We collect guests from the station, run errands.'

'Are they equipped to drive in these conditions?'

I felt sweat bead my hairline. I'd been trying not to fret about the chances of me driving away tomorrow morning, but with the storm the way it was, the route would soon become impassable. Council ploughs had swept up here the previous week, shunting the fall into tumbledown pillows that marked the edges of the road in chest-high walls, but, if Ezra persisted, the ploughs would struggle to get back, never mind my two-wheel-drive Nissan. The hotel's SUVs were 4x4 at least, but I'd seen the site team having to attach snow chains to the tyres in bad weather. I could borrow one, I thought, anxiously improvising – leave my car here in the morning. Mitchell could sell it and forward me the money.

'Miss Yorke?' Gaines prompted.

I clenched my fists, trying to warm them. 'Possible. But it'll be hard going,' I said, leaning into his shoulder to make myself heard. I could smell the sweat on him. We'd need to cut a steep path up the drive, turn right then follow the mountain road as it snaked its way along Farigaig. Plenty of tight turns to negotiate plus the added complication of treacherous edges; something my companion knew all about. He'd been lucky to escape with just a smashed knee. 'There's a chance, but the longer this goes on, the less I like it.'

'You have the keys, though?' I nodded. He turned to look at me. 'I need to be sure we don't lose our escapee; that he doesn't become a greater threat than he already is. I'd like you to hand over the keys to the garage and the gunroom.'

I'd been used to helping the police before. It's hard to avoid, growing up with a brother like Cameron. In my twenties I'd filled out written statements, brought biscuits out on Mum's best china (Mum always insisted on best for authority figures, as if the plates would somehow make up for the behaviour of the boy) and I'd persuaded and cajoled when necessary, often from the back seat of a patrol car. I found myself swallowing back a strong sense of unease as I worked the keys from their loop. The hotel SUVs might be my only way off the site in the morning. 'I'm going to need these back,' I said. 'I'm responsible for the safety of the site as well as the guests.'

He ungloved his hand, held out a weathered palm and I handed them over. 'Any other way off the site?'

'Not unless you fancy taking the boat.' I pointed beyond the gardens – a grey blanket of snow under fog – to the line of thick ice that marked the loch's edge. 'The jetty's almost a mile along the shoreline.'

Loch Alder was deep freshwater in gunmetal grey, filling the valley between our twin mountains. Out of midge season on sunny summer days, the two mountains provided shelter, stilling Alder's waters until they mirrored high cotton clouds and whirling birds. Watercolour artists came for the views and guests took boat trips or bathed using the pocket-beaches for picnics. But during harsh winter weather, Alder froze into stillness, the ice creeping inwards from the inlets and thickening sufficiently to encourage hardy skaters. Over the last week, it had accreted into smoked glass at the shallows, two inches thick and snow-topped so that, to the untrained eye, the loch had shrunk. Towards its centre, a black sliver of liquid still shifted like a jagged wound.

'Frozen. Not a great option,' Gaines said, grunting as he pushed away from the wall and made his way to the door. I nodded my agreement and watched the big officer fumbling at the gunroom key with clumsy fingers. He bundled it into the lock, twisting hard to break the ice gathering in the mechanism, then pushed the door open.

I was here again for the first time in a year. A ripple of shame passed through me.

Our breath clouded as we struggled in to the entrance hall, shutting the storm out behind us. Gaines re-locked the door against the storm. I didn't like the implication. There was ice on the inside of the windows, I noticed, before the exterior light cut out and we hunted for our torches in the darkness. Gaines was first to his, playing a beam across the floor. In the half-light his eyes looked heavily bagged. His mouth was set in a permanent, tight wince. To our right was a door that gave access to the garages, but we made for the stairs.

As we mounted them, I felt my past actions shift inside me. Last time I'd climbed these stairs had been in the darkness of a late December shift over a year ago. Cameron was a fortnight dead and I'd been broken and scared. My night shifts back then had been long battles with despair and terror. I was his sister; what if I was targeted too? I'd thought. I needed protection.

The hotel's Christmas lights had been glitter thrown

across the wet tarmac that night. The bar had been closed, the guests all asleep, and I'd been working that foggy netherworld between midnight and dawn, a time when the black pines above the loch's edge seemed to be in constant fricative communion, the wind buffeting branches together so they'd echoed beneath the voices of owls. I'd been alone but somehow it hadn't felt like it, such was the fear of anticipation that had pulsed in me. I'd crossed the Mackinnon's empty reception to the front doors and, leaving the guests safely in their beds, headed for the garages . . .

Now, Gaines and I creaked upwards to the electronic door of the gunroom, a heavy sheet-metal thing with a keypad. I prodded in the date of the hotel's construction just as I had that night over a year ago, and we switched the lights on. The gunroom was a windowless space under a pitched roof with a burgundy carpet. In its centre, directly beneath the strip light, was a glass-topped display cabinet the size of a pool table.

A dozen hunting rifles lay end to end on a scarlet baize. Their walnut stocks were polished to a gleam.

7

There were drawers inset along the sides and Gaines unlocked them and pulled them open.

I knew their contents from that frantic December night; recalled hunting through them in the dark, my fingers trembling painfully. One was a set of black scopes. Some were telescopic and some were red-bead; one drawer Gaines dismissed as smaller air-rifles, one was filled with neatly packed, palm-sized cardboard boxes. The police officer grunted his approval and began flipping lids, carefully pulling out Styrofoam inserts patterned with plugs. In each hole, a neatly stored bullet pressed nose-down.

There was a manifest detailing the exact contents of the drawers. A year earlier I'd had to adjust it so that it didn't look like anything was missing, burying the absence further back in the records so that the current stock looked accurate. I knew it would only take a cursory line-by-line search of the lists to detect my mathematical trickery and I'd been ready for the discovery, but it hadn't happened. In the months that subsequently passed, I'd never quite felt the tension ease.

Even so, I'd often thought of returning the stolen rifle, but the idea of a second secret foray into the darkness and a second tampering of the manifest was too much to take. Now my notice was handed in, my options had dwindled to nothing. I'd conceded over Christmas that the gun would remain safe where it was, hidden long after I'd gone. Only I knew the place. Maybe one day someone would come across it. Until then, it would stay, a permanent reminder of my fear in the days immediately after Cameron's death.

'Have you been hunting before?' Gaines asked as he opened and raised the glass cabinet lid. I blinked, breathing hard, and shook my head. 'I have a licence and training so I'm safe to use these,' he said. 'But you aren't, so I want to be clear: on no account must you use these weapons. Just me. Understood?'

'Understood,' I said, my throat dry.

'Remingtons,' Gaines continued, half to himself, as if recalling moorland shooting parties of his childhood. He pulled at a handle on the right-hand side and revealed an empty slot. 'Four rounds in the internal chamber,' he said, carefully inserting cartridges, clicking them into place and closing the gun. He placed the stock up in the crook of his shoulder, felt the weight of it, then held it before him. 'Safety catch here,' he said, examining the gun before holding it vertically. 'Good. Thank you, Miss Yorke. We can't be too careful.'

I gave Gaines a slow nod, trying to set aside my memories, and instead make sense of what had just happened. There was a lot implied in my companion's short, unnecessary demonstration of the rifle and I didn't like any of it.

'When we get back to the hotel I'd like you to stay safe,' he said as he looped the gun strap over his head, zipped his bag and re-shouldered it. 'I'll have another go at getting a phone signal. You'll be staffing reception, checking the hotel stays secure. Understood?'

I tried to speak but no sound issued. I hadn't spent a lot of time with police officers in more recent years, but Gaines was stirring troubling memories. Memories from much further back.

Having a brother like mine had meant setting aside many of one's own aspirations. Other girls got boyfriends; I was handcuffed to a delinquent. Mates drifted away to their steady jobs and gap-year plans; I returned home each weekend, the exhausted carer of an adolescent criminal. While my best friend Jessie was celebrating her twenty-fourth birthday, I was borrowing her boyfriend's car so I could look for my brother, driving the streets of Newcastle city centre, kerb-crawling in the rain like a sex pest. I still remember the tick of the heater, the rattle of the broken windscreen wipers, the shame and desperation of that long night.

Then, one day, the eight-year nightmare abruptly ended.

Like everyone else back then, I'd been following the Troy Foley story. It was hard to avoid coverage of the notorious gunrunner, at large for so long, finally trapped in an undercover sting by officers in Hackney. I scoured the news in ghoulish fascination as more of his gang-members were arrested. Every day brought new revelations; Troy Foley bought handguns and ammunition clips in Atlanta and arranged for them to be shipped to the UK packed inside the shells of air-conditioning units, it was discovered. Later it emerged that, once in the UK, the units were delivered to addresses associated with gangs in Bristol, Manchester and Glasgow. One by one, co-conspirators were flushed out as the investigation progressed.

Then came the announcement of the arrest of Cameron Yorke, 21, of Corbridge, Tyneside, in connection with the distribution of illegal firearms. My brother was described by an investigating officer as one of Troy Foley's 'key facilitators' in establishing county lines gangs. Reading about my criminal brother in a national newspaper was a gut punch from which I never fully recovered.

With Cameron under arrest, years of high-alert tension should have ended but, immersed in dysfunction for so long, I no longer knew what normal was. I'd already studied troubled teenagers and mental health; written an MSc dissertation on conduct disorder and pathological defiance, volunteered at community mental health centres, even mastered the criminal justice system and youth detention. I was so focused on the troubles of others I hadn't given a thought to myself for years. After my postgraduate study, I was lucky to have Edinburgh University take me on as an associate lecturer. My field became the psychology of faulty decision-making; Cameron's invisible hand steering my choices even then. I had three years teaching – the happiest and most fulfilled of my life – but when they moved him to Porterfell, I gave up my university role and followed. Someone had to check in on him every week, make sure he was safe. I'd thought it was all about protecting him. I didn't think I'd end up having to protect myself.

'You need to be alert,' Gaines was saying. 'Stay smart. And don't let anyone in. It could be a long shift at reception. Do you have some personal possessions that might make things easier? In your quarters?'

I croaked an answer, thinking of my travel guides and phrase book, and the officer nodded, re-locking the cabinet. We crossed to the door. 'The storm's due to ease around midnight,' he said as we descended. 'So that's another, what, three hours? I'll make contact with my colleagues, and if we're patient and careful we'll be able to resolve all of this.'

He locked up, pocketed his new keys and we hacked a return journey across the car park towards the back door of the kitchens. One way to try and re-centre, to master my thumping pulse, was to walk slowly, head lowered in a stoop, and count breaths. That's how I got to noticing our tracks. The ones we'd made on the way up had been fresh and sharp-edged only ten minutes ago. Now they were vaguer disturbances; softening memories of footprints. Half an hour more and they might be nothing more than ridge-and-furrow undulations, soon gone entirely. As we approached the lee of the main building, they sharpened once more. Out of the wind they lasted longer.

My mind struggled with a sudden memory as I floundered through the darkness. Something of significance that had passed me almost unnoticed.

Approaching the service entrance, I got it. The snow at the base of the garage doors was a long softening line of folded white, pushed away from the building as if someone had opened the up-and-overs. The doors were the type you pulled up from the bottom and they tipped outwards from the base, pushing back the snow before sliding into canopy runners overhead. That line of snow had been protected from the wind in the shelter of the building. We'd experienced plenty of snowfall in the last few weeks and February temperatures had preserved much of it in persistent drifts, but the site team had gritted recently, meaning this was recent fall, the line newly made. I tried to recall the comings and goings of the afternoon. Plenty of staff had left the site as we shut down. The catering team had hired a people carrier and had been bundling their luggage in after the lunchtime shift. The van windows had been down and the radio was playing. The driver had pipped his horn cheerfully as they'd departed, driving up between dirty banks of last week's snow. Clouds had come soon after and Ezra must've been heavy by four; I remembered hearing the howling of the wind. Mitchell left at five. Perhaps the line of pushed-back snow was his doing; he lived in a converted farmhouse three miles along the road, close enough to walk to work, but with the weather bad, it was possible he'd taken one of the SUVs home. The guests didn't have access, and, anyway, they'd come in their own vehicles – the soft snow-shells of our two final guest cars were huddled together in a corner of the car park. So had it been opened this evening? I looked back towards the garages, wondering whether I should hack back for another look. The building's movement-sensitive light was off again and it squatted in darkness, thick-shouldered and low against the hill, waiting.

Those marks in the snow were a puzzle but some things were certain – someone had been into the garage, likely late afternoon or evening, and likely when no one noticed a light in the darkness of the storm. And it hadn't been me.

8

'Miss Yorke!' PC Gaines held his rifle loosely, one hand cupped to his mouth as he waited at the service doorway. I'd stopped walking, it seemed, and was staring at the snow we'd churned up on our outward journey. 'Miss Yorke!'

I raised a gloved hand and ploughed my way towards him, digging for my remaining keys and letting us back inside. Dripping meltwater at the reception desk, Gaines fruitlessly tested the outside line again, then tipped his head in the direction of the office. We made our way in. He leaned his newly acquired rifle carefully against the filing cabinet, clicked the desk lamp on and lowered himself into a chair, hissing through gritted teeth.

'Want me to check your knee?' I asked as I took the chair opposite, swapping my torch for the first aid kit.

Gaines shrugged his coat off stiffly, then began flexing his fingers back to life, channels of pain creasing his forehead. 'It's OK,' he managed. 'Miss Yorke. Thanks for your help so far.'

'Call me Remie,' I said.

'Donald,' he said. 'Don. Hi.' As he gave a reluctant smile, I got a momentary glimpse at the person behind the professional mask. A pub man, I thought; a social drinker, a bad golfer and, by the absence of a ring, I reckoned a divorcee. I was looking at a steady career officer who was facing the most challenging night of his service. 'Remie,' he said, leaning forward, 'you're in charge of reception now.' The neckline of his shirt was damp, his cuffs grubby and his knuckles blood-stained. I watched him work his bandage off, check the wound beneath. 'I'm going to make another attempt to get through to my colleagues and let them know what's happened.' He removed his bandage and balled it up. I handed him a fresh one. 'We'll get you what you need from your room then I want you to come back and stay here. It's better if you don't sit in direct line of sight of the doors but stay close enough to see, just in case.'

'To see what?' I asked, my skin prickling. 'Listen. Who is it I'm looking for, exactly?'

'Our runner's a dangerous man.' Gaines picked up his rifle.

'Dangerous how? Armed?'

'I don't know, but I lost my weapon during the accident so it's possible. And he's high-supervision.' Cameron's supervision status had been low. High meant murder. I felt sick. 'He's violent and he's manipulative, that's all you need to know,' Gaines continued. 'Now, I want you down here keeping an eye on reception so let's gather your stuff. And on the way to your quarters,

I'd like to check in with Mr Parik. See how he's getting on with those radios.'

The basement flood was worsening. Standing at the top of the stairs, I dipped my torch beam into the fusty darkness and watched it dance stars across a film of fluid. Gaines winced at each steep step down. The corridor was a long puddle of black water.

Gaines lowered a foot in and tested the depth. 'Shallow,' he said. If it concerned him as much as it did me, he kept it to himself.

We sloshed through, the air cloying and cold. Somewhere, the hotel's burst pipes must be disgorging liquid. I heard the rumble and splutter of the old Victorian boiler. The events of the last few hours had brought the virtue of perspective and now Jai's likely mistake with a voice memo didn't appear so sinister. Hopefully he'd have a communication breakthrough to share, I was thinking, as I pulled open the door to the site-team's basement room, sending water in a backwards wave over the toes of our boots.

The space beyond was empty.

Gaines splashed over to the desk. 'The two radios have gone,' he observed.

I glanced about. The wall-clock read 9.05 p.m. Everything else looked as we'd left it, except the soaked rug had been lifted partly afloat. The liquid lapped against the feet of the desk. 'Maybe the water spooked him,' I offered.

Gaines cupped his neck with both hands, ran them

up through his greying hair, and swore. 'I was clear he shouldn't move. Very clear. This makes things complicated. How can I ensure his safety if he won't stay still?'

First Coben, now Jai. Two empty rooms. My blood chilled. I didn't like where my imagination was going so I said, 'Maybe he'll be back.'

The officer scowled. 'Let's get upstairs.'

We rode the lift again, and soon I found myself back at my top-floor room.

Standing on the threshold with Gaines, I felt myself wince with embarrassment. I was thirty-three and sleeping in a single bed. There are so many things one should have achieved by my age and everything in my top-floor room, tucked in under the pitched roof with a desk, a sink and a shower cubicle, said I hadn't.

My small suitcase, already packed and zipped shut on top of the bed, held a hoodie and sweats, t-shirts, jeans and walking boots. Its open partner held the remainder of my clothes, a tumble of travel books and star-gazing guides, a thousand euros and my passport. The bedside table told another sad tale; more books, my ten-year-old pro-turf hockey ball, a bright-orange Bauer I got to keep after a hat-trick in a grudge game against Kelvinside, and my stick leaning against the wall at the bedhead. My desk drawers, still to be cleared, were full of letters from Cameron – very short ones, awkwardly typed – and papers left over from the appeals process. My bathroom was home to a make-up bag, a toothbrush and a hairdryer. That was it.

'Most of my stuff's in storage,' I explained, squirming.

Gaines grunted. 'All packed to go, I see.'

'It's my last night,' I said. 'I'm flying down to Heathrow tomorrow.'

Gaines gave me a look, eyes dark beneath bloody brow ridges. 'From Aberdeen? No chance.'

I took a slow deep breath. 'Once I'm down into Inverness the roads will be fine.'

The officer shrugged. 'Grab anything you might need,' he said. 'A book, a flask for tea. That hockey stick might come in handy. You still play?'

'Not so much any more.'

He pulled his phone out. 'It'd be best if we could stay in touch. When the storm clears we might have a chance. We should swap numbers just in case.'

He checked and dictated his and I punched it in, awkward in case he saw my contacts. My phone held about a dozen numbers. One was Mitchell, one was Chef, one was a company called Safe Storage in Aberdeen. The others were colleagues from the psychology department at Edinburgh, names that triggered the ache of longing. There were two old friends in there as well; girls who'd stuck with me through my late teens while Cameron dismantled normality. One was Mum – a missed call notification next to it; she'd rung this afternoon but I hadn't picked up – and the last entry wasn't a phone number at all. It was the six-digit number Cameron had given me on my final Porterfell visit. I scrolled past it and the others and read my phone number out to Gaines. I was so concerned to conceal the sad state of my contacts I never paid much attention to the officer's phone.

It was only later it struck me how new it had looked.

'I'll be trying to contact my colleagues and checking the site remains secure,' Gaines continued. 'If there's anything – I mean *anything* – that looks amiss, get in touch. Even if we can't speak, a text might get through. And try Mr Parik's room, let me know he's safe.'

'I will.'

We hovered in the blue-black glow of the lift. 'Good luck,' I croaked.

'Heathrow,' he said with a smile as we parted ways. 'Dream on.'

I tracked the officer's wide-shouldered frame as he moved off into the dark. Then I went back to my room to get my hockey stick.

9

Back in the reception office, I brewed coffee and sat with the soles of my boots against the radiator, waiting for my hands and feet to rewarm, my stick across my lap. It was a Gray's Midbow, bought second-hand during my final year at uni, a mess of scuffs and scratches. Back then I had this habit of picking at the grip-tape; worrying away at the silicone with my thumbnail during half-time team-talks, my mind on Cameron. Distracted, I found myself doing it again; anxiously working my nail under the tape; picking away at it like a scab.

I hadn't used the stick for nine years. I felt a sudden, painful stab of memory, strong and sharp as a stitch. The last thing I'd struck with the stick in my lap was a young man's fingers.

I'd been trying to protect Cameron. I guess back then I thought that a sudden, brutal explosion might be enough to wake my brother up, to change the course of his life. I had been wrong. The only life that changed course that night was that of the victim. I'd broken the bones of his right hand.

~

Cameron's sixteenth birthday weekend was the last time Mum and Dad were together. I'd driven home as usual on the Friday night – though I'd scrubbed hard, I'd never quite cleaned the passenger seat of Cameron's blood from the night a year before – unpacked my bag in my childhood room and played hockey back at my old club on the Saturday afternoon. Mum and Dad hadn't known where Cameron was on the Friday night. We shared dinner, watched TV and tried not to talk about it. They were visibly relieved when he rolled in at six that Saturday evening. The fact he remembered his big sister was home for a family celebration was praiseworthy by that point, which demonstrates how things had declined.

We went out for pizza in town. All through the meal, Cameron seemed anxious, as if he was waiting for something better to happen. Hoping we might rediscover the closeness we'd had on the night of the stabbing, I tried talking to him. All he did was knot the tablecloth between his fingers and check his new phone incessantly. The phone had already raised a few eyebrows at home because it was one of three he carried around at that time; a habit he never convincingly explained away. That night he drank a couple of beers, never more than disconsolate, and his smile was forced when we toasted to his birthday. His hair was cropped short and he had developed a repeated, nervous mannerism of running his fingers in lines across his scalp, from the back to the front. His nails were bitten to the quick and his fingertips yellowed by tobacco.

Back at home it all exploded. Dad settled back with the TV remote, his legs thrust out before him, feet crossed at the ankles, and suggested a DVD. Cam, hovering at the kitchen window facing the street, explained he was going out. Dad's face fell, Mum lost it. Cameron leaned back against the worktop, his eyes glassy, gaze fixed on the middle distance and his hands making fists in his jeans pockets while Mum shouted about family being more important than friends on special occasions.

'Your sister's home!' she admonished, shaking a finger. She'd done her nails especially and the sight of her, angry in her make-up, cardigan and careful hair, was impossibly sad.

'And I've got work I need to do!' Cameron shouted.

Mum had clearly heard this one before. 'Sitting in vans?' she asked, her lips pursed. 'You ever checked what's in the back of them?'

Cameron laughed. 'Mum, you have no idea how the world works. Not the first fucking clue.'

'What's going on?' I asked.

'He's getting mixed up with that gang again.'

I felt a slow sinking inside, hoping it wasn't true. Cameron laughed bitterly, pulling back the kitchen curtains and checking the street, before swiping that fancy phone awake and checking for messages.

I said, 'Is this true?' I knew the gang Mum meant. I'd had sleepless nights ever since Cameron chose them at fourteen. Local lads, wild kids with chaotic childhoods who did as they pleased. One in particular, Danny Franks, was a rat-faced boy with an absent father and a mum who'd been arrested for benefit fraud. Franks had started with property damage and moved on to petty theft then soft drugs. He'd turned nastier. There'd been a rape allegation, a car crash that was rumoured to be insurance fraud. I'd lost track since moving away but my weekends at home had featured occasional updates; police cautions, an arrest, a spell of community service. 'Is this Danny Franks again? Cameron, he's bad news.'

'Not you as well,' he said, making claws of his hands and running them along his scalp, his chewed fingers trembling. 'Mum wasn't happy when I didn't have a job. Now I've got one, she's still not happy,' he said. 'I need a smoke. I'm going out.'

'They're a bad crowd!' Mum put in.

I held a hand up to her. The night of the previous year; the one with the blood and the naming of the stars, had given me a slim hope I might get through where Mum couldn't. 'Wait, Cam. One minute. What is it you're doing?'

'Forget it,' he said, making for the hall and pulling a coat from the peg.

'That's it,' Mum shouted. 'Run away from your responsibilities again!'

I sent her into the lounge and shut the door, then grabbed Cam before he could leave. I'd been peace-maker and go-between for long enough to know how to handle explosions like this one. 'You shouldn't be spending time with that lad,' I told him.

'Rem, you don't understand,' he said, pulling his

jacket on. 'No one does.' Again the claws across his scalp. Blood-rimmed, yellow-skinned fingers. And an expensive diver's watch I didn't recognise. The three phones and the watch together signalled some sort of escalation. I didn't like it one bit, but I was losing what small measure of influence I'd once had.

'I can help,' I said. 'You could come and stay with me for a while.'

'Fuck off,' he told me wearily, then turned tail and left, banging the front door so hard it bounced open again. In the same moment I glimpsed my hockey stick leaning amongst the coats and boots in the hall where I'd left it, and outside, the van in the street. Franks was behind the wheel with the driver's door open. I could hear the thud of his music. By the time I was down the path to our gate I could smell the weed, see it clouding the inside of the windscreen. I was burning with wine and fury, my Midbow gripped tightly in both hands.

Franks was laughing before I broke his fingers.

He'd turned to Cameron through a haze of smoke, his voice raised so I could hear. 'Bro, when did your sister become such a milf? I wouldn't mind some bump and grind with *that*.'

His right hand loosely gripped the apex of the steering wheel. I closed the distance with the van.

I'd played a lot of hockey. Edinburgh University Ladies had ten outdoor teams; I used to shuttle between the first and second XI depending upon my form. I could strike hard and with accuracy, so when I brought the stick down against Franks's exposed hand I smashed his metacarpals to powder. He sent up a howl, the keening scream of a child, and he cradled his ruined fingers.

The rest of the evening was a blur but I still remember Danny Franks's wobbling cries, all agony and disbelief, even now. I have a half-memory of Cameron driving him to accident and emergency, of a blazing argument sometime the following day as I packed my bags. Mum and Dad split some weeks later. I went back to Edinburgh and waited for the police to call.

They never did.

~

Ezra bullied the upstairs casements, rousing me from my recollections. I listened to the wind whump flat-palmed against the glass of the lobby. Upstairs somewhere Gaines was searching for a signal. Jai was AWOL; Coben was missing. For a brief and foolish moment I thought things couldn't be worse. Then there was a noise from the reception desk. It was the intercom.

Someone was outside, buzzing to get in.

Panic fluttered at the base of my spine. I'm not sure how long I sat there in the office before I managed to get my body moving, but when I did, I rose slowly, muscles aching and blood thumping hot and stupid. *It might be the storm. An electrical fault. Better get Gaines.* The phone slid in my fingers as I selected contacts and hit his number. Hopeless silence as I waited; not even a dialling tone. The clock read 9.15. I tried sending a text – *Someone at the door. Come down* – and watched the data upload slowly to the quarter-mark, then hit an invisible wall and stop dead. Nothing was getting through.

The second buzz made me drop the phone. It spun end over end and I had to scrabble under Mitchell's desk, fingers thick and clumsy as if still snow-gloved. The line of sight was such that whoever was hitting the intercom out there couldn't see this display of terror, but if I wanted to retreat, following Gaines upstairs, I'd have to emerge and cross the lobby and be seen. I pocketed the phone, crossed my arms and ran my hot palms down the polyester sleeves of my jacket, trying to dry them. Hockey-stick memories made me jumpy. But the stick could be an advantage. I gripped the Midbow's handle and worked to steady my hands, a familiar movement I'd done a thousand times out on cold Edinburgh Astroturf pitches. Those nights felt a long way away now.

Alex Coben, I reassured myself, returning from her walk, relieved to have made it back. Or someone else. A prisoner, cold and desperate. Gaines had arrived almost two hours ago so any new visitor had survived at least that long, with wind-chill driving temperatures to well below minus ten, no coat, no food, limited shelter. Hitting the intercom at the doors of a desolate and empty hotel was surely a final act of desperation. Chances were they were in no state to pose a threat; more likely they'd need immediate medical attention. I imagined someone staggering blindly in and curling into a helpless ball, frostbitten fingers screaming as they warmed up. I scooped up the first aid kit and took a second to steady my breathing.

When the third buzz came I was ready. I crossed from the office to the reception desk, took my seat, leant my stick against the desk and placed the kit down. 'The Mackinnon,' I said into the intercom. 'it's close-season at the moment. Can I be of any assistance?'

I had to give it to Gaines, the darkness worked in my favour. The only disruption to my view of the outside world was the evenly spaced blue dots of the reflected floor lights. The rest was dark enough for me to make out shape and movement.

There was someone at the intercom.

It's surprising how much you can read from a silhouette. This wasn't Alex Coben. This was a man, smaller than our first visitor, stooping close to the doors for shelter, the hood of a black jacket pulled low over his eyes. He wasn't exactly casual – there was an urgency in his posture and movement – but neither did he look like a couple of hours in a blizzard had brought him to his knees. I found myself revising my frostbite scenario. He'd drawn back a little from the intercom, I noticed, and was squinting into the glass. The angle prevented me seeing his face.

I watched him lean in again, press a thumb to the intercom. His voice, when it came, was dry, tired and English. Flat-vowelled, northern. 'Ma'am, I need to come inside.'

I cleared my throat. 'I'm afraid we have a situation here. I've been given instructions not to let anyone in.'

'Police officer, ma'am.' His accent suggested that he called the hills between Leeds and Manchester home. Police came out *pulleece*. Ma'am was *mamm*.

Relief bloomed. A second officer, maybe Gaines's partner – he hadn't mentioned a partner but it'd been a three-car convoy, *why hadn't I asked about the other car?* – had followed him down from the mountain road. I had to stop myself leaving my desk immediately, keys in hand. 'OK,' I said, suppressing joy and staying professional. 'I'll need some ID if I could. Hotel policy.'

The figure pressed a badge against the glass. A mugshot against white plastic; I was too far away to see it clearly, but even if I'd been able to it wouldn't have mattered.

What the guy said next drove the air from me.

'Gaines 4256. PC Donald Gaines, Police Scotland. There's been an accident up on the mountain road.'

10

My thoughts tumbled through glue.

I spluttered, managed to croak, 'Say again?'

'PC 4256 Gaines, ma'am. There's a situation I'm trying to deal with out here and I need some assistance—' He was speaking calmly but the hiss between my ears made concentration almost impossible. Words drifted through the crackle, the sound of the wind distorting his explanation. '—and I'm afraid the situation is complicated, ma'am, by the fact that we no longer have the whereabouts of our detainee. I need to come in.'

My heart shrunk as small and tight as a hockey ball. 'Detainee?' I managed.

'If I could come inside I can tell you everything you need to know. As things stand, the weather is making things problematic and I need to request backup, but I have no phone signal.' He leaned back from the intercom, his face unreadably dark. He raised both arms to shoulder height, palms out in a questioning shrug, then leaned in again. 'Also, ma'am, I'm in need of first aid. I sustained an injury when my vehicle collided. Open the door please.'

'I can't.' I tried to ignore my prickling skin and put some steel in my voice. 'What if you're not who you say you are?'

There was a silence. I watched the figure considering his options; saw the shape step back from the building – lighter on his feet than Gaines – and crane his neck to check the upper storeys, hands on hips. Then he leaned in to speak again. 'Ma'am, I'm putting my warrant card in the mail-slot here. It's just my card. Come and collect it, then check it. I'll stand where you can see me.' He looked up expectantly. I guess I was slow to respond because he hit the button again. 'I can't harm you from out here. Just check the warrant card.' He pointed.

We had a mailbox to the right of the doors. I had a key. It was a simple enough plan; I couldn't think how it might go wrong, so I stood and crossed to the doors with my hockey stick. I tried to look natural, strong, upright, but my hips seemed to be floating above someone else's legs. It took three goes to get the key into the lock and turn it, opening the chamber. There was nothing in the box except his card. The air inside was chill, like the decompression space between diving bell and ice-black water. I took the card. It was the size of a driving licence, the plastic cold to the touch.

I turned it over. It had been some years since I'd seen a police warrant card. There was a passport thumbnail of a slim-faced man with a high forehead, light hair and eyes a little too close together to be handsome. I looked through the glass. The man outside was standing in the centre of a churned circle of snow. The storm plucked at his coat so that he had to hold his hood back. The wind plastered his hair to his forehead, where a ragged gash had begun to scab over. An ugly bruise was colouring his temple and right eye. Very similar injuries to Gaines. Sustained in the same road accident, I guessed. I checked the card then looked again. It was an unsettling experience. The photo on the card was the kind of greyscale head-and-shoulders shot any decent printer could generate from a screen-mounted camera; the sort typical of temporary visitors' pics slipped into lanyards in every civic building the country over. Images like these, I realised, rendered any idiosyncrasies inert, as if the face was a landscape whose interesting edges had been rubbed smooth by snow.

Outside, the man shrugged a little self-consciously, a smile tugging one corner of his mouth. He said, 'It's me,' through a reassuring grin, then crossed to the intercom again. 'Cold out here, ma'am,' he said. His expectation of compliance was compelling; he simply waited to be obeyed, rubbing his gloved hands together then tucking them under his arms.

'One second, officer,' I said. 'I have to check something.' I turned and, without looking back, returned to the desk, placed the ID card on my keyboard and reached for the phone. Strange how context changes our opinion of someone. I wanted to speak to Jai. I dialled his room number, and when the door buzzed again, I ignored it. The phone rang three times and with each ring my heart dropped.

Then Jai picked up and I spoke through a rush of gratitude. 'You're OK. That's a relief. We thought you'd disappeared.'

'The basement started flooding,' Jai said. 'Wasn't going to ruin my trainers. Anyway, I got the radios working and figured I had a better chance of good reception up here.'

'Any joy?'

'No. Then I bumped into Gaines, and he told me to stay in my room.'

'When?'

'Are you OK?'

'Can you get him? He's one floor above you looking for a phone signal.'

'I know. He took one of the radios. Went up to try and raise help, maybe ten minutes ago. But he told me not to leave my room.'

'Could you go and check, please, Mr Parik?'

'Jai.' There was a pause, a sigh. 'OK. Hang on.'

I stared at the ID card and listened to indistinct sounds of movement. I heard Jai's door click shut behind him. I hit the intercom button and said, 'One moment, sir.' The officer outside said something but I returned my attention to the phone.

Jai came back out of breath. 'Can't find him. I'm out of shape,' he puffed. 'Bought a rowing machine on Black Friday but what do you know, haven't got round to using it. What's up? What's happening?'

I licked my lips. They were puckered and dry. 'There's a second stranger at reception.'

I could virtually hear Jai's thoughts. When he next spoke, the levity was gone. 'Who is it?'

'It's another officer. He's claiming to be PC Don Gaines.'

I listened to Jai breathe. 'You're kidding,' he said. 'I mean, you're kidding, right?'

'No.'

'You've let him in?'

'No. I need you to come down and help me decide.'

'Gaines? For real? Wait there, I'm on my way.'

As soon as I replaced the phone in its cradle, our visitor buzzed the intercom again. I picked up. 'Thanks for waiting,' I said in my hotel-voice. 'I just needed to check something.'

'I understand. But this is an urgent matter, ma'am. Googling me won't help.'

'I wasn't. Internet's down.'

There was a pause at this. Outside, a vortex of snow tunnelled upwards. 'I don't suppose you have a working phone?'

'The internal line works but our outside lines are dead. Sorry.'

I saw the guy rest his forehead against the frame of the revolving doors. 'Right,' he said. A squall of wind at the snow-bullied windows. He pulled his hood low, grounded his stance and braced against it. When it passed he hit the intercom again. 'I would like you to let me in.' I detected, beneath the surface of this patiently delivered request, the first signs of irritation.

'I'm just waiting for a . . . colleague.'

I heard the lift announce itself and the doors part. Jai padded into the lobby. His hair was down and he had his Yankees cap on. 'Where is he?' I nodded towards the door. 'Can I see him?'

I raised the ID and Jai crossed to take it. He studied it, then looked at the doors. 'Are you going to let him in?'

I found myself raking my thumbnail across the Midbow's grip, compulsively unpeeling it bit by bit, sticky glue smudged across my fingertips. I forced myself to stop, tried to think things through. 'I mean – should we? I don't think we have any choice. It's a man in a storm and it's sub-zero out there.'

'Yeah, but does he check out?'

Something flared. 'I don't know! Black coat and hood, black boots, looks something like his picture . . . what do you think? He could be anybody.'

'You mentioned a prisoner,' Jai said. 'It could be the prisoner.' I nodded and Jai added unnecessarily, 'What if he's dangerous?'

'Well,' I said, 'I've got this.'

'A hockey stick? Are you serious? Porterfell has hundreds of high-supervision inmates. Guys serving long sentences.' He thrust a finger in the direction of the door. 'Out there could be one of them. I thought the cop had insisted on going to the gunroom. You went to the gunroom, right?'

'I'm not licensed.'

Jai huffed in disbelief. 'Does it matter? We have to be able to defend ourselves. Surely you told him that. Did he offer you a weapon?'

I told him about the demonstration, about Gaines's insistence he only arm himself. 'He took the key as well,' I said, squirming inside. 'So that no one else can access the guns.'

Jai gazed towards the revolving doors. I watched his Adam's apple drop and climb as he swallowed. 'We'll have to go back and break in,' he said. 'You got some sort of crowbar? I could jemmy the door.'

Things felt like they were slipping out of control. 'It's high security,' I said. 'Solid. We can't just wander out there and knock it down.'

He gave me a look, mouth half open. 'Remie, it's your last night. And there's an escaped prisoner out there.'

'We don't know that for sure.'

'I don't like this.'

'I don't either, but we can't leave that man in this storm,' I said. 'Ever heard of confirmation bias?' Jai gave me a blank look. I found myself whispering, as if the officer outside might overhear. 'The tendency to inter- pret information in a way that confirms prior beliefs,' I told him. 'Telling your story first doesn't make it any more true.'

'I don't follow.'

'We know there aren't two officers,' I told Jai. 'So one of the strangers is someone else. Gaines seemed real enough, but what if the guy outside,' I said carefully, 'is for real?'

A vein pushed at Jai's temple. '*He's* Gaines?' he hissed, examining the doors, then turning to check the corridor behind him. The decorator's trolley sitting in the black space leading through to the silence of the garden room; the kitchens; the bar. I had a sudden memory of the first Gaines and me, switching all the lights off as we travelled the hotel. Trailing darkness behind us. 'And we've already let the wrong guy in?'

My skin was hot and my scalp tight. I nodded.

11

Jai ran a thumbnail up and down between his front teeth and stared at the floor, blinking. 'We should bring him in and lock him up,' he said. 'Question him.'

I felt a prickle of anger. 'Jesus, this night,' I hissed, then drew in a deep breath, flooding my lungs and trying to re-centre. 'If he's police, we could get in trouble,' I said, thinking of my flight, picturing a pair of uniforms frogmarching me back through the departure gates to the concourse.

'We have to protect ourselves,' Jai scoffed. 'All we've got is a hockey stick.'

I stared at my companion. His suggestion felt wrong and I wrestled with it, trying to pinpoint my concerns. 'What if the man outside is armed?'

'Well, then he's the cop,' Jai said, before scowling and adding, 'Unless he's stolen the gun and the uniform.'

The buzzer came again. We looked across the lobby at the man in the snow. He was mouthing something at us. Indecision didn't seem to be an option any more. I pressed the intercom button with trembling fingers. 'I'm coming over to let you in, sir. But I'm going to be putting you in the office.' I hefted my Midbow and turned to Jai. 'Please come over with me.'

Jai swallowed and nodded. We crossed the carpet. My pulse throbbed as I unlocked the doors. Once again a figure pushed its way into the revolving quarter-circles and emerged, blue-skinned and rimed in ice, into the dark warmth of the lobby. Our second visitor was a sandy-haired, bearded man, late-thirties but looking older. His figure was slimmer than the night's first visitor; slightly boyish, more my height and build. I took in a black storm jacket with button-down pockets, a thick stab vest, black trousers and police boots. He blinked grey eyes and pushed back his hood. The man had struck his head hard – or been struck, I noted – and his forehead was a puffy blue-black mess. Torn skin had bled and clotted, the skin around his eye and the bridge of his nose was already darkening. I held up the hockey stick.

He regarded the raised weapon expressionlessly. 'PC 4256 Gaines,' he said. 'You are?'

'We'll need you in the office for a short while,' I explained. My voice came out brittle. 'I'll leave you with a first aid kit and get you some food. But I'm afraid there's something we have to do before we can . . .' I couldn't find a diplomatic conclusion and let the sentence hang, indicating the room with the glowing desk lamp.

'I don't understand. I have to contact colleagues and alert them to a situation we've got here.'

'I need you in the office,' I repeated.

The man widened his stance. 'Ma'am. I'm a police officer. All due respect I have a job to do here.'

My pulse hummed as I wondered how to escalate. Thank God for Jai. 'Sir. Miss Yorke here is just taking necessary precautions. You're not our first visitor tonight. It shouldn't take long to establish what's going on. In the meantime, she's right – we have to be careful and safe. You'll just need to wait in the office.'

'And you are?'

'Jaival Parik, sir.'

'We'll be as quick as we can,' I said.

The man folded his arms and jutted his chin as he regarded us. I got a strong smell of meltwater and diesel; imagined a smashed vehicle hissing in the snow, its gutted engine steaming. We held our positions in a silent stand-off. Eventually he conceded. 'Have it your way.'

He unzipped his jacket as he walked, and began taking it off one shoulder, his back and neck taut with pain. I took in a white shirt tucked beneath a thick belt; no Don Gaines muffin-top here, this man was thin and muscular. Night-stick, empty shoulder-holster. Gaines One – the man I'd been thinking of as the real Don Gaines – had arrived without a weapon and told a story about its absence. Now we had a second officer in the same position.

I showed the man into the reception office, indicating the desk. He turned and sat, regarding us. The effect was of marked difference; the last man to sag into that chair, bleeding and grunting, had been a Don Gaines with fear pulsing off him in waves. This Gaines was lithe and neatly built, calm despite his injuries; possessed of a tight-jawed determination. 'You've had another visitor? What do you mean by that?'

'A man arrived nearly two hours ago now,' I said from the doorway. I watched his expression and added, 'A police officer.'

The man's bloody eyebrows knitted and he grimaced. He spoke quietly, calmly. 'And where is this man now?'

I stood at the door, my keys already hanging from the lock, wondering how much I should reveal. 'He left to search for a phone signal.'

The new visitor swallowed. Thin neck; protruding collar bones beneath his shirt and tie. 'Out in the storm?'

I shook my head. 'He's up on the third floor.'

'*Inside* the hotel?' He looked beyond me, evidently searching Jai's face for clues. 'What does he look like, this man?'

'A bit like you,' I said. 'But bigger build. Few inches taller. Older.'

'Did he show you his warrant card?'

I held my neutral expression as I thought back. Gaines had pressed it up against the window by the doors when he'd first arrived. I'd crossed to let him in. Had I checked the card close-up? *Sure I had.* Except I couldn't bring the picture to mind. Was it possible I'd forgotten? I cleared my throat. 'Of course he did.'

There may have been a fragility in my voice. The visitor arched an eyebrow then winced at the pain of it. 'Did you check it carefully?' I didn't know how to respond. He'd pressed something up against the glass. It might have been anything. The officer waited, pushing a pair of pills – from the same strip Don had used – through the foil of their blister pack. He grunted. 'Do you have some water?'

I nodded towards the coffee machine, where there was a cup left in the jug. The officer turned, poured, and popped his pills. I sifted options, hot hands slippery on the grip of the hockey stick. Should I be open and tell him everything or was it safer to selectively share? I swallowed painfully. 'He said he was PC Don Gaines of Police Scotland.'

The officer was sipping coffee. He stopped, looked up. His eyes flickered with something, but in the half-light it was difficult to tell what it was. 'That explains a lot.' His voice was uncompromising, direct and flat. He placed his mug on the table and rose. 'Listen. This man is dangerous. I need to find him. If you could let me get on with my job.'

'Wait,' I said, reaching for my keys. 'Just a few moments please. I'm going to lock you in.'

I watched him through the glass as I turned the key, his expression caught between frustration and outrage. *'Lock me in?'*

'I just need to talk things over . . .' I began.

'No, you need to listen to me,' he growled through the glass of the door. 'There is a man in this hotel. And he is a dangerous man. My job is to protect you but I can't do it from inside this office – don't back away, miss, this is important – neither of you know how much danger you could be in. But I know.' When he resumed, his voice tremored. 'Please. Do not leave the lobby. Take a moment by all means but stay close where I can look after you. OK?'

He pushed his blond fringe back with a thin-fingered hand and his shirt sleeve climbed, revealing an indistinct tattoo in the hair of his left forearm. These were the binaries I'd be trading in, I thought. Tattoo/no tattoo. Warrant card/no warrant card. The thought drew a line of sweat down the small of my back.

I nodded. 'OK,' I said to him.

We retreated to the desk at reception and Jai perched against it. I pulled up the chair and we waited in the glow of the office light. We'd just taken a prisoner. Jai dug the hand-held radio from his pocket, twisted it on, and I watched, picking at the grip-tape of my hockey stick as he studied the dials, his serious face uplit. Over his shoulders, across the lobby, the revolving doors were locked shut. Ezra threw an armful of chipped snow against the panes.

'Anything on the radio?'

Jai shook his head, tipped his cap back so the brim stood up. 'It's working,' he sighed. 'But we're not going to be able to get a decent signal. It depends on where the transmission tower is, I guess. Aberdeen? I don't know.' Jai twisted a dial and showed me the readout. A channel-number appeared on a small yellow screen. There was an icon – one arrow above the other, each pointing in opposite directions, the universal symbol of two-way communication. 'See? But whether anyone can hear us is another matter.' He pressed the shoulder button. 'Hello. Is anyone receiving? Can you hear me?'

We waited, listening to silence. Jai tried again. 'Hello? Anybody? We're at the Mackinnon Hotel. We need assistance.'

We stared at each other, waiting. Jai placed the radio on the desk. 'I've been trying on-and-off since I got it working,' he said. 'But nothing so far. I gave the other one to the cop. The first cop.' He bit his thumbnail. 'Wish I hadn't now.'

Did that mean the first Gaines could hear us calling for help? There was nothing we could do, but the thought chilled me all the same. 'What about other channels?'

'Been scrolling through them, seeing what I can get. It's a dead-end at the moment. Our only hope is that the storm clears a little and we pick something up.' Jai looked out into the night. 'Doesn't look like it's going anywhere yet. I don't like this. So what do we do with the guy in the office?'

I drew in a long breath. 'While you were gone,' I said, 'Gaines told me more about what happened up on the road.' I splayed my fingers against my thighs and stared at my hands in the half-dark. 'He told this story of transporting a prisoner, but the vehicles losing control and crashing. He woke up in his car.' Jai listened, his face in shadow. I'm not entirely sure he was frightened; fear was something that lived at the edges of the eyes and in the shape of the mouth and he wasn't transmitting those signals. I was getting anger, frustration – not so much fear. I didn't have time to wonder, though. I carried on. 'He wouldn't tell me who the missing prisoner was but he said he was dangerous. He

MARTIN GRIFFIN

warned me against letting anyone in. Our new visitor –
well, he's unarmed as well.'

Jai nodded. 'First impressions, he strikes me as genuine. Can I see his ID again?'

I hooked the card out of my back left pocket and placed
it on the reception desk between us. Jai stared at it.

'You think it's fake?' I asked him.

And as he examined it, a memory surfaced.

~

I'd seen my fair share of dubious IDs before; another
consequence of Cameron's life choices. In the years
following his fateful sixteenth birthday night, he began
moving freely through Newcastle's shadier bars and
clubs and, back home from Edinburgh each weekend,
I'd often get summoned to collect him from some dive
in Benwell or Scotswood. One night in particular stands
out in my memory: the night he had the camera. After
I'd broken his hand, Danny Franks had drifted to the
edges of my brother's circle and his absence had meant
a job vacancy; one Cam had stepped up to fill. It meant
my brother was earning good money and spending it
freely. It was a Saturday, late enough that I'd had a few
glasses of wine and been forced to sober up on toast
and black coffee before taking my battered Volvo out
to fetch him.

Cameron had been drinking at an estate pub, a fifties building with ugly white concrete cladding and
rotting woodwork. The windows were fogged with

condensation from the body heat, and the cracked tarmac was sprouting weeds. Out front was an abandoned flower bed and a disintegrating picnic table. The door was around the side.

I leant against the wall, avoiding the gaze of the doorman, an imposing guy with a vast belly and Motörhead tattoos, and waited.

It must have been half ten when Cameron emerged. He was high, drunk, or both. He had a broad-brimmed trucker cap on, a pair of Nikes and an Armani t-shirt festooned with gold studs. And he had this camera around his neck; a digital SLR. He'd evidently been amusing himself with it inside and emerged, wobbling, to take a picture of the doorman. The man obviously knew him – jokes were exchanged and Cameron got a friendly cuff around the ear before swaying towards me. I was next in line for the treatment. The flash stunned me. Those first harshly lit shots must have captured me wide-eyed and disarmed against the whitewashed wall of the building. He took many more as I led him to the car, and by the time I got him to the passenger seat he was laughing uproariously as he reviewed the night's pictures.

'It's mine,' he said when I quizzed him about the camera.

'Come off it, Cam,' I said, driving him back through the city centre. 'They cost a lot of money, those things.'

He responded by taking pictures of me until I threatened to make him walk the rest of the way home.

'What's going on?' I asked him.

Cameron grinned. 'Mum kept going on about college. Then it was about getting a job. You know what she can be like. Now I've got myself some money, she's not happy either.'

'Maybe you should be saving some,' I said, one of many futile attempts to persuade him to manage his cashflow. 'You could move out, get some independence.'

'I don't need the hassle.'

'But the phones, the watch, now the camera. Where are you getting the gear from?'

'A mate.'

'It'll all be stolen,' I told him.

He responded with mock astonishment. 'Jesus, you think?'

I blushed furiously as I drove, not knowing what to do or say. Part of me was angry at the injustice of it – I had a job, rent and responsibilities and yet I was the one in the battered car and the supermarket shoes. 'What do you even need it for?' I asked, petulant.

'Picture IDs.' He dug in his jeans pocket and fanned a hand of cards. 'Gym membership,' he grinned. 'Casino. Snooker club. College ID for bars and tattoo parlours.'

'You could get a college ID by actually going to college,' I put in.

'Fuck's sake, don't start that again.'

'But you're bright, Cam,' I said, hating the nagging tone I defaulted to every time I began a talk like this. 'You'd do well. And you'd enjoy it.'

'Just *stop*.' He sighed, stared out at the night as I drove. 'You have your life,' he resumed, 'I have mine. I've got work, I've got money. What's your problem? That I didn't get it the right way? The Remie way?'

I squirmed in the intervening silence, feeling guilty. I'd studied papers about mental rejection – disavowal, they called it; denial to avoid trauma. That night, driving my brother home, I realised that was me. He was never going back to school. If I was going to help him, I'd have to modify my approach. When we pulled up at some lights I asked for the cards and he handed them over. They were professionally finished, all with neat head-and-shoulders shots of my brother. Unbelievable.

'People only ever glance at them,' Cam told me, taking them back. 'Everyone's so trusting, you know?'

'One day,' I said, 'you're going to get caught.'

He laughed and said, 'Probably.'

~

Jai passed me back the card, shrugging. 'Looks to me like the guy in the office but might not be. What did the other guy's ID look like?'

'Gaines?' I steadied myself. 'I don't think I checked it.'

Jai looked up at that. Another gritty flash of hail peppered the glass. He smiled incredulously and said, 'What? You didn't check?'

'He held it up to the window,' I said, flushing. 'It looked OK. But I didn't check it up-close. I didn't realise what we were getting into, did I?'

We lapsed into silence. Jai studied the card one last time, handed it back to me, and fell to rotating the first aid kit slowly with his index finger. 'And this first guy. He's somewhere upstairs with a radio,' he said. 'What did you think of him?'

I mentally ran through everything I'd seen of the first Don Gaines. I'd got to know plenty of police officers through Cameron, and Gaines seemed like he fitted the mould. That plodding, methodical exhaustion struck the right chord for me. 'I think he's probably genuine,' I said. 'A decent man. You?'

Jai thought. 'I have a harder time trusting cops. Used to live near Neasden Temple when I was a kid – this would be the early nineties – and coming back from prayers, me and my brothers used to get all sorts of grief from one copper in particular. Big beefy guy with a red face and a beard, they used to stick him on traffic outside the school on the Brentfield Road. He'd pick on us. Snide remarks and such.'

'That's awful. Sorry to hear it.'

Jai shrugged. 'Sometimes I wonder if we deserved it. Maybe we cheeked him, I don't remember.'

I looked back towards the office light. Our new visitor was different from Gaines, that was for sure. Younger, an awful lot fitter and stronger, seemed quicker-thinking, more professional. This second visitor was driven, expected compliance. Where Gaines had peaked and his career was drifting, this man was still climbing. Yet there were only maybe ten years between them. 'The problem is,' I said, 'I know Gaines better. The first one, I mean.'

Jai ran a hand across his neck and tugged at his beard.

'So we should get to know this new one. There might be questions we could ask him.'

'Got any in mind?'

Jai exhaled, shook his head. I stood up. The officer was up at the glass wall of the office, leaning against the door frame. He'd poured himself more coffee and was cradling the mug in the palm of a hand. His breath, warmed by the drink, clouded the glass as he raised his voice. 'I know what your little conference is about,' he said, and waited until we'd approached before resuming.

I wasn't ready for what came next. His voice was muffled slightly by the glass so that, for a second, his words came dream-like, so unexpected as to be unreal, then as sharp as a sudden slap.

'This is about Troy Foley,' he said, eyeing us both in turn.

I felt my jaw drop, found myself blinking, my thoughts broken.

12

'Excuse me?' Jai asked.

'You're worried I'm Foley – which I'm clearly not, by the way; you have my ID – or that the guy upstairs is Foley.'

I must have managed a 'What?' because the man in the office repeated himself.

I heard the words again, this time more slowly, detecting a flicker of doubt in the officer's eyes as he spoke. 'Troy Foley, the escaped prisoner,' he said. 'We were meant to be transporting him to Glenochil.' He waited. 'I'm sorry, I must be confusing you.' He cupped his coffee, steam rising over bloody, knitted eyebrows. 'I would have expected any visiting officer to have appraised you of the situation.'

'He did. A little.' I felt like I'd been punched. I blinked my vision clear, struggling with the revelation. 'You're saying Troy Foley was at Porterfell.'

The officer behind the glass nodded. 'They were meant to be holding him temporarily after he kicked off at Barlinnie. But he's ended up doing a year there, and now he's repeated the trick – involved in a brawl last week and then another one as we transferred him this afternoon. You know of him then.'

'I followed the story like everyone else,' I said, dry-throated, feeling Jai's gaze on me.

'Smuggler, gang leader, gunrunner,' the officer said. 'Now listen. I want to be crystal clear on this, OK?' He waited until he had a silent nod from both of us. 'Those things you've seen in the papers, those descriptions of him – they're true. All that charisma, that man-of-the-people stuff? True. Foley makes my blood run cold, but when I've interacted with him, he's been charm itself. It took us so long to get him, partly because he's so unlikely, so convincing. He wriggles free, implicates others. He can talk. He puts on a good show, he's got connections, and he's got expensive lawyers.' The man sighed. 'I'm sorry to be telling you all this.'

'Gaines didn't mention a name.'

The officer raised a finger at that and spoke sternly. 'Go back a bit. You mean *Foley* didn't. He introduced himself as Gaines, but that's me. He showed you something you took to be police ID, a classic trick of his. Bet there was some sort of diversion as the card came out. He'll have been showing you something else. Probably did it quickly and from a distance. He wants you to be thinking of him as Gaines; he'll be counting on the advantage that arriving first has given him. I can see now why you've taken the action you have.' He nodded decisively to us both. 'And I can see I'm going to have to work hard to win your trust. Listen, I'm going to make things easier for you.' He withdrew his baton from its beltloop and placed it gently down on my desk next to the painkillers, his exaggerated gestures almost theatrical. 'I'll leave my truncheon here,' he said, taking a step back, holding an arm out, directing our attention. Then he raised the edge of his jacket to reveal an empty holster. 'No gun. I tried taking a short cut through the woods on the way down. Big mistake. The snow's unstable up there, ended up falling. Lost my way and lost my Glock.' He left his coffee on the table beside his baton and returned to us, his hands clasped loosely behind his back in a pose I'd seen adopted by officers lining parade routes. His greyeyed gaze was placid, though pain tugged at the edges of his mouth. He ran his tongue along his teeth and continued. 'You have my warrant card, I'm unarmed. I can't do anything else except emphasise the urgency of the situation. As manipulative as Troy Foley is, we need to remember he's a dangerous man with a track record of violence.' He brought an open hand, fingers fanned, up over his smashed forehead. The torn skin above his left eyebrow oozed black blood. 'My injuries meant I was off the pace when I recovered consciousness. I had to check the crash site and I lost further time after my fall in the woods. I'm sorry you've had to co-operate with an impostor for so long alone, it must have been confusing and stressful. But I'm here now and we need to work together. You have to trust me.'

His skin paled and he leaned against the door frame, face slewing close to the glass. Beads of sweat clung to his eyebrows, pink with blood. An officer with a significant head injury was battling concussion to persuade us to free him. I dug into my pockets for my keys, then stopped. 'One second,' I said to the man in the office, then took Jai's right arm above the elbow and pulled him away into the dark. 'He seems like the real thing to me. But Gaines seemed the real thing too. They can't both be.'

Jai's face was clouded. 'I like the guy. He just put his stick on the table,' he said. 'Whereas the first thing the other cop did was arm himself. I trust this one way more.'

I thought about Gaines and an idea slotted into place. *The first police officer's odd half-demonstration of the rifles.* I described it to Jai. 'He was warning me,' I explained. 'Trying to help me. An escapee wouldn't have done that. The first man can't be Foley.'

'But he took your keys, remember, and left you with nothing but a hockey stick. He got you where he wanted you. Just the sort of manipulation this second cop has been describing.'

'No, I think he was showing me how to use the rifles just in case.'

'What, so this second guy is bogus?' Jai exhaled upwards, arching his back and scanning the ceiling. 'Better for the first cop to arm himself under the guise of protecting us all, then confiscate the keys, don't you think? The new cop said Foley was persuasive.'

'Old cop new cop,' I said, sighing in frustration. 'It'll be easier if we just call them One and Two.'

My companion adjusted his cap, rubbed at his beard. 'Right. So is there any other way we could confirm this guy's identity?' He nodded towards our makeshift cell. 'Gaines Two, I mean. What about station codes? Individual police stations have codes, I think.'

Back at the office window, Gaines Two was waiting wearily. The baton was still on the table behind him. He raised his head as we stepped into his pool of light. His face was a map of contrasts, raised and bruised black around the eyebrows and nose, pale along the jaw and around the lips. He was gritting his teeth. 'Your CCTV system is not fit for purpose,' he said.

'It's due an upgrade.'

'It needs more than an upgrade. There's only six cameras and four are outside. Three of which are full of snow. It's not going to help us track down our escapee. Time is running out.' He looked at us both more coldly now. 'I don't want to have to charge you for obstructing an investigation.'

'We're not obstructing anything,' I said. 'We're being careful.' He scowled at this, turned for the table and picked up his coffee, muttering something indistinct to himself. 'I have a question for you,' I pressed. 'What station are you based at – and what's the station code?'

The officer raised a bloodied eyebrow. 'Seriously, ma'am?' He waited, and when I didn't speak, 'Inverness. Four-digit code but I don't remember it.' There was no sign of shame or embarrassment. 'Officers don't remember station codes. I've relocated from Bradford. Only been with Police Scotland for a couple of weeks.

And ...' he touched the tip of a finger to the edge of his wound '... I've just been involved in a vehicle collision. I'm concussed. You don't need a lecture about head wounds, concussion and memory, I'm guessing?' He licked his lips. 'Listen. I can't condone what you're doing – it's a big mistake. But I understand your predicament. I'm asking you, at least make yourselves safe. You should be locked in your room, ma'am. And you, sir. Please don't take it upon yourselves to track down this other man or involve yourself in any way.' He leant forwards. 'First and foremost, I need to protect members of the public. Are there any other guests?'

'One more. She's called Alex Coben, but she's not in her room and we don't know where she is.'

Gaines gave a frustrated sigh. 'OK. So we need to establish the whereabouts of this Alex Coben. Which was her room?' I told him, explaining I'd already checked it. He took this in with a nod. 'So she's out walking, I guess. Could be trapped by the weather somewhere. This just gets better and better. No one else we need to look out for? Site staff?'

'Hunting season finished on Friday. They all left this afternoon. Jai's due to check out tomorrow.'

'Mr Parik is a guest? You introduced him as a colleague,' Gaines Two said, before relenting. 'Understandable. You needed a second opinion. OK. So describe what your first visitor did. Exactly, in detail.' He watched me closely, gaze intense.

Under the spotlight of the officer's attention, my

previous actions seemed comically naive. I flushed. 'We checked the safety of the site. He wanted to visit the gunroom. He asked Jai to get the radios working.'

The officer drew his head back. 'Gunroom? He armed himself?'

'I thought he was a regular police officer. He arrived without a weapon. Said he'd lost it in the accident.'

Gaines Two interleaved his fingers, staring at the floor. I watched the rise and fall of his shoulders. A vein pushed at the base of his neck. When he spoke next, he was anxious. 'I don't like this. I can't protect you if I'm not armed. Where's the gunroom?'

I described its location, and told him about Gaines One – *was I to think of him as Foley now?* – and what he did with the keys. 'He took them,' I said, wincing at how foolish it sounded. 'Made me take them off the loop and hand them over.'

The officer cursed. 'So he's got sole access to the weapons? This just keeps getting better.' A sigh. 'Listen, I wouldn't be doing my duty if I didn't labour the point. Troy Foley is a dangerous criminal. If you can get yourselves to a place of safety, just until the storm passes, I'll take it from here. Lock yourselves in your rooms. When I'm certain you're both safely out of the picture, I'll track down our visitor. I can handle this.'

It sounded a plausible plan and an easy way out. The temptation to hand over the whole mess was strong. 'Give us a minute,' I said. The officer began to protest but I spoke over him. 'We'll be back shortly.'

He sighed. 'Seems ridiculous I'm having to bargain

my way out of custody. Our runner's been at liberty for nearly three hours now. Time is *of the essence*.'

I nodded my understanding and we retreated to the reception desk for one final conference.

Outside snow swirled like a fluid cage.

13

'Let's run through this,' I said, pacing. 'One and Two both arrive without weapons, but with different stories. One immediately arms himself. And Two wants to do the same.'

Jai rolled his lower lip. 'Let's look at it another way. Troy Foley's a prisoner. He breaks out of the transport when the vehicle crashes. He wouldn't have a weapon at all, he'd need to steal one. Maybe something went wrong. Maybe the story of the fall in the woods is true.'

'OK,' I said. 'What about appearance? They both look like police officers to me. One of them must be dressed in uniform with a stolen ID. That kind of stuff might be in the boot of the squad car, I guess.'

'What about the time of arrival?' Jai asked, examining the radio again. 'Gaines One arrives first, obviously. Is the driver of a police escort likely to sustain smaller injuries, to recover more quickly and get down here faster?'

'It could take longer to escape if you're handcuffed to the inside of a prison van. Which suggests Gaines One is real and the man in the office is Foley.'

'No. This guy had a story about checking on colleagues, radioing for help; it sounded legit. Unless he was hanging back on purpose.'

'I don't follow.'

'I'm asking if there's any advantage to arriving second? Some reason Gaines Two might have waited to make his appearance?'

I sighed. 'None as far as I can see. Whoever comes first has the chance to lay out their story, and that becomes the truth the second visitor must challenge. Anchoring bias, it's called. We rely heavily on the first pieces of information we're given on a subject and people fail to adjust as new information arrives.'

Jai examined me silently, eyebrows raised. 'You sound like you paid attention at school.'

'Psychology used to be my thing.' I sat, rotating the reception chair in back-and-forth arcs, stretching my thighs. 'Warrant cards? They both have them.'

'But only one is genuine. That means Gaines One is really Foley, right? He hasn't got a proper ID; he holds something up, hoping you won't check.' Jai pointed back at the office, 'But Two has his own card with him.'

I considered this. 'Lights?' I offered. 'One wanted them all switched off.'

'Right. Because he didn't want the cops following him down here? Or because he's scared Foley is pursuing him. Plays both ways.'

'What about priorities?' I tried. 'One wants to contact colleagues . . .'

'And Two wants us in our rooms so he can track

down the first visitor. Should he be wanting to contact his squad?'

'Has Gaines Two got a phone?' I wondered, thinking about prisoners' personal possessions being boxed up and stored for the day of release. But most prisoners used smuggled-in phones, especially those involved in organised crime. 'Gaines One had one,' I said. 'We swapped numbers.' Then a counter-thought landed like a blow. One's phone had been new; just the kind of thing you'd acquire if you were using multiple burners. Despondently, I relayed this to Jai.

'Did you get a look at the screen?' he pressed. 'Wallpaper? Family pictures?' I shook my head and he hissed a sigh through clenched teeth. 'Not enough to prove anything, though, is it?'

I rubbed my eyes, stared out into the night. 'What about uniform? Anything to differentiate the two?'

'Black cop-stuff for both.' Jai shrugged.

'OK, let's examine the behaviour. Gaines One was clear and decisive. He asked after radios and telephones. He wanted the lights extinguished and the site secured.'

'But we don't know enough about this second guy to compare. To me though, Two seems more ... real. Tougher and fitter.'

'Prisoners can look that way too,' I pointed out, remembering my regular visits to Porterfell. 'Nothing to do inside but train.' We listened to the wind. I might have been guilty of hoping, but it sounded as if it was weakening a little. 'We can't wait forever,' I said eventually. 'Whichever way we cut it, one of them's dangerous.'

Jai wiped his mouth with the back of his hand. 'I say we let our prisoner go and the two of them can fight it out,' he said. 'We should go to our rooms, safe and sound like he suggests. I mean, I don't know about you but I've got a family to think of.' He looked at me casually, took a breath. 'You'll be the same, I guess.'

I felt a flare. There it was again, a reminder of this man's peculiarities. He couldn't keep the questions from surfacing. I spun my chair again, watched the storm. 'No,' I said, dispassionately. 'On the move a lot.'

'Ah. The hotel people send you all over?'

'That kind of thing,' I lied. Jai rolled his lower lip between his teeth and gave me a look I couldn't read in the dark. 'We can't talk this over forever,' I said, getting up.

'So we let Gaines Two out, right? Send him off into the dark, hope he and Gaines One cancel each other out,' Jai said.

I still wasn't sure. There were so few pieces of concrete information at our disposal, and what certainties we had seemed insubstantial, slippery, impossible to piece together. One thing was certain: if we took a wrong step, we'd be dead.

We crossed to the office. I unlocked the door, opened it wide and stood back for the officer. He was assessing the site plan. 'This the gunroom here, right? Above the guest garage.'

I nodded. The officer stayed at the threshold for a second, assessing us both. 'So,' he said, opening his arms, hands palms up, 'Foley's dangerous and I have to track him down. I need to arm myself.' I tried to think but couldn't find a way through a tangle of competing possibilities. Gaines Two broke the silence. 'I'm going to need my truncheon, at least.'

'You said you want us in our rooms. That sounds like the best way to do things. I appreciate this,' I said.

'No problem. I'll escort you. You mentioned Foley had headed upwards to look for a phone signal. When exactly was that?' He checked his watch. 'It's nearly ten o'clock now.'

Nearly ten? Time had drifted, become elastic. Gaines One had been gone over an hour. That was too long, surely. 'It's been a while,' I conceded.

The officer frowned as he assessed the corridor that took us to the lifts. 'We keep it dark,' he said. 'Take torches. I don't want him knowing where any of us are.' He turned, slipped the truncheon into its buckle. 'Did you give him access to any rooms with his own key?'

I faltered. 'No. I think – no. I showed him into some rooms but I kept the key card.'

'So he's not hiding behind any locked doors.' Gaines shared his gaze between us. 'We stick together. Don't go wandering off. Mr Parik, we'll drop you first.'

'Second floor,' Jai said, his voice dry.

The officer nodded. 'I'll go in front,' he said. 'Follow close behind, stay alert.'

Gaines was all caution, knees bent and baton up. I held the torch, throwing light in broken stripes ahead of him. We passed the paint trolley and climbed the stairs, our visitor craning his neck to check the landing above before we crept upwards. The stairs, wide and curved with a deep-green carpet and gold-edged runner, split into two beneath two heavy-framed Victorian portraits, then doubled back on themselves. We climbed again, pausing at the top to assess the landing and the corridors either side. I kept the torch beam low, a pale pool around our ankles. Jai's corridor ended in a bay with a window seat, an antique tallboy and a couple of leather recliners. My torch turned the panes into opaque steel-grey sheets as I picked out the cushions and polished wood.

Gaines turned to assess the way we'd come, and Jai swiped his card. Opened his room. 'Where do I find you if I need to?' he whispered.

I indicated the service stairs but Gaines said, 'You won't need to leave your room, Mr Parik. Sit tight until I come and let you know we're safe.'

Climbing up to the staff rooms was unnerving. The torch threw light on the steepness of the service stairs. The space was austere and unadorned. Movement was limited here; I followed Gaines, eyes on the heels of his boots as he climbed. On the third floor, the wallpaper was charcoal floral swirls and I moved unsteadily forward through its grey jungle towards my room at the end. I slowed, my heart thumping high in my throat. 'I'm at the end there,' I said.

Gaines raised a palm to halt me.

Halfway along the corridor, there was a handprint on the paper, shoulder height, smudged. It appeared black in the light of our torches but I knew we were looking at blood. The carpet seethed liquid at our tread. I directed the torch at our feet. We were standing in a pool. I retreated a step, raised a boot off the carpet and held it there. We watched as it dripped.

'Water on the carpet,' Gaines Two said, 'blood on the wall.'

We examined the handprint. Wide splayed fingers blurring downwards, as if a wounded someone had held themselves up. Or been pulled off their feet. I felt an invisible finger draw an icy line up the knuckles of my spine and swung round, my skin crawling. The corridor was empty. I chided myself – *breathe, Remie* – and returned my gaze to the wall. The print looked like it was the right size and shape to be Gaines's hand. Gaines One, I corrected. I checked the pool on the floor and then, instinctively, panned up to the ceiling. Maybe another pipe had burst.

'Where's the water coming from?' I asked, keeping my voice low.

We huddled in the dark, listening. No dripping; no leaks. Just the bluster of the wind at the windows. Things were calming down a little out there. I'd noticed it in the lobby and up here it was evident too. Perhaps Ezra was at last blowing itself out. 'Meltwater?' I offered. 'If he came inside covered in snow.'

'We passed a door without a room number,' the officer whispered. 'Just there.'

We pivoted, our boots squelching on the wet carpet. 'Roof access,' I said.

Gaines nodded. 'He went up there and came back down, bringing snow in with him. What's he up to?'

'He's got one of the hotel's radios. He's trying to get a signal,' I said. 'Call his colleagues.'

Gaines gave a sneer. 'Colleagues?' he said. 'He needs someone to get him off the mountain. God knows who we'll have heading our way if he makes contact.'

Gaines Two eyed the roof-access door, crept closer and examined its push-down bar. In the light of my torch I could see a blur of blood on the metal. It looked like Gaines One had tried the roof, returned and pulled the door closed. The blood suggested an injury while he was up there, not in the corridor below. He'd come back inside and closed it himself rather than pushing the door shut and waiting outside on the roof space to ambush us.

The police officer stretched his fingers, took a breath. Then he pushed the bar down, using the edges to keep his hands clean. The door opened a crack. No wind. He shouldered it further. I could hear pillows of snow crumple behind the metal as he pushed. The force required suggested Gaines One hadn't been here recently. *How long had he been gone now? Ninety minutes?* Icy air and drifts of snow-mist in the torch beams; the foot of a stairwell. The second Gaines stepped out into the cold and climbed a steel staircase. It was quiet enough to hear the metal ring beneath his boots. The wind had calmed. I followed him up, arriving at a fenced gantry giving access to the flat roof between the steep tiled areas beyond. The snow was ankle-deep at the top and churned up. Someone had been here. I watched fat flakes fall through the night air, landing and blurring the edges of the previous disturbances, and judged the markings to be recent.

Gaines Two panned a torch across the jumble of angled roofs. 'Help me get a sense of the site,' he said, one hand over his eyes to keep the flakes off his lashes. He didn't need to raise his voice. The wind had dropped sufficiently to hear the noise of nesting crows in the wood, their harsh cries echoing.

I pointed up the hill into the fog, picking out the to-and-fro lines of the hotel drive, a crossways thread through massed black pines. 'You came down through the woods there. Main road across the mountain is a mile beyond the rise, and Porterfell that way. Above the treeline here, the peak of Farigaig.' The sound of my voice was a surprise in the still blackness. I turned left and pointed across the spine of the old roof. 'You can't see it, but the car park and reception are down there. Below us are the terraced gardens, tennis courts, then the loch's edge,' I explained. 'The grounds extend a mile along the shore to the perimeter fence.'

Gaines was about to say something when we heard the trees. He turned away from the frozen water and narrowed his eyes, assessing the wooded foothills. 'What was that?'

A dull moan – weirdly animal. Then another. Between the cawing of crows, the trees seemed to be groaning.

'I don't know,' I said, standing next to him. Side by side we were the same height, Farigaig tower-ing above us.

'It doesn't sound good.'

We waited. For a while, nothing. Then it came again; a shifting creak. I looked up through the steep pines, trying to establish the source, but it reverberated and scattered. A crack and a sudden pop threw echoes, then nothing but birds again.

The officer ran his fingers over pursed lips. 'The hill from the road is steep. Lots of snow.'

That was true enough. I'd explored the grounds plenty since I'd moved in, and the wooded section between the hotel and the mountain road was challenging terrain. The drive needed a series of switchbacks to allow vehicles to descend safely. Hikers and ramblers tended to follow the water's edge rather than head up; the woods up there were a tangle of precariously perched cedar and pine, vast boulders and cliff edges formed by exposed rock. 'It's a climb rather than a walk,' I said. 'The snow doesn't sound too stable.'

'Ever heard it moan like that before?'

Pointing my torch towards the woods, I shook my head. My beam fragmented twenty feet from us at the edge of the roof, illuminating nothing but falling flakes. Inside I was scratchy and brittle; my heartbeat skittish. The woods groaned again. Out in the dark, moving snow tore and echoed.

'Let's get you safely to your room,' Gaines said.

Back inside at my door, I turned. 'I'll be OK now, officer. Thanks.'

He shook his head. 'Not quite yet, miss. I need to check your room is clear.'

MARTIN GRIFFIN

A flush of embarrassment again. My single bed, my suitcases. I unlocked and opened the door wide. He took a cautious step inside and I followed.

'That balcony door locked?'

'It is.'

He cast his eyes across my bed, my suitcases. 'What's this?'

'All packed,' I said, checking my watch. 'I leave in nine hours.'

Gaines Two retreated into the corridor, checked the darkness again. 'From Aberdeen? Good luck with that.'

'The snow will clear,' I told him, determinedly.

He gave a distracted nod, attention already on the stairs. 'Stay safe, miss. And thanks for your help tonight.'

As I watched him go, I thought about the website of the avalanche service, the one that trapped the Mackinnon in a cage of red-topped pins, and tried not to think about what that might mean for my flights.

14

Alone in a locked room I paced, elevating my phone in every conceivable position, praying for a signal and fretting about the weather.

Sometime later I stopped, aware my senses had heightened. There was a noise at my window. I checked the glowing display of my bedside clock. 10.40 p.m. I crossed to the balcony, opened the door and the storm came bullying in, bringing a dusting of snow with it. Pulling my coat back on, I examined the hotel grounds from my vantage point, trying to establish the source of the sound. There was a figure on the terraced lawn beneath my room, looking up.

It was Gaines. The first Gaines.

Which meant that Troy Foley was standing beneath my balcony. He had a snowball in his right glove and his arm was raised and ready. The shooting rifle was in the snow between his boots. Gaines Two had said he'd try something – that he'd have some excuse to re-establish contact. This was it. 'Remie,' the man called, lowering his throwing arm and panning his torch upward.

I raised a hand as the beam dazzled. 'What's going on?'

'Can you speak? I have some questions.'

There was a fire escape running down from my balcony. If I refused, he could climb to me, though the knee injury would make it hard. I wondered if there was any conceivable advantage to feigning ignorance of his real identity. Perhaps there was. I descended carefully, pulling my gloves on as I went. Ezra, playing trickster, whirled and bumped at the old ironwork, shaking it in its rivets. My mind was churning. Foley was a man who gave the impression of co-operation, a consummate actor. On the final flight of steps I assessed the officer waiting in the snow in this new light; his awkward bulk, his trousers torn at the knee, the uneven lines of his tracks.

He waved, seemed to be smiling in relief as he raised his voice and said, 'I'm glad to see you again. I knew you were on the top floor but I lost my bearings. I've been flinging snow for the last five minutes. At the wrong windows, it turns out.'

I pulled my hood tighter. 'Where have you been?'

His expression, even contorted by a grimace, told me he'd noticed I was different. 'Are you OK? Has something happened?'

I was keeping my distance. I could tell it troubled him. 'We had a visitor,' I said.

Gaines's eyes widened. 'My detainee? Are you unharmed? Where is he now?'

I shook my head, spoke over the wind. 'Not as simple as that, Don. He's a police officer, or he says he is. And he introduced himself as you.'

That landed a blow that opened the officer's eyes further. 'What? How?'

'He's got an ID card.'

'That's my warrant card, Remie.' Gaines One stooped and collected his rifle then studied the storm, blinking, rubbing his injured forehead with the back of a glove. 'Must have taken it from me immediately after the accident as I was unconscious. He's got my gun too. Shit,' he spat.

I shook my head. 'No gun.'

'That can't be right.'

'Said he'd lost it on the way down from the crash site.'

'He stole my gun then lost it? I don't buy that. He's got it concealed somewhere.' Gaines One's jaw moved as he ground his teeth. He rotated his big body a full turn, examining the loch in the distance and cocking his head to listen to the trees as he returned his attention to me. 'Remie, I didn't want to tell you this but the situation is changing all the time and I have to level with you.' He beckoned. I took two reluctant steps forward and his face grew angry. 'Come on, Remie, I don't bite. You need to be careful with this man. Where is he now?'

'Looking for you. He told Jai and me to stay in our rooms.'

Gaines seemed flummoxed for a second. Then he adjusted. 'Maybe that's a good thing. Maybe I can recapture him.' He scanned the darkness again, twitchy. 'If he's told you to go to your rooms he knows where you are. I don't like that. Remie, this man is called Troy Foley.'

'I know,' I said, sparing him. 'He told us.'

Gaines One looked – or played – shocked once more. He was convincing. 'What, he admitted it?'

'No. He said you were Foley.'

'Jesus Christ. Don't. Believe. Him.' The wind had dropped so we could hear nesting crows conducting guttural conversations in the canopies above us. I wondered if this really was the beginning of the storm abating. 'Remie, I'm PC 4256 Don Gaines, Police Scotland. I have two kids called Emma and Joe. My wife is Jackie. We had Christmas together for the first time in three years and the kids loved it. I got aftershave, we watched the Queen's speech and played a crazy boardgame I didn't understand. I'm an ordinary guy, Remie. The impostor, he won't be able to tell you any of that stuff because until this afternoon he was behind bars in Porterfell.' He was checking the grounds as he spoke, eyes turning desperate. 'He's dangerous, Remie, and he'll tell you anything.' An idea struck him, and he straightened. 'I'm guessing he knows about the gunroom.'

Something about Gaines One felt awkward, as if he was trying a little too hard to be himself. 'Yes,' I said. 'He wanted a rifle.'

'Of course he did. I take it you didn't . . .'

I shook my head. 'He doesn't have the code to the electronic lock. And you're the one with the keys to the building.'

'Even so, he knows where to find you at the moment. That means you're in danger,' said Gaines One. 'What about the other guest. Coben. Has she turned up yet?'

'I'm afraid not.'

'I've been checking out the hotel grounds since I last saw you. No sign of her. I've had no luck with the radio either. But I did see a distant outbuilding along the shore of the loch.'

'The boathouse.'

'Right. It wasn't on the site map in your office.'

'No. It's a mile along the shore beyond the perimeter fence. I have a gate key.'

'And Foley doesn't know about it? Good. You and Mr Parik will be safe there if you need a place to hide. The route through the woods – is it passable?' That wasn't easy to answer. We'd shut it to the public a few weeks ago because of an unsafe bridge. Perhaps it would stand another crossing. In the end I nodded, brushing away the snow that had gathered in my eyebrows. 'Good. Has Mr Parik had any luck with the radio?' I told him no and he cursed. 'Well, there's no way you'll get a signal down at the boathouse; you'll need to stay high and keep trying. The weather feels as if it might be improving. Move Mr Parik out of his room and put him somewhere else. If you have any concerns or fears for your safety or his, any emergency at all, collect Mr Parik, take him to the boathouse and stay there.'

I tried to impose sense on the conflicting advice. Strung out and exhausted, I opted for the appearance of compliance. I'd do the hard thinking later. 'OK,' I nodded.

'Remie, one last thing – and this is very important – don't tell anyone you've seen me. My only advantage at the moment is that Foley doesn't know where I am or what I'm planning, so be careful you don't ...' Gaines One faltered, looked up at Farigaig, his eyes scanning the treetops. 'What was that?'

The same sound I'd heard on the roof was back again. How to describe it: a hollow and reverberating *clack*. As I listened I caught another sound, this one the irregular punctuation of a gentle *whumph* that made me think of towels tumbled down hotel laundry chutes.

Gaines One made a perplexed inspection of the pines, shoulders taut. 'What are we hearing, Remie?' he asked. Nothing but the dark whisper of snowfall, the rising moan of the wind. Then it came again, a tattoo of cracks and pops skittering through the upright trunks. We both went very still. 'When I was walking down,' he said, eyes on the trees, 'I tried cutting through the woods. It was too steep, I turned back. But there were huge cliffs of snow up there in the pines. Big shelves came away under my feet.' He blinked rapidly at the memory. The snow on his brow had softened the broken edges of his wound, and a line of blood, black in the low light, was snaking down his cheek. He brushed at it with the back of his hand. 'And we've still got another couple of hours of snowfall to come before the storm eases. The heavier the pack gets up there, the more likely it will split and fall. We've got trouble. Move quickly, Remie; put Parik in a different room. Keep trying your radio. If it all goes south, head for the boathouse, try to contact me. I'll come back for you.'

I wished him luck and he limped into the dark, rifle

cocked. I climbed the fire escape up to my room, my back aching, my feet numb and my head a mess of insecurities. I locked my door behind me and warmed myself at the electric fire, while I tried to make sense of what I knew. All I had was a tangle of competing problems and possibilities, none of which came with any evidence attached.

Mostly what occupied me was the ghostly groaning of the snow. I was thankful when the wind rose and blocked it out. Though I knew better than most that blocking something out doesn't make it go away.

15

I thought about my encounter with Gaines One, turning it over, examining it for inconsistencies. The family-at-Christmas story would've seemed the most normal of accounts. Now, in the light of new advice, I saw it for what it was; elaborately constructed artifice, expertly performed.

Unless it wasn't.

I paced, wondering about the advice Gaines One had given me out in the storm. Moving Parik to another room seemed watertight. But on the other hand it was guidance given by the man who'd been sure to establish exactly which guests were in which rooms; a man who now knew where to find me, since I'd emerged onto my balcony and descended the fire escape to meet him. I looked at my tawdry attic room, considering what that meant. Try as I might, I could see no disadvantage to moving Jai. I was psyching myself up for a torchlit trip to the guest floor below my room, when there was a knock on the door.

The sound made something in me leap and cower. I hovered at the electric fire. 'Hello?' I called, injecting as much confidence into my voice as I could.

'It's me.'

'Jai?'

'Yeah. Let me in.'

I crossed to the door. Jai was smiling and holding the radio up. 'We've got something. I heard a voice, Remie. Someone's out there.'

'My God.' Relief glowed beneath my ribs. We had a way out.

He nodded. 'Can't get her right now but I heard her a minute ago.'

'Did you ask for help?'

'Tried to,' he said. I closed the door behind him and we gathered by the fire. 'But she was coming in and out. I'm not sure she heard me. We need to find Gaines Two, tell him.'

'It's not that simple,' I said, and, when he looked at me quizzically, I described my recent encounter with the first Gaines. 'He told me not to tell anyone I'd seen him,' I finished.

Jai brooded. 'Well, he would say that.'

'But he sounded genuine. Told me about his wife and kids. Said Gaines Two had stolen his ID.'

'That's what I'd say too, if I was...' he faltered. 'Wait, he had you on your own, he was armed, and he didn't shoot. Doesn't that make him the real cop?'

'I thought that at first,' I said. 'But I've been thinking, surely I'm more useful to him alive. I know the hotel, the grounds, the route down to the boathouse. He needs me on side, at least for now.'

'What does that make me? A potential hostage?' Jai

crossed my room, heading for the balcony door. Once again I felt a disruptive tremor of concern. His eyes were all over my stuff. I wondered again whether Jai had his own agenda and how much I could trust him. I couldn't shake the feeling that even he, my supposed ally, wasn't telling the truth. I watched as he examined the darkness outside with his back to me, his shoulders hunched with anxiety. 'Where is he now?'

'He could be anywhere,' I said. 'Tell me about the radio. I want to hear the voice. Can I call?'

He turned and handed the receiver over with a frustrated sigh. 'Go ahead.'

I watched Jai pace and pressed the button. 'Hello. Can anybody hear me?' I waited, hope blossoming. 'Hello? Anybody? We need assistance. We're at the Mackinnon Hotel. We have a situation.'

The thing emitted a dull beep, then a volley of digital glitch. Nothing. I pressed the radio's shoulder button and repeated my plea. Then again. Fourth time, a voice, a spirit from the white-noise, spoke. I felt tears needle. A female voice, a real person. I couldn't make out the words.

'Hello?' I said. 'Can you hear me?'

'Is this the Mackinnon?' asked the voice.

'Yes!' Jai and I exchanged a grin. 'I can hear you,' I said. 'If you're near a phone, please call the police immediately. We urgently need assistance and our lines are down.' I depressed the button, waited.

'Thank God,' the voice said. It was only then I realised what a dry and desperate thing it sounded. The glow in me dimmed.

I repeated my plea. 'Can you please acknowledge our request?' I finished. 'We need to know assistance is on its way.'

'I need your help,' the voice said.

'No, we – sorry?' I faltered, twisted the volume knob to maximum and the voice came drifting up through interference like a diver through loch water. 'My vehicle was involved in a crash. Mountain road between Porterfell and the hotel. Need assistance.'

'Who is this?'

'Talbot. Serco prisoner transportation.'

I felt my scalp tighten. *'Prisoner transportation?'*

A fuzzy nothing, followed by, 'Correct. Crashed in the storm. I'm injured and I need help. Please send someone up.'

'I'm – we don't have any trained medical staff on site.'

The voice came back, tight and tired but smiling. 'You run the bar. Recognise your voice.'

The radio felt slick against my hot fingers. 'Who is this?'

I wasn't looking at Jai as the voice answered my question, but I imagined what was said might have tugged his eyebrows upwards. 'Shelley Talbot,' the woman on the radio responded. 'Used to be a guard at Porterfell. I'd drop by for a drink on Fridays.' I remembered her. She'd pull up on a noisy motorbike and we'd swap complaints about the weather or share inconsequential news. 'Met you at the prison a few times too, when I was an officer. You used to visit,' she added. 'You're Cameron Yorke's sister.'

I'd made the journey from the hotel to the prison

every other Saturday morning. There's a toughened glass window where you tip out your pockets and deposit your bag and purse then pass through a full-body scanner, where an officer meets you. Shelley Talbot had greeted me a number of times. A squat woman, cheerful with dyed-red hair. She'd escort me to an austere room of tables and chairs, battleship grey with a wall-mounted TV. Expressionless guards stood with their hands behind their backs, eyeing inmates talking in low voices to harried-looking loved ones. I'd take my seat and wait for Cam. A buzzer would indicate change-over. Cameron's rubber-soled plimsols would squeak on the polished floor as a guard led him in. We'd sit across from each other. When the session ended, and I'd watched him return through the double doors back to his cell, Shelley would show me out.

I pressed the radio-button. 'I remember you.'

Shelley laughed, a brief strangled sound. There was a pause before her voice resumed. When it did, she sounded winded. 'Christ, am I glad to have got through to someone I know. Who was that other guy?'

'We have a guest working on the radios. We've got a police officer here too. Gaines.'

'Gaines.' Another pause. 'I know him. Solid dude, Gaines.'

I let that sink in for a moment, then brought the radio close. 'Shelley, this is going to sound mad, but would you mind describing him?' This time the pause was so long I had to check she was still there. 'Shelley? Sorry to ask.'

'Not feeling great here,' she said, her voice shifting in the static. 'Need the cop's help. Yours too.'

'Shelley. Is there any way you can stay warm?'

Silence for almost a minute. Then, 'Still here. Trying to get out. Van fell driver's door down so I'm going to have to climb. Cab's flooding.'

'Please repeat. Flooding?'

'Pools of meltwater and mud,' she hissed. 'Going to have to try and move. There's a ...' the remainder of her words were reduced to a garble, then her voice vanished entirely.

As quickly as Shelley had emerged, she was gone again. I called her over and over, adjusting my position in the room. I opened my balcony door and risked stepping out into the night to try again. I got nothing. *Shelley Talbot.* She'd become a regular fixture in the hotel bar on a Friday, and as I thought about her, repeating her name into the emptiness of the static, she became more real. She always complained about the music at the hotel bar; *folksy shit*, she called it, with a good-natured curl of the lip. She had a soft spot for aged malt whisky and a disdain for *lager-drinking city-boys* – by which I think she meant men with office jobs in Inverness. She had a particular fondness for a photo above the bar, an old shot of a dozen or so staff members gathered formally along the jetty, the loch waters lapping the newly made wooden uprights. The water's surface is crowded with barnacle geese. I imagined it was taken in the '30s; the Mackinnon was a hunting lodge back then, so the chaps have rifles shouldered over woollen jackets; plus-fours, waistcoats and flat caps. She talked with infectious enthusiasm about her motorbike; she loved travel. I hadn't asked, but I'd been the recipient of Shelley's personal recollections of a trip to Easter Island when she'd clocked I was working the last fortnight of my notice period and heading to Chile.

Yes, Shelley Talbot loved to talk.

16

No response on the radio. I felt hot panic crystalise.

'This is serious. Jai, we need to help her,' I said, picking through and discarding a host of possible plans. I checked my watch. 11.15 p.m. 'It's maybe two miles up the drive and along the road to where she is.'

'Two miles is going to feel like forever,' he said. 'It's brutal out there. How are we going to get up to her? And once we do, how do we get her back?'

'We could pull her through the snow? I'm not sure. Look, the hotel's got a whole supply of outdoor clothing downstairs. If we kit ourselves up properly, we should be OK.'

'And Shelley could help us,' Jai added, piecing things together. 'She's a witness. She knows Gaines. She's got a hell of a story to tell, I'll bet. What have you guys got in the way of medical equipment? Splints? Bandages, morphine?'

I shook my head. 'Small stuff in the first aid kits. A couple of defibs in the cellar. Nothing major.'

Jai adjusted his Yankees cap, removing it, pushing back his hair, replacing it again. 'She asked for the cop.

Maybe we send Gaines – Gaines Two, I mean – up there; we could wait it out while he does the dangerous stuff.'

'But that leaves us down here,' I pointed out, 'alone with whoever Gaines One is.'

'And is that worse than fighting our way through a storm with whoever Gaines Two is?' Jai gnawed at his thumb. 'I don't know. We should go, I guess. This Shelley, she knows Gaines, right? She witnessed the accident. She could have seen things.'

It was good to hear Jai so supportive. The guarded part of me kept coming back to the voice memo in the bar. Had it really been in error? Or was Jai on the hunt for a story? I tried not to dwell on it. Shelley Talbot was in trouble and we were the only ones who could help her. 'What if we try driving?' I offered. A bit of practice on treacherous roads wouldn't go amiss; I'd be skidding down the mountain into Inverness tomorrow morning, after all. 'The hotel has a couple of SUVs out in the garage. Snow chains too.'

Jai examined me, then gave a confessional shrug. 'Listen. I'm not the best behind the wheel,' he said. 'Picked the hire car up at Edinburgh station the other day and I didn't know how to start the thing. Had to go back into the company's office and ask. It's only small but the dashboard looks like it belongs in a trans-atlantic jet.'

'Don't drive much?'

'I've got the Tube. I've got Uber.'

'Little different up here,' I said.

'Turns out it the engine doesn't start unless you've got the clutch pressed in. Who knew?'

A bleak thought occurred. 'Wait. Gaines One took my garage keys.'

Jai rubbed a thumb back and forth against his front teeth. 'Is there another way in?'

I shrugged. 'A window maybe.'

'Better than nothing. Maybe we can get Gaines Two to drive. We'll need to tell him what's occurred. He was on my floor a few minutes ago,' Jai said. 'I heard him knocking on doors, came out to see if there was anything I could do.'

'He was knocking on doors?' That threw me. I scrabbled for pieces again, trying in vain to build a picture. Was Gaines Two down there trying to establish where Alex Coben was? Or which exact room Jai was in?

'Yes, one by one,' Jai said. 'I think he's looking for the other guest. Alex Coben? He wants to figure out whether she's still in the hotel somewhere.'

'I'm pretty sure she went walking after breakfast,' I said. Problems felt as if they were tumbling over me, one atop the next. 'She hasn't come back.'

'That could be bad. She could be lost or frozen to death. Did she look like she knew how to handle herself?'

I shrugged. 'I think so. Pretty rugged, an outdoor type.'

Jai considered this. 'The weather closed in at – what, three or four this afternoon? If she knows what she's doing, she'll have taken shelter somewhere.'

Jai was probably right; Coben had looked like the kind of experienced hiker who could handle herself in difficult conditions. Those muscular arms and rock climber's hands. Mentioning her, I found myself recalling more of Alex. Snapshots of her that I'd forgotten about when Gaines One had asked. 'She was into her maps,' I said. 'I had a conversation with her about it.'

Alex had wondered if we had anything larger scale than the OS maps guests borrowed from reception. I'd had to ask Mitchell for help. Turned out that detailed maps could be requested from the OS but Alex hadn't been interested.

'I wanted to see all the pathways,' she'd told me. 'Public rights of way but other routes along the loch's edge and through the woods.' She had a very direct manner that I put down to her having English as a second language. I hadn't been able to place the accent. Polish, maybe?

'We have geological maps?' I'd offered.

'Not what I need,' she'd said abruptly.

'The map room gives a large-scale overview of the area,' I'd told her, and she'd spent some time photographing sections of it. The rights of way interested her, because afterwards she'd come back down in leggings and muddy trainers and, studying the shots she'd taken on her phone, gone to run the perimeter of the hotel grounds.

'Well, there you go,' Jai said as I told him. His tone was confident. 'She knows the surrounding area. I bet she's got as far as that pub up at the crossroads.'

'The Clachaig.' It was five miles towards Fort William and there were clearly waymarked routes up to it.

'That's the one. She'll be warming her feet at the fire up there.' Jai scowled and added, 'Lucky cow.'

I'd spent a lifetime wishing myself somebody else – someone with a less complicated family, a partner, a place to call my own; most of all, someone with a normal brother, a kid who'd become an ordinary decent man. But right then I was with Jai. I'd have given pretty much everything I had to swap places with Alex Coben if she was sipping red wine in the snug up at the Clachaig.

We locked up and moved carefully along the staff corridor, then took the service stairs down.

Gaines Two was indeed on Jai's floor. Having made his way along to the end, he was standing at the leather chairs outside room sixteen – Alex Coben's room. The curtain had been pulled aside and he was studying the terraced gardens and loch edge, or perhaps just looking out at the storm. His silhouette was small and neat.

He turned. It was hard to read his face in the dark, but his voice was tight with barely disguised anger. 'God's sake, I told you to stay in your rooms. We're in a dangerous situation here. I don't want you two in the way when I track our runner down.' He gave a gruff sigh. 'The building's clear so far but I've still got a floor to search and the grounds extend a long way.'

'All along the edge of the water,' I confirmed.

Then I explained about the voice on the radio.

'Really?' he said, aghast. 'I mean that's good, I just didn't expect it. Who is it?'

'A woman who was injured in the same accident as you.'

Gaines Two blinked, drew his head back. 'I'm sorry?'

I repeated myself. 'The woman on the radio knows you.'

He released a breath. 'How? She a member of the prison staff?'

'No. She's in transportation.'

'Right,' he said. 'Don't think I saw the driver of the truck tonight. Was it Pucketti? Newport?'

'Shelley Talbot.'

'Talbot. Yeah. She OK?'

'Injured. Sounding desperate.'

'She's going to struggle in this weather,' he said, then after a moment's thought, he grimaced. 'You gave Foley a radio, is that right? We don't want him discovering Shelley. Poor Talbot. What a nightmare for her. She's a good officer. Decent family. Got a school-age kid.' He sighed in frustration. 'I'm afraid I'm going to have to go and get her. With Foley still at large, she's in danger, particularly if she saw something . . .' His gaze took us both in. 'I'd like the two of you with me. It's a rough journey, I know, and dangerous. But my alternative is leaving you down here with an escapee on the loose. Even if you stayed in your rooms, I can't be sure of your safety in those circumstances.'

My discomfort was evident, even in the darkness of the corridor. I knew, even better than the man before me, that Gaines One was indeed prowling the site armed. And that he knew where my room was – he'd been beneath my window in the snow just half an hour ago. *Don't tell anyone about me. It's the only advantage I've got.* From that perspective, Gaines Two's request made perfect sense. He was doing his job, keeping us from harm. But on the other hand, what if *he* was the impostor, and we were being asked to accompany a manipulative murderer on a dangerous nocturnal trek? Would he use the conditions to somehow evade us? He wasn't armed, but that didn't mean he couldn't harm us ... or Shelley. Thinking of her clarified matters. Here I was, able-bodied and uninjured, but Shelley was out there in the storm, dying. Shouldn't I be doing what I could to help her? Isn't that how life with Cameron had conditioned me, after all?

Gaines Two watched us think. Unintentionally or not, he had us cornered; there was no chance Jai and I could convene and plan alone like we had before. The silence lengthened as I sifted through the binaries. Gun, no gun; phone, no phone ... One, Two. Psychologists refer to false-dilemma syndrome; a stress-induced faulty logic where people only think in either-or terms. Was that me? Instead of thinking in opposites, would it help to consider what united the two strangers? Neither had tried to kill us ... yet, which meant both considered us somehow useful. *How? For what?* The two of them had told us the same story, they shared the same name. Thinking of them both as potentially Gaines helped keep a lid on my nerves. The alternative – one of these men was Troy Foley – would have shredded any steadiness I still clung to.

The silence made thinking impossible. 'OK,' I said, my voice dry. 'I want to help.'

'Mr Parik?'

Brows furrowed, Jai nodded.

'It's for the best,' Gaines said. He touched his head wound, wincing. 'It's going to take us some time to get to her. We'll need to be well prepared.'

'We can try using one of the hotel SUVs,' I suggested. 'Foley took my garage keys but I still have an ignition key.'

'Any way in to the garages apart from the door?' Gaines asked.

'A window around the back, I think. It's worth a try. And if that doesn't work we'll have to walk it. It's good we're going together. Neither of you know the terrain as well as I do.'

'I had a hard time coming down,' Gaines agreed.

'Right. But I spent every Sunday last summer along the foothills here,' I said. 'From the loch up to the road. The woodland climb is steep but passable. There are maps downstairs, I can show you.'

'Maps?' Gaines Two said. 'Good. I'll need to check them over.'

Too late, I thought of the boathouse on the loch's edge. Its omission from the hotel's site plan rendered it invisible; a safe place to hide, as Gaines One had pointed out. The moment we began looking through walking guides and OS maps, anyone could spot it. I'd just levelled the ground, surrendering the only advantage I had over either of these men. The thought twisted uncomfortably.

'We'll need outdoor gear too,' Gaines said. 'Base layers, boots, hats and coats. Does the hotel have stock for guests?' I nodded. 'Gather together what you can.

Get the maps. Do it safely, bring them to reception, lock yourselves in the office. I've still got one more floor to search but I'll be quick.'

We left him and descended the service stairs. The wind struck the panes and the old hotel creaked at the seams as we went.

The map room was a windowless ex-pantry converted into a high-ceilinged, ground-floor space. The room was dominated by the map on its main wall, a huge topographical diagram of the hills and fells all the way out to Fort William in the west – the one Alex Coben had photographed. Beneath it, shelves were loaded with walking guides. The storage spaces beneath them were home to the Mackinnon's complimentary winter gear; a boot room's worth of footwear and gaiters, folded waterproof clothing, balled-up socks, scarves and hats. I examined the walking poles stacked neatly upright, the tripods and snow shovels with flat, oar-like blades. There were looped climbing ropes and crampons hanging from hooks in the wall above neat piles of boxed-up binoculars and highland wildlife guides. There was even a wardrobe of quilted jackets and coats, each with a stitched number and a system for checking them in and out. I swept up armfuls of outdoor gear and carried them to the lobby where we used the open space as an impromptu dumping ground. Gaines Two, back from his search, unfolded maps. Jai took over the assembling of outdoor gear and I retreated to the reception desk with the radio while I worked on the torches, unscrewing their big rubber-coated bases to replace the batteries.

I repeated my call. 'Shelley? Can you hear me?' I waited, nervously checking my watch. Almost midnight. 'Shelley? We'll be on our way shortly. Hang on.'

I panned bright new beams along the lobby carpet then set the torches on their bases to illuminate our pile of outdoor gear, calling Shelley again and watching Jai separate and sort the hats, arrange walking boots by size and choose himself a yellow snow coat. Gaines unfolded two OS explorer maps. The Mackinnon fell on the border between the Loch Laggan and Invergarry maps; not quite of either world, the prison and the hotel occupied an edge-land trapped between. Good navigation necessitated the use of both guides. I called on the radio again. Waited and tried again. Ten minutes passed. I left the radio and selected my clothing instead, choosing snow boots, a pair of waterproof trousers and a winter jacket. I borrowed a pair of outsized gloves in pink and blue, hunted down a hat then walked across the lobby with my gear, piled it at my feet and stared out into the night.

The radio crackled. 'You still there?'

'Shelley!' Warm relief pulsed through me. 'Are you OK? Where've you been?'

'Tried to get out,' she grunted. 'Bad idea. Think I'm concussed. And I'm cut up somewhere 'cause I'm bleeding.' Her voice, racked with pain, subsided. She grunted as if trying to move herself. 'Cab's flooding,' she said.

'Shelley?' The others were at my shoulder now, listening. 'We're coming to help,' I said. 'Hang on in there.'

'I'm somewhere on the main road,' she breathed. 'Not far from the top of the drive. Gaines'll know. Hope he made it out in one piece. Christ, it's cold. Painkillers. Bandages. A whisky would be welcome . . .' she continued to speak but her voice sounded slurred and the signal dropped out.

'Just need a few minutes with the maps,' Gaines Two said to us both. 'Figuring a quicker route up through the woods. You two try and track down anything else that looks useful.'

Back in the map room we kicked aside walking gear and sifted the harnesses, crampons and ropes. I didn't know anything about climbing rope. The stored coils looked alarmingly thin – I guessed that was standard – and also huge; forty or fifty feet neatly tied. I unrolled a couple of batches to compare them and gave Jai a pleading glance.

He shrugged back. 'You really think we'll need some? I'm not . . .'

The radio crackled again and I stood aside and left him to it. 'Shelley? You OK?'

I heard a tight laugh, pained. 'Surviving. Just needed some company. Something to concentrate on.'

'I'm here. Just pay attention to my voice. We're gathering together some equipment and supplies and then we're driving up.'

Each exchange was punctuated with crackle and hiss.

Shelley shifted in the fog of it, then returned. 'Driving. You must be mad.'

'It might not get us all the way but we'll try. Listen, Shelley, I know it sounds strange, but could you describe Gaines to me? The police officer?'

Jai lifted a coil of rope, his gaze a question. 'I don't know. Get some whisky from the bar,' I told him. 'There are half bottles under the counter.'

'Remie?' came the disembodied radio-voice.

I took a moment to steady myself. 'Go on. Describe him.'

'You need to be ...' Shelley slurred. I didn't catch the rest.

'Please repeat?'

'... careful. Be careful coming up, do you copy? Watch your back.'

'I will. Shelley?' For a long minute I was left thinking about what she might have meant. 'Shelley?'

Gaines Two called from the lobby. 'Remie, let's get moving. We're up against it here.'

'One second!' I shouted back, then pressed the shoulder button. I was going to lose my description. 'Shelley?' In the silence that followed, something cold crawled up between my shoulder blades.

'Remie, we have to go!' shouted Gaines. 'What's wrong?'

'Hang on!' I called back, bringing the radio to my ear and holding my breath. I could hear Gaines Two crossing towards me.

Suddenly the radio shuddered with digital noise. 'Didn't work out,' said Shelley Talbot.

Before I could make any sense of her words, Gaines Two was at the desk. 'Everything all right?'

'You're going to be OK,' I said into the radio, then addressed the officer. 'She's not too good. Sounds a bit delirious.'

'We're all set,' the officer said, pulling on a black ski coat. 'Let's go.'

Jai returned from the bar and we assembled in the lobby, zipped our coats up and checked our torches. I chose a backpack and Jai handed me the booze; a half bottle of single malt. I wrapped it in a walker's fleece, tucked it into my bag, clipped the lid shut and shouldered it.

I'd been moments from getting a description of Gaines. The thought felt like a blade.

17

We thrashed across the car park, Gaines Two leading, me bringing up the rear. The storm sealed us into our separate worlds and I used the time to reflect, sifting through the few certainties I had. Shelley was struggling. Alex Coben was still missing. And since we were crossing to the garage my thoughts returned, for the first time since I saw it, to that mysterious pushed-back line of snow. Every time I conjured an explanation that seemed solid and dependable, it collapsed under examination. The fact that Gaines One had taken my keys to the garage and the gunroom – initially explainable – was now suspect. Keeping others away from the guns was an indication of his intention to protect, but denying us the garage keys also prevented us from leaving, left us trapped.

Back at the garage, the line of snow had softened to an undulation. Gaines Two ignored the up-and-over and rattled the knob of the side door, ran his fingers along the jamb, exhaled through his teeth then did the same at the garage door. 'These are locked tight,' he said. 'You mentioned a window.'

We followed the wall around to the back. In the shelter of the building I could hear our bootsteps creaking in the harder pack gathered beneath the eaves. The air was stilling a little. Above me in the plantation, echoes conversed, a colony of crows chattering.

Gaines assessed the small window. It was above head-height, just large enough to give access to a squirming body. 'Miss Yorke,' he said, 'it's either me or you fitting through there.'

We assessed each other. 'I'll try.'

'If Mr Parik and I lift you, do you think you can break the glass?' He handed me his torch. They leant against the brickwork, gloves cupped, and boosted me up. I began gingerly, tapping the base of the torch on the window, but ended up unceremoniously hammering. The glass gave on my third attempt, and I used the heavy rubberised grip of the torch to clear the aperture, then leaned in and worked a bolt free. I panned my light, getting impression enough to know I could lower myself in, then wriggled through the gap. I knew the garage interior well, felt for the workbench, landed in a heap and brushed myself down. The light switches were on the wall by the up-and-over door, so I padded across and clicked them on.

What I saw threw my head into further confusion. It took me a dizzying second to make sense of the new development.

There was a tap on the garage door and, head still spinning, I hauled the door open to the elements. The night had stilled further. No longer a violent swirl, snow drew ghostly vertical lines. The two men brushed it from their coats and assessed the interior, evidently as surprised as I had been.

'Does this belong to the hotel?' Gaines asked.

'No,' I told him. 'This is not one of ours.'

We studied it from the threshold, its strangeness somehow best assessed from a distance. We were looking at a black SUV; one that gleamed beneath the overhead lights as if it were virtually new. It was the kind of 4x4 farmers swore by around here; I'd seen its type on the high roads – usually caked in mud and bristling with mountain bikes – or off-road, churning over moorland tracks and fields. Its big wheels raised it high off the ground, making it good in snow. The driver's door was wide open.

'It's got no plates,' Jai said. The space above the front bumper was empty. Two screw holes in the polished metal. 'Looks brand new.'

Gaines Two moved forward slowly and on the balls of his feet. I didn't like the story his stance told but followed nevertheless. Closer to, I could see the car had been on the road. Its high wheel arches were fogged in mud and meltwater, its headlights clouded with grime. Made sense; someone had to have driven it down here, it hadn't fallen from the clouds. I thought about the line of snow along the front beneath the roll-up doors and imagined a person with access to the garage keys reversing the big SUV in earlier today. I could make out the dried remains of the tracks left as it was parked. Next to it were the two hotel vehicles, looking drab and tired beside their shiny neighbour, and beyond them a workbench beneath a wall of tools hanging from hooks.

Jai circled the SUV from behind and peered into the rear windows. 'Subaru Forester,' he said.

'Ring any bells, Miss Yorke?' Gaines was at the open driver's door, the big vehicle dwarfing him.

I went fast-forward through the frenetic activity of the afternoon, trying to remember if I'd seen the SUV arrive; a driver drop a parcel or borrow a key; a guest request additional parking ... but though I turned over every stone in an attempt to generate a reasonable explanation for what I was seeing, I couldn't find anything satisfying, nothing but a patternless puzzle, all noise no signal.

Then it struck me. For a second I was felled and breathless. A truth I didn't want to acknowledge had been staring me in the face. Often all it takes is a trigger to reveal it, a one-time-only deal that comes like an electric shock. I had it right then in the garage.

I imagined myself as Troy Foley and followed the line of reasoning. If I was an escaping prisoner, what might I need? A change of clothes and a weapon. An injured motorcade officer could provide that. What else? Shelter. The Mackinnon provided that – but only if the crash happened at the right moment at the right place: the gap between maps. Ten minutes too early or late and you're in the middle of a hundred square miles of empty mountain. And if the timing was right, what else was needed? A means of escape. Like a stolen 4x4 hidden somewhere nearby. A cold flush swept downwards through my body.

Foley had an accomplice.

Since he was in the back of the prisoner transport, someone else would have had to engineer the accident. That same someone would then need to break open the rear doors and free him. Would he have been hand-cuffed to the interior of the van? I imagined so, which meant Foley's accomplice had the means to release him. That same person could have delivered the Subaru to the hotel garage hours before the accident was due to happen.

Which meant the whole thing was premeditated. Foley causes trouble at Porterfell, knowing he's on a final warning. The motorcade sets off . . . the accomplice must surely have been planning in the days running up to the escape; whoever it was would need a safe place from which to work. *The Mackinnon.* That just left the cold mathematics. I wasn't the accomplice. The rest of the hotel staff had gone and that left only two other people here. One of the hotel guests had to be here under false pretences, to help Foley escape. It was either Alex Coben, who had vanished at breakfast, leaving an empty hotel room, or . . . Jaival Parik. The man who had been recording me on his phone last night. The possibilities hollowed me out. I dragged in a deep breath.

'Empty,' Gaines Two was saying, pulling out of the car's interior and stretching his back. 'This thing is either fresh out of a showroom or it's been given a very thorough valet.' In his flat northern accent, valet came out *vallet.* 'No keys of course. I doubt we'd even get touch-DNA from this.'

'Wait,' Jai said. He'd tried the boot and, finding it open, had raised it. 'There's a bag.'

Gaines looked up, eyes gleaming.

'What the hell is happening?' I asked. Croaked might be more accurate; my throat had thickened until it felt as if I was breathing through a straw.

'I don't know,' Gaines said, working his way along the car to join Jai. 'When Foley arrived earlier tonight, did he come on foot?'

'Yes. At least – yes, I think. I didn't see him arrive exactly.'

We stood side by side at the rear of the vehicle. There was a small holdall in the boot space; black, the size of a gym bag. I could see there was something in it.

A recollection, sharp as acid, cut through the cold.

~

Cleaning out the back of a van with Cameron. He was working for Foley's gang by then, though I didn't yet know it. I was lecturing at Edinburgh and I'd come back home to help Mum out; she and Dad were taking a break and she was in pieces, clearing his stuff out, knowing, I suppose, that he was never coming back. I stayed for the weekend, kept her spirits up. We bought canned supermarket margueritas and watched game shows together.

Then Cameron called. My response by then was almost Pavlovian; I made frantic notes, wheedled a location from him, reassured Mum and made sure she had something to do – she got gloomy if she thought too much – then

144   MARTIN GRIFFIN

sharpened up with black coffee before packing my car with bottled water and driving to find my brother. I'm not sure I even knew where we were that night. He'd broken down on the way back from London and managed to get his van off the A1 and into thick countryside. It was sluicing down with rain and I eventually found the vehicle in a lay-by. I recognised the plates, the off-white paintwork overlaid with road grime, and pulled in next to an empty farm vehicle to text him. Then I waited, listening to the rain drum the roof, wondering what the hell was happening. He emerged from the cab in a black parka and filthy desert boots, crossed towards me in the pouring rain, then took a seat next to me. He smelled of energy drinks and cannabis. His hair, growing out now, stood in greasy tufts and his fingers jumped as he dried his palms on his jeans. He was nineteen by then.

'You bring the stuff?'

I nodded. 'All in the boot. What's happening?'

He clawed his hands and ran them across his head front to back, drawing red lines on his scalp. 'Broke down. Had to transfer the stuff to the other vehicle. Gotta clean this and leave it. We've two hours until they pick up,' he said, nodding through the rain to the van he'd abandoned. 'Can you give me a lift back when we're done?'

Back when he was thirteen or fourteen, this would have been my cue to lose it. *I've been driving for hours, where the hell are we, what have you been doing* . . . but we'd passed the outrage, anger, the disappointment by this stage. Those words were a script we didn't need to perform any more, so instead we played more subdued parts, him brusque but apologetic, me silent and paranoid. 'What if someone sees us? What if the police come past?'

'Pull your car up behind the trees here,' he told me. 'If we work fast we can get this done.'

'What are we cleaning?'

He eyed me. 'Prints, fibres.'

That night was the first time he'd asked for something so big and it felt significant. I knew it implied something organised; a courier network. Secret logistics. Long way from a white van and Danny Franks. 'Let's just get it done,' I said. We crossed to the vehicle, shut ourselves in the back to stop the rain pouring in, and I distributed the cleaning gear. Wearing stupid marigolds, we scrubbed at the metal interior with bleach and wire wool while the rain drummed on the roof, then moved onto the cab seats and dashboard with sponges and spray cleaner.

Every chance I got with Cameron – and they were increasingly rare by that stage, two years on from the night with the camera – I still broached the topic of escape, of the possibility of reinvention, and that night was no different. 'You need to stop this,' I said. 'If you carry on there's only one place you'll end up.'

He'd been swabbing the interior walls, hangdog and exhausted. He didn't reply until I pushed him again. Eventually I got, 'All right, for fuck's sake, will you leave it?'

'If you could save just a little each job. Squirrel it away; I swear that stuff adds up. And before you know it, you'll have enough.' I'd been trying the savings thing for a while by that night. The year previously he'd been retaking his

GCSEs but dropped out of college because it was getting in the way of work. When I'd given him grief, he'd confessed the money was too good to turn down and, ever since then, I'd been tediously preaching the benefits of laying cash aside. 'Take your pay,' I continued, 'and put away just ten per cent. You'll never notice it isn't there. No one needs to know but you.'

He looked up from scrubbing. The rain had stopped. 'We've been through this, Rem.'

'Yeah, well, have you done it yet?'

'Sort of,' he said cryptically.

'What does that mean?' I knew this was a key moment, a potential turning point, but by then I'd worked with enough troubled youngsters to know whatever gains I'd made needed support and consolidation. I couldn't push further. When he didn't answer, I said, 'That's great, Cam. Seriously. You won't regret it.' I tried to coax a smile from him but he was wiping down surfaces. 'Even if you've just made a small start,' I said, 'it will build up. You're taking steps, Cam. I'm really proud of you.'

He did look up then, his expression complicated. And that was when we heard the other engine. 'Shit,' he hissed, genuinely terrified in a way I'd never seen him. I realised Cam was scared for *me*. 'They're early. Get back to your car. Go.'

I ran back through the puddles. A big truck hissed through standing water, throwing grey wings as it passed. Then a black Lexus pulled in after it. I watched, heart pounding, from my car, the lights off, the windscreen steaming as I warmed the interior, glad of the presence of the muddy farm truck parked beside me. A figure emerged from the Lexus; a slim figure, female, hooded in a puffer jacket and heavy boots. She didn't look my way. The woman spoke to Cameron, made a call, then opened the door of her car and beckoned her passenger out. A man emerged and crossed to the van, made an inspection, then took the keys from Cam. The truck nosed out onto the road, then accelerated into darkness. I watched its headlights dwindle. The woman got back into her car and followed.

Cam was left in a lay-by, hugging himself, shoulders up and jacket soaked. He still looked thirteen. I drove him home under a clear night sky, and all the way he leant forward as far as his seatbelt would allow, and watched the stars.

After a long period of silence I asked, 'What are you thinking about?' I don't know what I was hoping I'd get in reply. Something like *a way out of this*. Or, *saving some money like you suggested*. Or *I'm sorry*.

Instead, he said, 'There's sixty-something telescopes out there, you know. People travel from all over the world.'

I'd been thrown. We were just south of Durham. 'Where?'

'The Atacama Desert,' he replied.

18

'Don't touch the bag,' Gaines Two told me. He stooped, examining it, then turned to me. 'Who has access to the garage?'

I swallowed, trying to get my breathing back to normal. 'I – the site team, me. Guests can pay an additional fee to park here.'

'Could this belong to a guest? The missing one, Alex Coben?'

'No. Her car's out there under the snow with Jai's. I've never seen this vehicle before. Someone must have brought it down here.'

'Someone with access to the garage.'

Jai played with his cap and examined the back seats through the windows. 'So why is it here?'

'Someone has put this vehicle here deliberately.' Gaines arched his back, the discomfort clear on his face. 'Perhaps with the intention of using it tonight. I can't be sure but I think this bag is safe. I'm going to try and open it.'

Jai and I stood back, watching Gaines steady his breath then very deliberately lean into the boot and inch open the zip. He waited, then unfurled the cavity slowly, pushing an exploratory hand inside. He withdrew something.

He stood. 'Clothes,' he said, holding up a fleece-lined sweatshirt in light grey. 'For a man. Size . . .' he checked the neck. 'Tags have been cut out.' Gaines folded the item, tucked it back in. 'Jeans,' he said. 'Looks like a base layer in here too. Hat and gloves. Someone's change of clothing.'

'But for this to be useful,' Jai said slowly, running a hand along the roof of the vehicle, 'the RTA earlier – well, it couldn't have been an accident.'

Gaines shrugged. 'That could be true. But I'm not here to speculate. Right now I have two jobs: protect members of the public; recapture Troy Foley. That's why we're getting Talbot and we're doing it together, safely. The story of how the incident occurred is someone else's concern.'

Gaines stepped back, arms folded, chin tucked in against his chest as he thought. I drifted down the driver's side of the car to the open door and leaned in, running my gaze along the steering wheel, the still-new shine of the dashboard dials, the brushed upholstery. Beneath the wiper-stick on the dash was a starter button. Someone somewhere would have the key fob whose presence would activate the engine. I reached a hand out, curious.

'Miss,' barked Gaines Two. 'I would ask you not to contaminate any potential evidence. Do not touch anything.'

The word evidence triggered a slow, crushing feeling. This was going to become a crime scene. I was going to become a witness. In hours, I was meant to be on a flight. I conjured the warmth and noise of the airport's concourse cafés; the high-spirited laughter in the check-in queue, the piped music. Families, hand luggage, newspapers and complimentary drinks, the sense of potential; the possibility of escape. Heathrow, Madrid, Santiago. I closed and wiped my eyes, squeezing back tears of frustration, and tried thinking of Shelley Talbot instead.

Gaines Two crossed the garage and stooped to open the roll-top door from the inside. The wind squirmed beneath the gap, chilling the interior, running icy fingers through my hair. Jai walked out into the dark and I followed. Outside, it became clear the woods were moaning again. This time, though, it was different. Over the echoing creak of wood, a drum-roll rumble.

Jai gave me an alarmed look. 'Is that what an avalanche sounds like?'

I craned my neck, squinting into the high darkness of the looming trees. It came from way further up the mountain and sounded like thunder. The hotel, squatting in against the side of the hill, sometimes felt like it was huddled safe in a lee of rock and forest, protected from the elements. Not this time. If that was some sort of slip, we were directly in its way; a tiny building caught beneath a plunging wall of snow tossing upended pine trees. We'd be smashed like matches. As we listened, the rumble grew in intensity, throwing an echo across the face of the mountain, gathering to a low roar. Then it faded and died, lapsing into silence.

Gaines Two joined us, the map open in his arms, the wind buffeting it. 'The snowpack's not stable,' he said. 'There's no way we're driving up in these conditions.'

As if in agreement, the snow gave another moan and the three of us stared up in unison, peering through the dark canopy into the night above. 'I don't like this,' Jai said, adrenaline stiffening his posture.

Gaines examined the map. 'We'll need to walk it.'

He didn't get any objections from the two of us. Any prospects I had of driving tomorrow were looking increasingly impossible. I pushed down the thought.

'We should be protected from the wind taking a route through the woods,' Gaines Two was saying. 'The drive is too exposed, and look – it takes us back and forth, rising in the wrong direction.' He indicated the road. 'At the top, we'd need to take a left and walk all the way along here. Miles. But if we find a woodland path—' he broke off, examining the cedar and pine that began at the far edge of the drive and covered the steep climb upwards.

Jai and I checked the map over the officer's slim shoulders while he ran a finger across the tight whorls of contour. I'd walked the woodland paths on my days off the previous summer; the trees grew close together, choking out any understorey so that paths were peaty and friable, often hidden beneath claggy carpets of needles. The hillside was steep. Not vertical, but difficult enough to mean a direct climb was impossible.

Contouring was the only way; following the paths that climbed in lengthy upward diagonals, making sure we didn't miss the switchbacks. Still quicker than taking the road. 'If we're careful,' I said, pointing at the map, 'we could take a route like this ... and emerge about here. Then follow the mountain road along. The crash site must be somewhere here, I'm guessing?'

Gaines grunted. 'Think so.' He looked up to check the pines again then pointed directly into them. 'So we follow the drive for this first section, then work our way into the trees up there. It'll save us an hour. But it won't be easy. I came down from the crash site that way. Nearly lost my footing. There are big rocky bits.'

I nodded. 'Exposed boulders,' I explained to Jai, 'sudden cliff faces. We'll need to work our way around them.'

Gaines folded the map. 'Let's get started,' he said.

We followed the drive to begin with, a half mile of relatively easy walking. At the point where the drive curved and turned, I looked back down at the Mackinnon. The distant glow of lights would have been obvious in ordinary circumstances; instead, all I got was an outline of brickwork through the easing snow. From ground level, back down in the car park, I'd always find my eye drawn to the bay windows of the dining room, the black-and-white bargeboards of the gables and the ivy-clad clock tower. But viewed from an elevated perspective the Mackinnon could be seen as a whole, and from here the place looked dark and small, dwarfed against the wild white foothills of Farigaig, less a secure stone-built lodge, more an inconsequential speck.

Gaines Two was fighting the map, the wind plucking at it as he made one final check of our position. I joined him and he pointed, moving his finger through the marked woodland up to the road. 'Like this?' he said.

I nodded in confirmation. 'The hill's criss-crossed by paths. Just depends how much snow has gathered in the trees.'

'It's going to be dark in there,' Jai said, pulling his torch out.

We looked up, assessed the blackness and nodded our agreement. The edge of the drive was a blocky wall of drift deposited by last week's snowplough. We struggled over it, into the softer deeper fall beyond, and waded over to the treeline, our torches stabbing the dark.

Then we plunged in.

The trunks were close, standing no more than a few feet apart. In exposed positions the wind was already dying; in here the air was ghostly and still. We contoured first, so the going was steady, the ground pine-needly beneath the snow. Soon, though, we forked right and began to climb. Each step required us to plant boots carefully, sinking with a slow crump to knee-depth. Heaving upwards, I experienced the curious feeling of simultaneously burning calves and numb feet. The incline was unforgiving. As we hacked our way up, I panned my torch along the flat, vertical faces of rock and found frozen cornices at their tops, snow overhangs that gave the illusion of safety but could break, sending the unwary into a sudden plunge. An owl hooted mournfully, mocking me as I panned my pitiful light, assessing the pack and considering the incline of the valley. We were high now. If I was unfortunate enough to lose my footing the only thing stopping a speedy slip through the dark would be striking a tree. No one would find my body for weeks.

Eventually we reached a plateau and gathered together in the dark, panting and steaming, listening to the calls of crows. We were level with the canopies of trees growing lower down the slope, standing in thick snow topping an outcrop of rock. We didn't venture near the edge. The snow was a brawl of awkward chunks, white shapes that looked as if they'd been quarried from a cliff face. It was deep too. Each boot sank into the snow to above my knee as I went, so movement was a wade more than a walk.

'I need a few minutes,' Jai panted. His hood was pulled tight around his face but I could see the shine of sweat on his skin.

The sway of our lights painted the forest above us an ancient grey, all ugly trunks and wild, shabby growth. We could hear the patter of fresh flakes in the canopy. The going ahead looked steep enough to require us to haul ourselves from tree trunk to tree trunk, climbing through the blackness on what looked like a non-existent path.

We rested. Gaines Two placed the fingertips of his gloves gently against his forehead and checked for blood.

He cleared his throat and spat into the snow. 'I'll lead,' he said, 'checking our footing's safe.'

I gave him a thumbs up. He began an ungainly thrash across the outcrop to the upward slope. I heard him grunting as he hauled himself into the trees, and I watched the will-o'-the-wisp of his bobbing light as he struggled upwards. Planting one foot after another, we hauled for half an hour, legs burning with effort. I often lost track of Gaines Two, just followed his footprints carefully, steered by the glow of his torch somewhere above, swinging and bobbing between trunks and branches in a way that implied hard-won progress. There were steeply rising dunes of white up on those slopes, some of them twice my height, solid strata of snow accreting upwards with subsequent falls. The snow broke and shifted beneath our boots as we climbed. Once, I heard a yelp from behind me and turned, flashing my torch beam wildly.

'It's OK. OK. I'm all right,' Jai spluttered from below me. I could make out a flash of yellow as he yanked himself upright, brushed his coat down and raised a hand. 'My fault.'

I waited for him, shaking snow from my gloves and wiping my hair clear. We climbed again. Eventually the ground began to level out and the woodland thinned. I leant against a straggly pine, its thin trunk snug between my shoulder blades, and fumbled for my torch. Here the canopy was dipping in the dying wind, which meant we'd reached the edge of the forest. It was nearly one o'clock.

Jai pulled up alongside me, his exposed skin steaming in the torchlight. He leant forward, gloves on knees. 'No chance we're going back that way,' he said. 'Imagine trying a descent in the dark.'

'No wonder he fell and lost his gun,' I gasped.

'Where is he?' Jai said, raising his head.

I panned my light through ghost trees and glittering drifts. Maybe he'd gone to check the road. A white wake of bootsteps confirmed my guess. 'Scouting ahead,' I said.

We rested up, clouds of breath misting the lower branches. I was disturbed by a crackle, but put it down to the chatter of trees. Then it came again and I realised it was my inside pocket.

The radio had sprung into life.

19

I dragged the handset from my pocket. 'Shelley. We're close to the road. I think Gaines has gone ahead, he's nearly with you. How are you doing? Shelley?'

'Well, I'm still here,' she said, her voice watery. 'Can't feel much any more. Except my leg. Throbbing like a bastard.' She laughed feebly. ''Scuse language.'

'Hold on,' I told her. I hauled myself up and waded forward. 'We'll be with you in twenty minutes. Can you walk? We'll pull you back if we have to.'

'Curled up in the wet. Can't move. Don't know how you'll get me from the cab. Windscreen maybe.' A pause. 'Did you bring whisky?'

I smiled. 'Single malt.'

'What I wouldn't give for a last ...' The signal became garbled, her voice an indecipherable rush of noise.

I didn't like the use of *last*, so I kept talking. 'Lost you there, but I'm guessing you're getting boring about whisky. I'm fine with the taste, Shelley, but the hang-overs not so much. When we're back at the hotel you can try some of our top-shelf cask-aged malts. Any preferences? Shelley?'

'We should go,' Jai put in gently.

'Trying to keep her focused.'

'I know. But we need to stick with Gaines.'

'Go ahead and check if you want. Just a few more minutes. Hey Shelley,' I adjusted the radio. 'Thinking back, we've known each other for nearly two years now. Imagine that. Bet you don't miss your days in Porterfell, eh?'

Trying to raise Shelley, I found myself suddenly transported back over a year. My final visit to Cameron – the last time I'd seen him alive. It's a meeting I rewound and replayed often, though at the time I had no particular reason to commit it to memory. There'd been no signs of imminent tragedy; the only thing that had made the visit different was the cryptic, confessional passage of talk in the middle of an otherwise pedestrian conversation. Listening to Shelley brought it all tumbling back.

~

Cameron was beginning to look different at twenty-three, shedding the boyish vulnerability I'd seen in him during those troubled teenage years and bulking out. When he leant forward his arms were thick and muscular, his shoulders solid and wide. His hair had grown out so it curled at the nape of his neck. His eyes were darker, his jaw heavily stubbled. He looked fit. By contrast, that morning I'd just finished a night shift and skipped break-fast to get to him. I was tired and hungry. I felt irritable as I dropped my bag and phone at reception. Shelley and I might have talked at the bar on a Friday night but inside the walls of Porterfell she was expressionless and silent as she escorted me into the visitors' room. It was a close, warm day and the enclosed space smelled of hot bodies and boredom. My stiff-backed plastic chair, particularly uncomfortable that time, creaked as I shifted position. Thin bars of light caught dust motes.

We were talking about the English class he was taking when, unprompted, Cameron said, 'Remember that night we cleaned the van?'

It hadn't been the only night I'd driven backstreets or empty country lanes to rescue Cam from some frightening predicament, but I recalled it with clarity nevertheless. The woman who'd arrived as we finished up cleaning; Cameron conversing with her, then a silent drive home, him stargazing all the way. Sometimes, as I replay that scene and countless others, I wince at the reg-ularity with which I seemed to be haranguing, cajoling, and insisting that he live differently. Always the drone of my voice, the grasping tone. I bored myself with those repetitive arguments; Lord knows what it must have been like for my poor trapped brother.

'We scrubbed the insides of that thing until it gleamed,' I said, mustering a smile. Behind my left eye, a headache throbbed.

He grinned. 'And you wouldn't shut up about how I needed to save, remember?'

'Save?'

'Put a little aside each time you do a job. "It'll build up",' he said, making air quotes with big, rough-skinned hands.

'I was obsessed about it at that time.' I smiled. 'I know I went on. I was just trying to help.'

'Well, you did. You did help.' And then he turned serious, moving in his chair, leaning forward and saying, carefully and quietly, 'I have a locker.' It was as if the air shifted and, despite my best instincts, I stiffened, found myself checking the room. Cameron cleared his throat and, when I looked back at him, gave me an almost imperceptible shake of the head. 'A locker,' he whispered deliberately. 'And inside the locker, a bag. Are you listening carefully? I've been a very clever boy.' I knew better than to reply. 'Smart Storage,' he said. 'Aberdeen branch. Small locker registered under your name. Bag inside.'

My pulse quickened. 'Smart Storage,' I repeated. 'OK.'

'You've always been good to me,' he said. 'If anything ever happens, I want you to clear it out. All of it is yours.'

'Cameron . . .'

'Let's not get sentimental, Rem. These are my savings. There's a digital key code. Are you ready?' He waited until I nodded, serious. 'It's a date. An important one.' He gave me the six digits. It was a February two years hence – a day with no special meaning, as far as I could see.

'Got it,' I said. 'But what's the significance?'

It was then he told me about conjunctions; about

particular dates on which, at the right time and from the right part of the world, the tip of the Earth on its axis and the alignment of the universe was such that you could see two or three planets together in the night sky. Rare and special, he said, and when viewed in the right conditions, unforgettable. His expression was calm and neutral as he continued. 'Don't forget that date, OK? I've pre-paid for the locker for the next eighteen months. After that the lease runs out so you'll need to extend or collect.'

And that was it; just as quickly as the conversational detour had begun, it was abruptly ended. Cameron smiled, ran his hands down the thighs of his prison-issue trousers and said, 'So, *Of Mice and Men* is named after a Robbie Burns quote, right? But it's set in American farming country. What's that all about then?'

Fifteen minutes later, the buzzer barked and my visit was over. We stood up together and hugged awkwardly. We'd only started hugging when he went to prison and, unpractised as we were, we never got very good at it. I watched the guard lead him out at the far doors, then picked my stuff up in reception and returned to my car.

I'd been able to remain quite stoic on most of my visits, but not this one. He'd listened to me. He'd tried to change, to put aside savings. He'd just been too late. I wept behind the wheel for what felt like a long time. The tears kept coming. When I eventually drove back to the Mackinnon my heart was sore, eyes puffy, but my head was clearer. Back in my room, I visited the Safe Storage website, memorised the location, saved the phone number and created a false name in my phone contacts, adding the six-digit code Cameron had told me about. Within a month he was dead.

~

The radio fizzed. Shelley was back. 'Didn't work out,' she said. To begin with I didn't know if she sounded obscure because I was lost in memory, or if it was something else. I shook my head clear.

'Say again? Shelley?' I strained to hear, radio against the hood of my coat.

'Screwed it up. Couldn't stay on the road.'

'The conditions, though. It's not your fault. Transportation shouldn't have made you drive in a storm like this.'

When her voice came again it was noticeably weaker. 'Need to tell you about your brother,' she said.

I felt my legs tighten and sway. 'What do you mean, Shelley?'

'I was there. Night he was killed.'

A shaft opened in my stomach.

I was struggling with a breathless response when Shelley continued. 'Last year, January time. Was a prison guard back then. It all kicked off in the rec room. Gang related. They covered the cameras . . .' I heard her grunt and swallow. More crackle, then she returned. 'Me and three others trapped in there. Carnage. Cameron was stabbed. Saw him bleed out. So sorry, Remie, nothing I could do.'

I made it to a tree, slid into a squat, the shoulder of my coat snagged on the stub of a broken branch. 'What else?' I croaked.

'Couldn't get a medic. They'd locked us in.' I heard Shelley shift her weight, curse at the pain. 'Been wanting to tell you for so long but . . . signed an NDA. Guess it's a little late for that now.' She faded quite suddenly. I waited for more. Digital interference like a burst of ironic applause, then nothing.

'Shelley?' I managed. I was simultaneously empty and ready to explode.

'Remie,' Jai said, leaning in and holding a hand out to pull me up. 'We need to keep moving. Got to find Gaines.' Then he saw my face and withdrew.

'Shelley,' I said firmly. I was thinking about the endless inquiry that followed Cameron's death, the written summaries I'd received in the post with their dense prose, the terse stonewalling that followed even as we appealed. No substantial conclusion can be reached, said the Porterfell authorities, due to a lack of evidence. 'Shelley, are you still there? I need to know, Shelley. Who killed Cam?'

What she said next caught me breathless. 'I saw,' she said.

I felt hot beneath my hat. My skin itched. 'Who?' I whispered. Nothing. I waited, scanning the road beyond the trees, watching the night air shiver, the flakes flexing and spinning. Jai stayed at a distance.

'Lost a lot of money,' Shelley whispered eventually. 'A lot. Couldn't stop. Needed a way out.'

I managed, 'Hang in there, Shelley,' my breath short and my throat coarse and dry.

'All my fault. Selfish. Made the deal.'

I didn't want to hear this stuff. Didn't want to make sense of it. There's such a thing as stress-restricted cue sampling: decreased vigilance leading to poor decision-making when operating in emergencies. That's what I was doing, moving too quickly to the wrong conclusions. This wasn't Shelley confessing to something. It couldn't be. On the other hand: someone must have orchestrated the accident. Someone must have parked the 4x4 in the hotel garage. Shelley was a regular at the hotel bar and – this bit felt damning – Shelley had been driving the prison transport.

I croaked, 'What deal?' and held the radio up to my ear.

She was very quiet now. 'Sold my soul.' She laughed quietly. 'Doesn't matter now. I'm finished.'

'Hold on,' I said. A blare of interference exploded in my ear and made me call out in pain, holding the radio away. I pushed it tentatively against my coat hood again, and heard her one more time.

The last thing Shelley said to me came through clear, her voice briefly steady. 'I want you to know,' she said, 'that Foley's boys killed your brother.'

20

I felt the sudden combustion of a passion I'd carried with me for thirteen years. It wasn't simple emotion – pain or grief didn't burn hard enough to keep you warm, but this thing inside me flared hot and wild. One of the two men calling themselves Gaines was responsible for the murder of my little brother and I was going to find out which one it was. Then I was going to do everything in my power to mete out punishment. I was going to make Cameron's death mean something. The certainty glowed in me like a sunrise, bright and strengthening.

I pushed through the snow and joined Jai at the road's edge. Ahead, Farigaig climbed into cloud, its snowy flanks glittering in stillness. The wind had gone and the landscape was at rest at last. I could make out the veins of drystone walls, the scars of drainage ditches, hummocks of tangled grass. We checked the road left and right. It was a shrinking thread of white, its outermost reaches being slowly subsumed. The forecast had been pretty good. It had just gone one in the morning and, above, the sky was beginning to clear.

*

MARTIN GRIFFIN

A mile in the supernatural stillness and then a vehicle in sight, one headlight illuminating the snow.

A single police patrol car. The rooftop beacon lights still spun slowly, strobing the night red and blue. As we approached, its bulk solidified; the bonnet a snub-nosed mess, its dead headlight a blind eye.

I felt Jai's hand against my arm and leaned in. 'Where's Gaines Two?' he asked. I shrugged in reply. 'Be careful,' he told me.

We stuck to the centre of the road. Periodically I felt the cat's eyes beneath my boots as we moved forward. Closer to, I could hear the tick of the hazard lights. Through its smashed windscreen, the patrol car looked empty. An interior light flickered, illuminating seats and headrests. Beads swung listlessly from a chain hooked over the rear-view mirror. Good Catholic boy, I thought as I drifted left, opened up a better angle and saw the boot was up.

I approached and Jai followed. With each step, I slowed, feeling a curious floating detachment as if my legs belonged to someone else. The thump of my heart became an insistent wham that sent clouds of silver spots blazing across my vision. I drew closer. There was something curled in the boot of the car, a snow-covered curve. Jai placed an open palm against my back and we stood together, assessing the scene. When he resumed walking, I stayed put. I watched him look down into the interior, lower a hand inside and brush snow from the shape, then I was stumbling forward to see.

There was a dead man in the boot.

It's curious how one's vision fails to make sense of what it sees. Having never set eyes on a body before, I found I couldn't fully comprehend it, as if I was looking at some alien object that defied all law and logic. Couldn't establish a shape. The body was stripped to the underwear and lay blue-skinned in a foetal curl. In the centre of the forehead was a drilled hole, red-edged and frozen. The lad would have died instantly. At least the cold didn't get him. He was young, lean and muscled, clean-shaven. His body hair was gathering fine flakes of snow as we watched. I had to lean against the side of the car and tip myself into a forward bend. If I'd eaten anything recently it would have come back up – instead, I dry-heaved then made it upright, gasping.

A dead officer. Troy Foley had shot him and taken his clothes.

'He's the right size,' Jai said, 'but he's too young. So Foley would've needed someone else's ID.'

His touch at my shoulder directed my attention. He was indicating the road's loch-facing edge. The prison transport and its escort had broken open the roadside walls of banked snow and dropped down the verge. A scribble of tracks graffitied the tarmac surface. Despite a cotton sheet of fresh fall, they told a clear enough story and we approached the drop carefully. I held a jittery arm across my eyes and looked down.

'Shelley!' I shouted.

The verge, a steep tumble of wild grass and heather, banked for twenty feet or so. The two sliding vehicles had unzipped the peat as they pitched downwards but

MARTIN GRIFFIN

the storm had been busy erasing the wound again. Where the ground levelled out, a big prison transport lay on its side in a pool of oozing liquid, its smashed pipes and ruptured tank bleeding into the snow. The van's sliding side door, facing upwards, was drawn back. The churned-up ground beneath was a peaty swamp edged by boot prints, suggesting someone had emerged. Next to the prison van was the second patrol car – Gaines's car, I guessed – tipped-up on its roof, choked by drifts. Its four skyward-facing wheels were rotating slowly in the dark, wind-driven. I planted my feet carefully at the top of the bank, standing knee-deep at the farthest reaches of the strobing lights like a watcher on the border of a new and unfamiliar country. Jai held an arm out and I took it. At the bottom we had to wade through knee-deep snow towards the crash site.

'Shelley!' I called again.

Reaching the transport, I sloshed along its underside, following the twin exhaust pipes up to the engine, feeling the last remains of its heat. It was an old thing, the rusting undercarriage coated in mud and oil. I rounded the front.

Gaines Two was on his knees, upper body through the smashed windscreen. Inside, Shelley was a peat-encrusted shape slumped against the driver's door. Gaines withdrew and wobbled to standing, his shoulders slack, his head down. I knew what that meant but I didn't want to believe it. 'I'm sorry,' he said. 'I tried to get her out of the van but she was so weak. Thought there was a chance we could make it back, that if we reached the trees the shelter would help, and we'd be able to carry her between us.' His voice was thick with emotion and he looked genuinely shaken.

Two bodies in ten minutes. The tipped van had lurched through the frozen surface of a bog, and from what I could see of the cab, Shelley had been radioing us from a half-filled chamber of ink-black slush. Her face was contorted in pain, her skin wax-white, her clothes stiff with mud and wet with meltwater. Her dyed hair was flat against her forehead. I could see the crow's feet at her closed eyes. Her presence seemed some sort of travesty.

'I'm sorry,' Gaines said again. He rubbed at his face. 'I tried.'

Short of breath, I turned to face the forest, my lungs torn paper bags as I tried dragging in cold air. The Porterfell escapee had been strangely notional up to this point; a twice-told scary story. Now, with two dead people on the mountain road, the night had lurched. My safety was a delusion and my true reality was sharp and bitter. I was meant to be working a final uneventful night shift before the start of something new, a chance to change forever; instead, this rapid escalation of some strange madness was really happening – I was stuck in a storm on the side of a mountain, and one of the two men I'd been helping was Troy Foley. The man responsible for my brother's death.

I gazed, dumbstruck, at Shelley Talbot's ragdoll body. Thinking felt impossible but I had to try. If Gaines Two was Foley, things had certainly worked out well for him. The one witness to his escape was now dead, and he'd engineered the time to kill her by getting here first. Had he orchestrated the hill climb that way – striding ahead of us to buy himself an opportunity? Or was he just an ordinary officer hastening to the assistance of an injured colleague? If this man was Foley, Shelley would have known she was a dead woman as soon as she saw his shape looming through the snow and saw her prisoner, dressed in a police uniform, returning to finish her off. Did that mean he'd try and kill us now too? Or were we still somehow useful? The possibilities were chilling.

I heard Jai exchanging words with Gaines Two. 'We need to go. We can't stay out here. The clouds are clearing, the temperature's going to drop further,' the officer was saying.

'Can we raise some assistance? We could use the car radios.'

A vague awareness of the two of them crossing the crash site to the upturned police car. Shocked into stillness, I stayed with Shelley, fear pouring through me until my muscles trembled at its flow. There had to be something of significance here; something that would tell me which man was which, but I couldn't find it. I wondered if I could tell if Shelley had been strangled by studying her, but though I tried, I couldn't look. Instead, I scoured my memory of Gaines Two's response to Shelley's initial radio call – had he been shocked? Fearful of discovery? I recalled him calm and decisive, a professional faced with difficult decisions, simply doing his best to navigate them. But Troy Foley, I reminded myself, was the master dissembler.

I was shattered and distracted and didn't notice Gaines's return. Suddenly he was right next to me. 'I'm sorry I couldn't do more,' he said, gripping my shoulder and gazing at me sadly. 'We did the right thing trying to help. There was no way we could know she was so weak . . .' he trailed off, turning instead to the upturned patrol vehicle. 'That one has a broken radio. Let's get back up to the road and check the other car. There's nothing else we can do here.'

Gaines Two turned to go. Jai waited and walked with me, and we both kept our distance from the officer. Up on the road, Gaines checked the interior of the second car while I studied the space illuminated by its surviving headlight, trying to think. Sideways snow chased through the darkness. The telephone poles thrummed in the last of the wind. To our left, Farigaig climbed in steep shelves of snow-capped rock. Across the road on the other side, the calligraphy of tree shapes at the edges of the light.

I heard Gaines curse as he emerged. 'Radio's dead here too. Nothing useful . . .' He suddenly stiffened and turned, the words dying in his mouth.

Jai took a distracted step forward, eyes on the darkness. 'Is that the snow again?'

Something was rumbling off to our left. I watched, transfixed, as a section of Farigaig at the edges of the light seemed to shrug off its covering. The surface slid in a broadening U-shape, a tongue advancing quickly like a foam-topped wave and a fan of slip following. The snow broke over the coping stones of a half-buried wall,

MARTIN GRIFFIN

charged out in a dissipating spread and wrestled itself into a brash breaker that crossed the road before slowing. Wind-spun powder-clouds misted the air, steaming off the back of the thing. The patrol car's headlight shot them through with diamonds. The moving bank ran with slipping snow, shallow fans resettling, then the noise faded and the last rollers came to a stop.

I watched, stupefied. The slip had started with nothing, emerged out of nowhere. Who could say what changes in temperature or vibration had been the trigger? It was as if some giant fluid animal had settled itself in front of us, its huge body blocking the road. The three of us stiffened in position, worried that further movement might bring the mountain down over our heads.

'Shit,' Jai breathed.

'That was relatively small,' Gaines Two said, and nodded at the woods, 'compared to what we might get. The section between us and the hotel drops at a much steeper gradient. There's a lot of unstable snow in there; it's a miracle we got up here without triggering an avalanche. If we get another on a bigger scale, the hotel is right in its path.'

Across the road, the slip was still settling, clouds of powder spinning to rest. It was like we were being penned in slowly but surely, each exit shut firmly against us. Our world was now just the few square miles around the hotel, and our landward borders were shrinking. Waiting for rescue was looking increasingly futile. We were going to have to find a way off the mountain, and – I felt engulfed by hopelessness at this – the road up here wasn't going to be drivable, now or in the morning. There was a possibility it was clearer further along, but how was I to get there with no vehicle? I'd been waiting years for the chance to leave everything behind, and now, hours from catching my flight, it seemed suddenly further away than ever. For the first time, I wondered whether survival might become the only goal that mattered.

'Dawn is five hours away,' Gaines said. 'The skies are clearing, the temperatures will drop. It'll be, what, minus five? Ten?' He removed his hat and ran a hand across his brow. His voice was low and he weighed each word. 'I think we could be in serious trouble,' he said. 'I need to get you two out of here.'

21

The option of returning via the woods was off the table. Instead we half-climbed, half-slithered over the back of the new slip and, once on the other side, followed the cat's eyes along the road, walking with nervous purpose. Only luck had got us up here; I wondered how much we might have left.

Nothing made sense and my thoughts were a knot I couldn't untangle. Needing to talk to Jai, I touched his arm and together we slowed our pace until Gaines Two was fifteen strides ahead. We were only going to get a moment; we'd need to make our exchange of words as brief as possible.

'You think he killed her, don't you?' Jai breathed.

My heart broke for Shelley all over again, crushed in her frozen cab, desperate for help. When I returned his gaze, he thinned his lips and whispered, 'But if he's Foley, he'd want us dead too. Wouldn't he have done it by now?'

'No gun,' I mouthed. We matched each other's footsteps, the crunch of our boots alarmingly loud in the fresh-minted stillness. Above us, the clouds were thinning. Our passing frightened something at the edge of the wood and it scurried away into ink-black darkness. Gaines Two was still ahead but we didn't have long.

'There's a thousand ways a murderer like him could do it. He doesn't need a weapon,' Jai pointed out. 'He could've killed us but he didn't. Which makes him genuine, doesn't it?'

I tried a double-check of Jai's reasoning. Was there something he'd missed? What could this man still want from us?

'You both OK?' Gaines had slowed and turned. We nodded mutely, our secret conference curtailed. He smiled. 'Good. Try and stay positive. I'll get you through this.' He stayed alongside us, keeping his voice low. 'With the snow unstable, I won't be able to risk getting you two out of here by road. We need to start thinking about other ways off the mountain. Miss Yorke, you know the grounds and the surrounding area. Is there anything you can share that might help?'

Any chance I'd had to marshal my thoughts was lost. I silently cursed, weighing up the costs and benefits of sharing. Did I tell him everything I knew about the grounds, the paths along the loch edge, the bridge under repair, the boathouse? Or would I be sacrificing advantage?

'Miss Yorke?'

'The hotel has a boat for cruising guests along the loch,' I conceded. 'A mile along the shoreline is a perimeter fence gate. Beyond the gate is the boathouse. If the loch ice isn't too bad, we might be able to take the boat west along the shoreline to the far tip of Alder.'

Giving voice to the idea seemed to solidify the possibility of using the loch to leave. At Alder's western tip was a jetty, which hotel guests used as a disembarkation point, and at the shoreline the road met a gravel car park at the water's edge. From there, it descended into Inverness. It was possible – tantalisingly possible – that the worst snow was gathered on the sections of the road up here, where we were currently walking, and that further down, the way had been ploughed and gritted. If I could tie the boat up at the loch's furthest point, I might be able to hitch a lift into town. It was two hours twenty into Aberdeen by train. My car wasn't the only way out of here.

'Tell me about the path to the boathouse,' said Gaines.

Maybe this was why he needed me. I'd have to be careful; releasing information slowly would better preserve my position. 'There's two. A longer one along the edge of the water, or a cut through the woods. We'd have to be careful on the shorter path,' I explained; 'there's a crossing that can be treacherous.' Barnacle Bridge was an old unstable thing spanning one of the steep woodland creeks populated with roosting geese. The spray from the tumbling streams made the wood rot, and the bridge was high above the rocks below. Such was its danger, we'd shut it for the winter.

Gaines Two nodded. 'So we've got a potential way out ...' He faltered, face buried in his coat and breath rising as he considered another thought. 'When Foley first arrived, did you mention the boat to him?'

I replayed my conversations with Gaines One. We'd examined the loch from the shelter of the garage doors when we'd been to collect the rifle. 'I told him it was there,' I said. 'He asked about the grounds and I told him everything. I thought he was . . .'

'Understandable,' Gaines Two said, nodding. 'Did he seem to have a particular interest in the boathouse? The vessel itself? He'd have dressed it up as something else.'

Gaines One had indeed seemed interested in the boathouse; in fact he'd urged Jai and me to go there to keep us out of the way and safe. Unless he was doing it simply so he knew where he could find us and finish us off. It made a sort of sense; the worsening weather had rendered his SUV getaway plan impossible, so his aim was to eliminate the police officer on his tail, then finish the witnesses and leave by some other way. Perhaps his whole search of the hotel hadn't been about looking for a phone signal to contact colleagues at all, I realised. Perhaps he'd been investigating the loch shore, looking for a way across the water. But if Gaines One really was Foley, he'd have killed us both as soon as he got his hands on the rifle. *Why hadn't he?* I kept coming back to the same questions.

'He mentioned the boathouse a couple of times,' I said. 'Suggested it might be a safe place to hide.'

Gaines Two considered this. 'Which makes it the one place you shouldn't go,' he said, 'until I've made sure we've dealt with him.'

We reached the top of the driveway. It would take us at least twenty minutes to flounder our way down the switchbacks. Even in ski gloves, my fingers were aching with cold, and my numbed feet made me feel like I was walking on ungainly borrowed legs. My nose was streaming. Breathing was difficult; each ragged inhalation like swallowing ice. Halfway down, Gaines stopped to listen to the shifting snow creak and echo in the woods. When he resumed walking, Jai placed a hand on my shoulder and we managed a quickly snatched exchange of whispers.

'When we get back, I say we head to the basement and lock ourselves in,' Jai hissed.

'If it isn't already underwater.'

Below us, the Mackinnon, normally a firework display of bright windows, was a dead-eyed outline. I thought of those corridors and rooms in a new and darker way. The bar, snug and kitchens, and the slowly flooding cellar – they were all now places of potential concealment.

Jai leaned in close. 'Listen. I have something to confess,' he said. 'I haven't been entirely honest with you.'

I felt an anticipatory tightening inside and wobbled on numb feet, readying myself for a blow. But Jai never got to finish. Gaines Two turned. For the briefest of moments I felt like we'd been caught, but though he noticed our closeness, he pressed on as if he hadn't. 'We're going to need to be very careful down there,' he said. 'Torches off. Foley could be anywhere and I don't want to alert him to our presence. I recall a movement-activated light above the garage doors? We'll need to give that sensor a wide berth.'

We resumed our walk, Jai and I following as Gaines skirted the inside corner of the drive down a bank of snow-choked heather and made it to the car park with the hotel grounds still in darkness. The snow here was criss-crossed with the softening scars of our previous footfalls; some imperceptible depressions, others raised ridges. We studied the building beyond, our breath billowing. I checked the sky and watched heavy storm clouds continue to thin. The moon wasn't visible but a gauzy patch of pale grey shifted quickly beneath its light; soon we'd be seeing bright points of distant stars through breaking strips. I studied the implacable black of the Mackinnon's windows with their stern brow-ridges. No sign of movement within, the place just as we left it.

'I can get my job done best if I know you two are safe,' Gaines whispered as we stamped our feet against the freezing temperatures, 'So you're going back to your rooms. You do not answer your doors for anyone except me, clear?'

'What about our missing guest?'

'Leave that with me,' Gaines replied. We moved slowly, skirting the car park towards the revolving doors at reception, together as a three. There was no opportunity to give Jai a moment to explain his cryptic half-confession. What had he been about to say? Back in the garage before we'd set off, I'd wondered if he might be the man who'd arranged for the SUV to be parked there; if he might be here to aid Foley's escape. The more I knew him, the less likely it seemed. But could it be true? Was he about to confess?

We'd just reached the fountain and the broad dark arms of the old larch when the radio bleeped into life. It was in my coat pocket. I pulled it clear with numb hands. It garbled at me again, a voice emerging. 'Stop where you are. Stand still.'

Gaines Two, a couple of steps ahead, turned, examining the radio in my hand with hard, steady eyes. 'What?' he managed.

My heart barrelled. I held the radio up in one shaking hand, a reluctant messenger. The three of us stared at its little yellow screen. Then it chirped into life and the voice came again. 'Don't move,' it said. 'I have a gun. I'm pointing it at you right now.'

The voice had a firm highlands accent. It was our first visitor. The man who'd called himself Don Gaines.

22

During the course of that nightmare slog through the dark, exhaustion and cold, those twin dissemblers, had stripped me of clarity. Who was the gun pointing at? Was I the target? My knees weakened. The simple act of adjusting my footing was painful and I nearly fell. Next to me, Gaines Two took a slow 360 turn, assessing the landscape; a quick scan of the garages behind us, the line of woods marking the edge of the turning circle, then a long examination of the Mackinnon. He seemed remarkably calm.

Now that the snow had eased and the wind had dropped, we had a good view of the building; over to our left, the service door to the kitchens, the big stone-mullioned bay windows of the ground-floor rooms, and ahead, the reception's glass and steel extension and the revolving doors. The ground floor looked empty so I lifted my gaze, checking the first-floor windows one by one, then the second and third. Black glass, closed sashes, drawn curtains. Rising above, the ivy-clad belltower was a silent sentinel. The top of the building; a jumble of pitched roofs, dormer windows and chimney stacks that was harder to read. I hadn't shown Gaines One the third-floor roof access door but he'd been up to my room and left the handprint on the corridor wall, so he knew where it was. Up there was a walkway beyond a gantry that criss-crossed the flat sections, allowing access to skylights, chimneys, pipes and gutters. He could be looking down at us, his position disguised.

Gaines beckoned for the radio. I handed it over. His eyes were quick, on the move, never leaving the hotel building as he spoke. 'Who is this?'

There was a long silence. I had a jittery, exposed feeling; I moved my feet in my boots, flexed my fingers. The three of us waited, watching, our breath a climbing column dissipating into the dark. Above us the cloud cover had thinned to a high, dying mist. Through the branches of the old larch, the stars had begun glowing hard and bright and the moon was an ivory blur.

The radio fizzed. 'PC 4256 Gaines, Police Scotland. I have a clear line of sight and I will not hesitate to shoot if you do something stupid. It's over, Foley.'

Adrenaline throbbed and I felt giddily light-headed. Both men together, one my brother's murderer. I was no nearer to knowing which was which.

'My God,' said Gaines Two, his voice flat and expressionless, hungry eyes searching the windows. 'Troy Foley. There's no way you're getting out of this alive. That prison transport was due into Glenochil hours ago. As soon as they lost contact with your vehicle, they'll have started working on backup. Look around you. There's no way off the mountain in these conditions.'

Eyes still assessing the building, he tipped his head and continued speaking, this time to me. 'He's clever and manipulative, Miss Yorke. He'll do everything he can to convince you I'm an impostor—'

The radio bleeped again, and the voice of Gaines One returned. 'Jesus, you're a piece of work,' it said, exasperated. 'I'm going to ask the two civilians to step away now. Remie, Mr Parik, listen. I want you to walk slowly into the shelter of the big tree to your right—'

Gaines Two depressed the button, shaking his head and interrupting. 'Don't you try splitting us apart, Foley. If they move, you have a clearer line of sight.' He turned to us. 'Don't listen to him. He wants to be able to cover each of us. Easier to take us out individually. Three clean shots—'

'I'm PC Donald Gaines,' the voice countered. 'This is what he does, Remie. He plays roles. He manipulates and confuses. Do you see what he's trying here?'

Gaines Two gave a growl of frustration, bringing the radio close to his lips. 'I'm not trying anything, Foley. I'm doing my duty as a police officer, keeping these people safe. You're the one with the gun.'

The radio buzzed. 'That's right,' said the voice of Gaines One. 'So I'll give the instructions.'

Gaines Two scoped out the garages again, checked the pines. I wondered why; it seemed pretty clear the man at the other end of the radio would be inside the hotel somewhere. He must have concluded the same because he returned his gaze to the building, facing the lightless windows.

The voice on the radio returned. 'If I hadn't asked Miss Yorke for the keys to the gunroom, you'd have armed yourself and killed the two people you're currently pretending to protect.'

It seemed too risky even to glance about but I managed to briefly meet Jai's gaze. He'd arranged himself stiffly, hood half up, snow in his dark hair. His hands were raised, palms out. He was looking at the empty windows and I watched him swallow, wincing at the dryness caught in his throat. What had he been about to tell me?

A group of birds, disturbed by some shift in the woodland darkness behind us, lifted into flight and wheeled above in a broken circle. The clouds had cleared and the stars overhead were a pin-sharp pattern on black silk. Gaines Two raised the radio to his cracked lips. 'The more you try your lies,' he said, eyes roving relentlessly, 'the worse it looks for you. You've no ID, you're dressed in stolen clothes and you've been sneaking around out in the dark while we've been working to rescue the injured driver of your transport. It all points one way, right?'

The world had shrunk to this space beside the fountain and the old tree, outside the revolving doors. Everything else was shrouded in nothingness. I felt for a second as if we were the only people left on the planet. Until, eyes on the Mackinnon's guest rooms, I thought I saw something. A movement somewhere inside, behind a third-floor window. I held my breath, checked the blank eyes of the upstairs rooms again. Couldn't detect it. Had I just seen the gunman?

'Get down on your knees, Foley,' came the voice on the radio, 'or I will shoot.'

Gaines Two grimaced, his jaw working furiously as he ground his teeth. He glanced at us both in turn, his expression apologetic. 'I can't think of a way out of this,' he whispered. 'Stay alert. Don't trust him.' Then he raised his hands and lowered himself slowly.

'Hand the radio to Miss Yorke,' said the voice of the first Gaines.

Gaines Two extended an arm in response. Our eyes met as I took the radio. He gave me a resigned look. 'I'm sorry I couldn't do more,' he said. 'Just be careful, OK?'

The dark hotel felt part of some grand simulation. I tried to blink myself back to sharp and steady truth but all I saw was a masquerade of signals, of uniforms and stories. I was numb with cold and shock but hot enough to be running a fever, trying to read every gesture and change in tone, weigh every word, check every window for further movement.

I realised the radio-voice was talking to me. Raised the handset and my answer caught in my throat. 'What?'

'I said, I want the man on the ground to remove the wallet in his pocket.'

Gaines Two, on his knees, called, 'I already showed Miss Yorke my warrant card, Foley!' He looked up at me, cocked his head and tilted his hands in a helpless shrug.

The voice of Gaines One continued, gentler now. 'Remove the wallet and throw it towards Miss Yorke. Remie – I want you to pick it up.'

MARTIN GRIFFIN

I turned to the man beside me. Watched as he closed his eyes, lips pressed hard together, and reached inside his coat to produce his wallet. He dropped it at my feet. I tried to blink away the black dots crowding at the edge of my vision, and dropped slowly to a crouch, focusing everything on the slow extension of my arm. I clasped the wallet and, rising to standing, felt a flush of dizziness that nearly knocked me over. Jai released a pent-up cloud of breath.

'That ID is mine,' said the voice on the radio. 'Foley took it from me.'

'Bullshit,' said Gaines Two.

The radio crackled. 'Inside you'll find a driving licence.'

I woke my hands with a series of painful movements and made a clumsy examination of the wallet's contents. I finally managed to pull the licence clear, gloved fingers dancing. The thumbnail picture was better than grainy but an overlaid watermark made it hard to discern the features in moonlight. White guy, lightly bearded. Hooded eyes, square jaw. It could certainly be a younger version of Gaines One, the Scot on the radio. But it could have been the second Gaines too.

'The man with you,' said the radio-voice. 'Ask him for his date of birth.'

'This is ridiculous,' spat Gaines Two. He'd returned to his obsessive check on the darkness around us, quick glances taking in the outbuildings and woods.

'Ask him for his date of birth.'

I turned to Gaines Two, on his knees beside me. 'Just tell me,' I said.

'It's a trick, Remie,' he said calmly. 'Don't you listen to him. Or you, Mr Parik.' He risked a quick check of Jai. 'His aim is to drive a wedge between us, get us doubting each other. He's an expert at this game.' He ground his teeth. 'When he discharges the gun, it'll take a moment to reload. That's when you run, OK? Hide.'

'Just tell me,' I pleaded, 'and we can prove it.'

He shook his head slowly. His forehead wound had split afresh and he wiped the blood from his eye in a distracted gesture. I could see from the rise and fall of his chest that his pulse was up and his breathing was shallow.

The radio bleeped. 'He can't,' Gaines One said. 'He can't because that's my licence. My details. Last chance, Foley. What's the D.O.B. on the licence you stole?'

The man on the ground grinned.

And I watched as his posture shifted; his shoulders dropping, his chin rising, his body seeming to coil in readiness. 'Fuck this,' he hissed in sudden and convulsive anger. His mouth slackened into a sneer. I took a trembling step backwards. 'Fuck *all of this*,' Gaines Two shouted in a bloom of breath and spittle.

One face had been cast aside, another revealed. Certainty at last. The man on the roof was a police officer.

And the one in the snow next to me was Troy Foley.

23

The harsh bark of Foley's upraised voice broke the night's silence. There was an applauding flurry of moonlit wings. Disturbed birds rising from the hotel roof; half a dozen ravens scattering like blown rags, drawing our eyes.

The three of us were transfixed, staring upwards. The hard edges of the building blurred as the silhouetted head and shoulders of a man appeared, standing in a gully between two pitched dormer sections. We craned our necks. I held my breath. Up there was Don Gaines. The big broad-shouldered officer, the night's first visitor. He stood, boots at the very edge of the roof, back against the sky, a hunting rifle tucked against his side under one arm. With his spare hand he threw something down to me. I watched it drop and land, sending up a halo of snow powder. I advanced to find a coil of rope lying there.

'I'd like you to tie him up,' Gaines called from above, then, turning his attention to his prisoner, continued, 'Hands behind your back, Foley. Try anything and I will shoot.' He limped a step away from the edge and raised the rifle, settling it into the crook of his arm and watching us down the barrel.

I picked up the rope and stood behind the figure of Troy Foley. The man on his knees had leaned forward, hands on his thighs. I saw a different person now. Maskless, he was narrow-eyed and calculating. 'Fuck all of you,' he said, over and over at a whisper. I flexed warmth into my fingers and held the length of rope between two fists. I found myself testing my strength, pulling the rope as taut as I could, loosening then pulling. Tourniquet.

Above me, Don Gaines was calling down to us again.

'Troy Foley,' he was saying, his raised voice remarkably steady, 'you're under arrest for escaping from lawful custody. You do not have to say anything but it may harm your defence if . . .'

I looked at the rope in my hands, then back up to the figure. The voice of the man on the roof drifted to the outer reaches of my attentional spotlight. I took a step forward, the length of rope loose between my fists. I was close enough to drop the rope in a bib across Foley's front. It would take only seconds to twist it into a loop, channel everything I had into my arms and pull the hardest I'd ever done. I could strangle Foley right here and now and Gaines, perched as he was three floors above me, wouldn't be able to see what I was doing until it was too late. I sucked in a shallow breath and positioned myself behind the kneeling man.

I was going to kill him.

Up on the roof, Don Gaines was completing his

arrest statement. '. . . you do not mention, when questioned something you later rely on in court. Anything you do say—'

I looked up, shaken suddenly awake. Don Gaines had stopped talking and was turning away from us. Something behind him had caught his attention. He turned back, assessing the three of us, a wordless outline, then spun again, this time turning his whole body, adjusting his footing and raising his gun at something up there with him.

Facing something we couldn't see, he seemed momentarily frozen. Then he lowered his gun and raised an arm in surrender. He held a hand out as if offering something to whoever was up there with him. His radio.

Then there was an ear-shattering crack.

I'd heard guns discharged before. Hunting parties up and down Farigaig and Bray shot grouse over the autumn and winter. But I'd never been up close and nothing had prepared me for it. The noise made my ears sing. I flinched, crouching; dropped the rope.

The big figure on the roof fell heavily backwards. His left knee gave. I watched, horrified, as Gaines spun out into the air, one shoulder pushed back by the force of the bullet, one arm extended, both legs locked. The rifle broke from his grip and for a second he seemed to hang above us, a swimmer seen from below, thrashing limbs in dark water, before he plunged. The shape struck the ground at the front of the hotel with a horrible crunch. An explosion of displaced snow, rising in white wings. The rifle, pitching end over end, hit nearby. Jai shouted in horror. I felt my lungs contract and gaped, airless, at the broken shape drilled into the drifts at the hotel's edge.

Feet up, legs wide like a beached bather, Don Gaines blinked a couple of times before his jaw lolled slack.

The volley of the shot was still echoing, rolling through the trees and up the hill. I had enough presence of mind to return my gaze to the roof, seeking out the source. Nothing. Then a flash of movement. I didn't see anything clearly because of what happened next – but I had a sense of a slight silhouette, momentarily backlit by stars then quickly receding. My insides pitched downwards and liquefied.

I was pretty sure who I'd just seen on the roof.

The figure was lithe, slim and strong. The upper body was bulked out by a puffer jacket but there was no mistaking the slim runner's legs, the cropped hair. And the rifle gripped at the trigger by strong, climber's hands.

It was our missing guest. Alex Coben.

24

Coben, the gunshot, what came after: those things will always be connected in my mind as a result. Illusory correlation, they call it. My skull thumped, jagged and raw. I was on my knees. What I took for the echo of the shot became something else, something swift and vengeful.

I looked up through the trees towards the drive and felt my body dissolve.

The mountainside was rising up, lifting itself on foaming shoulders, bursting forth into forward motion. It was coming for us in a great broiling wall. The pines submitted quickly, one after the other like dominoes, trunks snapping and shaggy tops plunging downwards, spinning end over end, thrown then consumed. The avalanche brought its own weather system; pushed an eddy of expanding fog before it. The rhythm of the fall shook the liquid in my body. My blood thrilled to it. The gel between my joints hummed. The avalanche moved like an animal, shattered limbs, scattered branches, noise and shuddering air. The fucking thing had jaws. Its big white mouth smashed into the stable block and ate it whole. It buried my car. Two vast spreading shoulders came booming down towards us, tossing trees, rolling rocks of snow like beachballs.

For a split second I saw the knot of our group silhouetted against the charging wall. Troy Foley on his knees, rising slowly, transfixed; Jai beginning an almost comic lope towards me, his knees high and pumping as he tried to run. The figure on the roof was turned at the waist, rifle loose beside her. Like a chased child shrieking at an incoming wave, I turned and fled, slow limbs thrashing through glue. The noise rose to a wild bellow. I was running through mist now, the fine drifts of spray at the base of a waterfall – the foremost edges of the chasing wave.

The slip ran its fingertips through my hair and I screamed.

Ten steps later it hit me hard.

I was smashed face down into the snow as if an open palm had struck me between the shoulder blades. Abominable noise; the grotesque bellow of the avalanche. My feet were lifted upwards as a rolling wall tipped me vertical. Some crazy childhood instinct made me pull my arms in and make fists. I had a sudden jab of memory; taking Cameron ice skating and warning him to fall with closed hands. The wall smashed me into a flailing spin, then over on my back, rolling me senseless.

I must've blacked out.

When I came round, I was lying in grey snow the weight of rock.

I tried to move my arms but they were pinned to my

side. Then I tried my legs, straining hard. To my horror, they were stuck too. I was rigid, frozen into a black and airless pocket. My lungs began to prickle, my body desperate for oxygen. Snow pressing against my face, in my mouth. I somehow dragged a breath in, sick with fear. If I didn't calm down, I'd pass out and the cold would kill me. My chest rose and fell quickly as I gasped. I felt my coffin shift almost imperceptibly in response. My body's terror had created a little more space.

My thinking became clearer. I started to move a shoulder, pushing against the weight of the snow, then a knee. I steadied my breathing and thought: *Heathrow, Madrid, Santiago.* Then I pushed again, eking out room in small degrees. Found I could turn my head, grab a breath of air from a cavity at my shoulder then resume my careful wriggle. It was exhausting; slow-motion drowning, loosening further space, bullying concessions from the drift; grunting, kicking, jerking. *Can't die now. Not after everything.* I repeated my mantra again and again. *Heathrow. Madrid. Santiago.* Sometime later I could turn on my side and press upwards with my left shoulder. The roof retreated. On my back again I hammered at the ceiling with wild hands, thrashed at the walls of my amniotic sac.

My left foot broke out first. I'd been digging in the wrong direction. I had to reassemble my sense of the world, an ungainly newborn, trying to remember how to raise myself up on my hands. My whole body broke through the wall of snow and I glimpsed stars. They made me think of Cameron and I was so grateful, so relieved to have made it out of my icy coffin that I started to cry, long hoarse sobs that ached as they came. I had a go at standing then gave up and lay on my back, tears still streaming. The world levelled out. My stomach rushed upwards and I had to roll over and throw up. The dizziness wouldn't pass. I lay in the storm for I don't know how long, kissed by snowflakes and spitting vomit.

Eventually I made it to all fours and my eyes came back into focus.

I was lying on my torch. I excavated it, brushed the lens clear and clicked it on. I'd been carried forty feet down onto the lawn beneath the turning circle at the hotel entrance. Much of the hotel was buried under a new landscape that shelved upwards in steep-sided blocks like wet sand. A following wind came bowling down its sides, carrying fresh swirls of fret. Somewhere in the woods above, there was a slow, low grumbling sound, the off-kilter creak of sliding snow.

I hauled myself upwards. Stars exploded in my head and the loch-facing side of the hotel – the section that hadn't been partly buried – tipped drunkenly as I wobbled upright. I panned my light across the hissing white tundra of the new world; almost began shouting for survivors until the thought that any sudden sound might bring further slips iced the words in my mouth. Instead I kicked snow over the contents of my stomach and tried walking. I kept having to stop and rest, hot pain lancing as I moved.

It's hard to describe the child-like disorientation of

finding your world remade. The turning circle and fountain – we'd just been standing there – were gone. And the old larch was down. It had fallen through the glass-fronted reception extension, felling a metal joist and shattering the floor-to-ceiling panes. Its stunted head was partially indoors. I moved forward cautiously. It was a disorienting sight, the big thick trunk and arms like those of a downed beast. I ran a hand across its flank, a curious mix of snow and shattered glass beneath my feet. I'd imagined tempered glass might break into safe particles but the Mackinnon's front had disintegrated into vicious slices and the spaces inside and out were decorated with sheared blades of the stuff. The revolving doors were a partially compressed mess, but getting inside the hotel wasn't going to be a problem with a tree-sized gash across its face. The shaggy arms of larch had dumped a carpet of winter needles across the glass-covered floor.

I retreated, assessing the rest of the slip. The car park, the stables and the drive beyond were crushed beneath a remade world. Poor Don Gaines had received a swift burial. He'd been helping me; all this time, trying to protect me and track down his escapee. And he'd come so close, in those final moments . . . I felt wretched, staring at the elevated slab of snow-country that had settled in fifteen layered feet over him, rising behind the fallen tree like a wall.

I saw Don Gaines fall from the roof each time I shut my eyes. What did the events at the fountain tell me? Had I been mistaken, or had I seen Alex Coben up there with him? I had. *So where had she been all this time? And who the hell was she?* Coben had been Foley's accomplice, it had to be. She'd reversed the Subaru into the garage sometime yesterday. Then she'd cleared out her room and gone missing after breakfast. She hadn't gone walking, though; hadn't been in the snug at the Clachaig as we'd speculated. She must have been hiding nearby. In the garage, maybe. She'd have been close when we'd broken in earlier – I must have been right on top of her as I'd wriggled in through the broken window. And the door of the vehicle had still been open; she'd left it that way as she'd hurried out of sight. Foley, playing Gaines, must've had his heart in his mouth as he'd feigned surprise at the presence of the vehicle and the case with his change of clothes. Another piece fell into place: she'd been interested in maps because she'd known the weather might close off her escape by road. *And the telescope.* She'd left the telescope in her room placed innocently like birdwatcher's kit, facing the loch. But it was the window at the side of the building that had been open because she'd been studying the prison from there; she'd doubtless watched the violence erupt and known the time had come to act. She must have found a way into the gunroom, arming herself. The garage, the gunroom … she had to have a copy of the keys from somewhere. Keys which gave her access to the whole hotel. Maybe she'd gone on the hunt for Gaines – *the real Gaines*, Gaines One – while we were trying to rescue Shelley. Then, eventually, she'd seen our torches weaving slowly down the drive as we'd returned.

All of which meant I really had climbed through the woods up to the mountain road accompanied by Troy Foley. He'd killed my brother, broken out of prison and then killed Shelley Talbot when he'd discovered she'd survived the crash, a witness to his escape. *And I'd helped him do it.* I pulled myself up and over the larch, burning with rage, broken by guilt. First Cameron, then Shelley.

I pushed aside survivor's guilt and tried to concentrate, assessing the foothills of the new slip, establishing its boundaries. One border, to my right, was the outer wall of the hotel. The slip had foamed in a frozen wave against the stonework, coming to rest above the level of the first-floor windows. Behind me, the vast corpse of the toppled tree, and, to my left, a softer border; the dark woodland. Huge grey tumbledown tongues of the stuff disappeared between the trunks of the trees. I tested the slip with a tentative foot. Troy Foley was under here somewhere. This thousand square yards of unstable snow, doubtless riddled with random caves below, and above, ridged with big white erratics; pockmarked with crests and cavities, was Foley's burial ground as well as Gaines's. I hoped he felt the same panic that I had experienced, the terror of being buried alive, before he succumbed, slowly, to the cold. I wanted him to suffer.

And Jai was under there too, his secret confession, whatever it was, buried with him. One thing was clear now: Coben was Foley's accomplice, which made Jai just a man who'd come up to the highlands for some walking. A decent man, entirely innocent. I tried to picture our positions as the shot went off and the avalanche came, to figure out if it was likely he'd survived. He'd been behind me, that was for sure. I began to dig. The passing minutes were inconsequential; I just shovelled snow, scooping out armfuls on my knees, standing and clawing it out between my legs. Progress was slow, quicker when I found pockets trapped under firmer slabs like open veins in limestone. Perhaps Jai was still alive, working his way through a connected intestine of chambers. Common responses to shock amongst disaster workers – alongside the trauma-specific desensitisation – can be mindless fugues or frenzies, and I think that's where I was during the lost time after the slip; I was just hacking at the thing from the outside in, desperate to find Jai.

I returned to sanity because of a sound.

I wiped my face, listening. *Clang, clang, clang.* Then nothing. I found my torch and panned it into the darkness beyond the crashed larch, feeling my skin tighten and the hairs on my arms rise. It was nearby. I moved ten steps along the edge of the slip and it came again: *clang, clang.* Silence. I waited until it came again. This time I was sure; it was an impact noise, something against hollow metal. I froze in the moonlight, listening to the creep-and-moan of settling snow. Long minutes passed with no recurrence. Then it came again. This time I was looking in the right direction. Beyond the tree, emerging from smashed blocks of avalanche, was the bent pole of a tall outdoor light – the one used to illuminate the turning circle and entrance, one of the ones Gaines had asked to be switched off when he arrived. It vibrated at

MARTIN GRIFFIN

the final *clang*, shed snow from its bulb-cover. I panned downwards. The metal upright was planted in ten or twelve feet of tumbled avalanche.

Someone was under there, hitting it.

I rolled gracelessly back over the trunk of the fallen tree and across to the pile, stooping beneath my own dissipating vapour clouds and pulling armfuls of snow clear. I worked more warily now, trying to recall exactly where each of us had been when the avalanche struck. This was likely to be Jai, I reasoned, but there was a chance it was Foley under there. I could be attacked as I liberated him. Had to be careful.

I was getting closer. I clawed and swept, lungs ablaze. Another five feet down. I pulled aside wedges, scooping at the hard-packed stuff. Eventually I rent through the outer wall of a desperate little cave. Something was moving in there. I saw a yellow coat and kept digging.

Jai emerged, half-conscious and banging his torch against the base of the light. I pulled the walls clear and yanked him by an arm, dragging him into the night air.

25

The presence of another survivor validated me. I wasn't alone and losing my mind. I felt my senses sharpen and, as they did, waking pain receptors communicated a howling barrage of information: cuts, bruises, sprains, bone-deep numbness.

'Jai,' I hissed when it had begun to pass. 'You're all right. I've got you.' He blinked bloodshot eyes, failing to focus. The side of his face was scraped raw and his mouth bled. His lips were blue, his whole body shaking with shock and cold. I pushed his hair away from his wounds. 'You're OK now,' I whispered. Instinct made me wriggle an arm under his shoulder and try lifting him into my lap as I knelt, but his bulk was limp and slippery so I settled for rolling him onto his back. He blinked tears. 'Hey, Jai. C'mon now. You're safe. It's me, Remie.'

He responded to my name, focusing now. When he saw me, he flinched and croaked, 'He might still be alive. He was nearby when we started running.'

I watched his shoulders shift as he breathed, then checked the slip, my scalp shrivelling at the thought of a hand thrusting upwards through the pack behind us, or Coben, out there somewhere, digging her boss free. But there was nothing. 'We need to get inside,' I said. 'These temperatures are going to kill us.' He managed a nod, hugging himself. I helped him up. He ran the back of a hand across his face and took a long shuddering breath. He blinked his red eyes open, gritting his teeth.

I gave him a second. 'Are you in pain? Is anything broken?'

Jai grimaced. 'Left arm pretty bad.' He straightened and tested his shoulder, then let out a long breath.

We leant against the downed tree, dropped to sitting side by side. My thighs were numb, my fingers swollen claws, my body at once clammy with exertion and shivering with cold. Jai brushed the snow from his coat, scooped it out of his neck, emptied his sleeves. We were in shock but we didn't sit for long beneath the billowing clouds of our breath, waiting for the world to make some sense again. We couldn't. Fear needled me into action, but rising upright left me howling.

When the pain receded I managed, 'We better get inside.'

Jai struggled to his feet and followed. I watched my companion trying to make sense of the hotel. He blinked at the crushed cage of the reception doors, studied the glass-edged hole drilled through the frontage then, leaning on the trunk of the newly felled larch, took in the tumbledown mountain of snow, the front edge of the avalanche rising up to an elegant overhang.

Up beyond that, it would be blasted moonscape; a ten-ton pile-up of Jenga-block snow-work. Behind us, the world still looked relatively normal. Loch Alder was still there, encased in its grey coffin of ice. There was something at once reassuring and frightening about that, but I couldn't put my finger on what. Jai needed a moment longer to regain his balance, then we hauled ourselves over the trunk, crook-backed and geriatric, and approached the wreck of the reception.

I checked the darkness in there, my imagination populating every fold with Coben-shapes. The screen of my watch was cracked and fogged, impossible to read. I dug for my phone. How long had I been unconscious? How long had I spent digging for Jai? Coben could've moved freely through the wreck of the avalanche during a lost ... I didn't know, I guessed an hour maybe. She'd been prowling, looking for Foley. Or setting traps for us. Inside the building, I imagined slim silhouettes, armed and hell-bent. My skin goosebumped. Coben or not, we had to get inside. Jai worked to wrestle a tooth of glass free, pushed aside a curtain of twigs and we proceeded, checking carefully as we stooped and crunched our way into the half-dark of reception.

'Jai,' I whispered as we straightened up. 'Did you see who shot Gaines?'

He shook his head. 'Came from the roof, I think.'

I told him about Coben. He stiffened in response. 'The other guest? *Shit.* She's an accomplice? Plus she's armed?' He turned to examine the night through the chaos of the fallen tree. 'You think she's out there? Or in here?'

'Haven't seen her. Guess she went to try and dig her boss free.'

Jai covered his eyes with a trembling palm. '*Fuck*,' he hissed. His breath came rapidly and he gave me a queasy look. 'We're not out of this by a long way.'

'I don't think so.' I knew I needed a plan but my thoughts were scattered and my attempts to piece them together felt slow and ungainly.

Then something changed outside. Whatever it was, it was enough to send a rush of heat through my system. Jai saw me watching and narrowed his eyes. I'd seen a faint glow against the broken glass. There was a light outside. Not the stable brightness of a streetlight, the low bob of movement between still-standing trees. A torch.

'That's her,' I said. 'She's searching for Foley.'

'Or coming for us. We have to hide.' Jai's face was creased with exhaustion. If his was anything like mine, it was bone-deep. He ran his good hand down his trousers, located and pulled out the radio. 'Still working,' he whispered, examining the screen. 'Let's try and call for help. Storm's gone; we might be able to raise someone.'

'The roof's best,' I said. 'Up where Gaines was.'

We left the crown of the fallen larch and crossed to the curved reception desk by the blue glow of its inlaid lights. I picked up my Midbow and hefted the stick in numb hands, then headed past the decorator's trolley down the long main corridor towards the lifts. Such was the silence, I could hear the whirring of the grandfather clock's springs and coils. I wonder what an observer would have made of us; two exhausted figures nursing bruises and scrapes, shivering against the cold in wet clothes, standing shoulder to shoulder and whispering.

'I was wrong,' Jai confessed. 'I'm sorry. I thought Foley was the first guy.'

'The second one would have fooled anybody. We couldn't have known,' I whispered.

Jai gripped his forehead and stared at the floor. 'We gave him everything he needed to kill Shelley Talbot. We told him about the radio contact, collected maps and walking gear for him. And he gladly took us along so we couldn't hook up with the real cop and try to escape while he was away.'

The regret came as a desperate ache. 'I kept her talking on the radio,' I breathed, 'giving him time to get to the crash site first.'

'You couldn't have known. If *I* hadn't heard her on the radio in the first place . . .'

'It's not your fault. We were manipulated, Jai. This is what he does.' I felt more certain with the passing minutes. 'Listen. Foley killed Shelley, not us. He killed the young officer we found in the boot of the car . . .' I swallowed hard. 'And he murdered my brother.'

You won't find a lot of psychology on the subject of vengeance. My colleagues back at Edinburgh would have argued it's a social phenomenon, the concern of anthropologists, and maybe at some early point in my life I'd have been inclined to agree with them. But the night I took a hockey stick to Danny Franks's hand I'd been burning with emotion – more than just a retaliatory impulse, I was alive with a passion, a desire for justice. Psychologists might disagree: simple pain or grief or shame, they'd say. But I don't buy it. Passions are more persistent and my new one was for some sort of closure, some kind of revenge. It had started on the steep climb to the mountain road when Shelley Talbot had confirmed it was Foley's boys who'd killed my brother. Now, with Gaines dead and Troy Foley exposed, it burned brighter than ever.

But there was something else in me, beating with equal insistence as I dug my phone out. It was 2.55 a.m. In eight hours I was going to be in Aberdeen for my flight at eleven. I'd made a promise to myself and to Cameron. Madrid by lunchtime, then overnight to Santiago. I was not going to be in the Burnett Road police station answering endless questions, writing out statements and reliving every horrific moment. Which meant I had to be careful. Where Jai might greet the possibility of rescue with joyous relief, I'd have to stay guarded. Plan a way out of this.

The torch in the darkness outside had vanished but I could feel Coben; sense her prowling the outer edges of the slip, finding a way to dig Foley free. We rode the lift to the third floor. On the way, I found adrenaline had begun to sharpen my senses so that the low light became a diamond-hard gleam as I showed Jai to the roof-access door. We shouldered it open, pushing fresh snow back, then closed it behind us. The night felt alive, electromagnetised, as if something about the aftermath of the slip had changed the fabric of the air. It smelt different; a petrichor of broken wood and rainfall that put me in mind, unlikely as it sounds, of freshly dug earth as we climbed the metal steps to the roof gantry. Up there I breathed deep, wondering if turned-over snow released suspended minerals or compounds, and noticing other things that had changed too; the darkness was fogged in silence, a thickly wadded nothingness punctuated only by woodland crow-calls. We stood beneath a canopy of stars. And looking ahead, up the hill, the world appeared broken and remade. Farigaig had shrugged its huge shoulders, and by moonlight I could make out a vast, broken V-shape that had opened up down the hillside. Inside the gash, moonlight washed over steep swathes of moorland heather, lightly snow-dusted. Further down I could follow the trail of destruction left as the mountain dumped its freight. The drive was intermittently exposed, but the hill above the hotel was mostly a cargo of smashed blocks. And the wave had gathered momentum, crashing over the garages and across the car park where, due to the angle of our view, it disappeared beneath us.

Up on the roof was a fenced walkway. Jai leant against it and set to work on the radio. Perhaps responding to the curious atmosphere, he kept his voice low. 'Hello? This is an emergency call. We need help. Repeat, SOS.'

The storm was gone, the night sky a clear, marbled dome. We'd be transmitting for miles in the silence. I listened to the night, fancying I might be hearing the sound of Coben digging somewhere in the snow below. The woods moaned and clattered as the world settled into its new posture. My heartbeat had slowed a little, until I remembered Jai's unfinished confession.

Haloed in his own breath, my companion was going at the radio. 'Can anybody hear me? This is an emergency call.' The receiver emitted a dull note, then a burst of white noise. Nothing. He went again, repeating his plea, changing channels, trying again. For minutes, the monotonous rhythm of bleep and hiss. I saw shapes in the stars and listened to Cameron's remembered voice point out constellations to me. Then finally a spirit from the white-noise rose and spoke. For a disorientating moment, I thought it was Cam. Relief rushed through me and I listened, alert and energised, trying to make out the words.

'Hello?' Jai said, stiffening. 'I can't hear you well. This is an emergency call. Can you send help? You have to send help.'

Another explosion of interference. Then a distant woman saying matter-of-factly, 'Confirm your position please.'

It was a female voice; one of those which immediately suggest calm authority. This was no civilian, this was a police officer. Which meant Inverness. The realisation brought a tumble of interconnected feelings. The giddy potential of escape; the chill certainty that I had to leave before help arrived. I had to be in Santiago by the correct date. I'd promised Cameron. My personal clock was ticking now.

'I'm a member of the public,' Jai said. 'I'm at the Mackinnon Hotel. We need help here.'

More interference. Then a reply; 'The connection keeps dropping out. So if you could—' followed by more silence until '—keep your finger pressed hard against the shoulder button and speak clearly. I repeat, is this an assistance call?'

Jai took a breath, looked at me with wide, grateful eyes. I took the radio from him. 'Yes. Yes! Assistance call,' I said.

'What's going on, please?'

'There's a man with a gun,' I said. 'A dangerous man.'

'Confirm gunman. Requesting—' I bit my lower lip and listened as the connection dropped and the radio fell silent again. This time the gap was longer, and the dead-air beep returned before I caught: '—further units, can you confirm your precise location?'

'The Mackinnon Hotel. Can you hear me? The Mackinnon Hotel.'

Jai leaned in until we were hunched over the radio shoulder to shoulder. Once I thought I caught an eddy of noise in the black emptiness, but nothing came back but the beep-beep. We waited another few minutes. I tried again, repeating our plea and location.

Then, sudden and sharp, a fizz followed by, 'Repeat: can you confirm your location please?'

'The Mackinnon Hotel!' I said. Kept repeating it, a tension headache probing behind my eyes. More minutes, more silence; frustration climbing.

Jai leaned against the handrail, his expression tortured.

He opened his mouth to speak but no words came out. Instead, his gaze softened and he stilled. 'What was that?'

We paused our activity, our breath dissipating in slow and fragile clouds as we listened. The noise of movement, nearby and inside the hotel. Too late I realised Coben had a radio too. She could hear us.

The two of us turned our attention to the roof door at the same time. It shuddered in its frame. Someone was pushing at it.

26

Fear pressed against the small of my back and I reversed, slithering. My muscles cramped and my heart gave a single, horrific kick that thrummed through to my fingertips. I pocketed the radio, grabbed my hockey stick and retreated along the raised steel walkway. We were hemmed in by pitched roofs to the left and right. The mesh-metal path was raised above the roof itself, high enough to be almost clear of snow. I could see evidence of previous boot prints. Gaines had been up here only an hour or so ago. Gaines and Coben. Ahead, the walkway took a ninety-degree right-hand turn.

'Where does this go, Remie?' Jai hissed, attention caught between the door at the foot of the stairs and the walkway, face drawn and cheeks hollow. I beckoned, not knowing what I was going to do. The path was still dusted with snow and our new tracks became freshly marked signposts as we retreated backwards. I'd never been up here; had no idea where to go. Beneath us was the top-floor corridor – anyone in the hotel directly below us would surely hear the metal reverberate as we moved above them – to our right, a pitched section of roof rose upwards to a chimney stack. I turned away from the roof-access steps and crept forward, the raised pathway no more than a couple of feet wide, slate tiles slippery with ice either side. The noise at the door behind me had gathered into a series of thumps.

'The tracks, Remie. *Fuck.*'

I paused, assessed the mess. We could sweep them away in arcs with our boots but the noise against the gantry metal and our direction of travel would be obvious anyway. 'Nothing we can do,' I hissed, turning back. 'Coben was up here to shoot Gaines. She knows the roof better than we do.'

Jai followed, breathing hard. We took a right. Another trench between pitched roofs. Already I was losing my sense of positioning. Ahead, the walkway took another right-hand turn, clearly circling the chimney to one side of us. We crept forward and turned again. Now we were on the far side of the island, hidden from view by the gritstone stack. I crouched and waited.

Life with Cameron had taught me the simple distinction between fight or flight was bogus. Up on the roof, I felt it with fresh certainty. The access door thumped once more – someone was pushing back a dense pillow of gathered snow with each shove – and I felt a fear so sharp and deep I couldn't move, a genuine freeze-response that locked me in a crouch on wooden legs. My heart slugged at me like a creature in utero. I stared at the toes of my boots for I don't know how long, my vision a watery mess. Some primeval instinct made me want to play dead – I had to fight the strong urge to curl up on my side and close my eyes. Then a vague awareness: the noise at the roof-access door had stopped. Didn't know when for sure.

Jai had tentatively risen to a hunched stand. He roused me, shaking me gently by the shoulder. 'Think we're safe,' he croaked.

We crept back the way we'd come. At the corner I stopped, hands in hot fists on my hockey stick, and dipped my head around in a swift movement. The rooftop walkway was empty. A spasm of relief. Nerves rubbed raw, I turned the corner and moved foot over foot back towards the gantry fence, as lightly and silently as I dared, until I'd opened up a line of sight to the door below. It was ajar. The corridor beyond was in darkness. I waited like a creature assessing a trap until Jai joined me.

When we spoke it was in breathless whispers; silent, mouthed shapes so we had to watch each other's lips. 'Where are they?' I said.

Jai followed my gaze. Every threat in our tiny, doomed world seemed coiled up in that black space between the half-open door and its frame. He watched, then turned to me and mouthed, 'They could be waiting.'

I shuddered at the possibility. It was a horrible thought; an ambush, a single shot in the head, and the last remaining witnesses to Foley's escape erased. My blue-skinned body splayed across the third-floor corridor carpet, stiff and glass-eyed until help arrived. *Help*. My mind cleared somewhat. Just moments ago, we'd raised somebody on the radio. But had they heard us say

the name of the hotel? If they had, there could be someone at Inverness station putting a rescue team together
right now. Part of me imagined waiting on the roof
until we saw the lights coming along the mountain road,
but a bigger part knew it was hopeless. The route was
blocked; would be until the morning at least. I thought
of Santiago, of the Atacama and my promise. I couldn't
be here when the police arrived.

Jai nudged me. 'Is there another way down?' he
mouthed. *Not unless you want to descend the way poor
Gaines did.* I shook my head. We studied the door some
more. Around us, broken trees reshared crows. Echoes
and pine sap in the wind. 'What do we do?' Jai whispered. 'Wait?'

We backed glacially away again and stood with the
hoods of our coats touching so we could raise our voices
to a hushed whisper. 'It could be hours until help arrives,
even if it does,' I said, my breath clouding the space
between us.

'Could we make it through the night out here?'

I examined the stars – heard Cameron's voice gently
explaining their patterns and relationships – then
returned to our huddle. 'Temperatures are going to keep
dropping. We have to get back inside.'

'Then what? We escape via the loch?'

'Let's concentrate on getting off the roof first.'

Then, a sound from below. It was a loud noise muffled
by distance. The crash and clatter of metal. Something
about its position suggested the kitchens, two floors
below us. It came again. We looked across the roof,

waited. Nothing else. Jai shifted position. 'Could that be them?'

I imagined the two of them pulling drawers clear, upending a medley of knives across metal surfaces. Paring and chopping knives, finger-length blades in protective sheaths, heavy wooden-handled butchers' cleavers. Were they planning on carving us up? I tried swallowing but my throat refused. 'Sounds a long way below us if it is,' I whispered. 'They've left us up here ...' I was about to ask, *why is that?* But I bit the question back.

Since the avalanche my thoughts had been fogged in fear and confusion, but clarity was returning. Up on the hotel drive, Jai had been about to confess something to me; something he'd kept hidden since his arrival. Well, I had a secret too. My brother's storage locker. The locker made sense of a problem I'd been wrestling with all along: Gaines Two was Troy Foley, so why hadn't he killed us when he'd had the chance? Jai had already pointed out that he didn't need a gun to finish us off, he could have silenced us whenever he wanted. But he hadn't, he'd kept us alive – *me* alive. *What if he'd spared me because he knew about Cameron's bag and the storage locker?* It was a possibility that triggered a world of subsequent questions. If it was true, it gave me power and leverage. I just needed time to think about how to use them.

'Remie? You OK?' Jai lifted his boots gently, one after the other, in a movement I knew meant painfully numb feet. 'We can't wait forever,' he observed. 'Not dawn for ages yet.' I pictured the half-open door at the bottom of the gantry steps; the top-floor corridor bristling with traps. Crouched figures, cocked guns. But if the noise from deep below us was them, we could be penned in by fear alone. Without realising I was doing it, I found myself creeping slowly back to the fence and assessing the dark space beyond the door.

'I think we need to get back inside,' I said. 'Come on.'

I lowered one boot at a time, the maw of the darkness below yawning. Jai followed. Each downward bootstep was a trial. The balls of my feet blazed with painful readiness. I reached the gap, tried blinking away black pinpoints in my vision.

I faltered twice before raising my stick, pulling the door back and stepping inside.

27

The corridor was empty, but not entirely dark.

To my left, a light was on. The door to my room was open a crack, and lamplight played out in a broadening stripe across the carpet. I watched, holding my breath and feeling unexpected strength conjure itself within me. Someone was in my room. I took a few steps forward, coiled tight, my Midbow in both hands, waiting to strike. Then I noticed the door frame. The wood around the lock was split, and the door had been forced.

I pushed it slowly inwards, heart pushing hard and fast beneath my ribs.

The room was empty and everything was normal. Except for my bags on my bed. They'd been turned inside out, my stuff disgorged. My throat closed and I swayed on watery knees, staring dumbly at the tipped-out cases. Tears sprang to my eyes. I crept forward and assessed the mess.

Jai hovered at the threshold. 'What's missing?' he hissed, checking the corridor with quick backward glances.

There was a black well opening in my chest. I

burrowed through the clothes and books on the bed, trying my best not to cry, but the tears came nevertheless, hot with frustration. 'A thousand euros,' I said. My voice cracked. I felt abused, ashamed. 'And my passport.' I ran a hand across my scalp, my head thick with emotion. 'My passport.'

'Shit,' Jai hissed.

When Cameron's appeal had fallen through, a cloying despair had drained me of any emotion. I still wonder how I got through the night shift after I heard the news. I must have moved mechanically through my tasks, numb and sightless, hardly breathing until, unbelievably, the sun came up on another day and I dragged myself up to my room and climbed, defeated, into bed. This feeling was different, though. It was a painful twist of rage, sharp-edged enough to hurt my insides. I wiped tears away with the backs of my hands. Both men had insisted on checking my room, both had taken in the shabby surroundings, the modest accretion of belongings on the bed; both had established I was leaving tomorrow so both knew my passport was packed and ready. But it was the second Gaines – Troy Foley – who'd taken it. Either that or he'd got Alex Coben to get it for him.

Scrambling backward through the evening's events, I recalled the last time I was up here: Shelley Talbot on the radio. Foley sending us downstairs, telling us he needed to finish his search. Me and Jai leaving for the map room and working to prepare our rescue attempt. Meanwhile, I guessed, Foley had climbed the stairs to the third floor, broken in to my room and taken my passport and money.

I was right, then. Troy Foley needed me alive because he knew about Cameron's bag. Which meant the night's events hadn't been random accidents – they'd been precisely orchestrated *because I was here*. And that prompted a bigger question. What was in Cameron's bag that our visitor so desperately wanted? My brother's savings were surely negligible compared to Foley's annual turnover. My bedside clock read 3.55 a.m. It was two and a half hours to Aberdeen; more in this weather. Time was running out. I pushed the sleeves of my uniform across my eyes, smudging eyeliner in gritty streaks, took in a breath and calmed myself.

Jai looked shellshocked. 'Why would they do this? If you're the one who knows how to access the boat, could they still need you?' He furrowed his brow. 'I don't get it.'

I kept my thoughts to myself. Even if I'd wanted to give voice to them – talk them through until I'd constructed a version of the night's events that made sense – I don't think I had sufficient air to do so. Jai continued thinking aloud. 'The loch water's treacherous, right? The ice, the currents. Maybe they need you as a guide. Whatever the reason, Remie, the truth of it is they need you but they don't need me. I'm a dead man. We have to leave now before Coben lures us in.'

I tried to think. I knew why they'd stolen my passport and with growing certainty came a coursing of energy. Foley and Coben were counting on my helpless terror.

What they wouldn't be expecting was courage, cunning or aggression. If I was to exact any kind of payback, at the very least escape, I'd need to out-think the two of them. Jai wouldn't understand. 'I'm staying,' I said. 'I need that passport.'

'Your trip to Santiago? Fuck's sake, you're dreaming. You'll be spending the next month in an interview room.' I didn't say anything and his face slackened as he saw my resolve. 'You're crazy. They're killers. Criminals.'

I knew on some level he was right. But I was resolved. 'One of them has it. I have to find them.'

Jai gaped. 'This is madness. Listen to yourself!' he said, his tone harsher and his eyes narrow. 'Nobody would risk their lives for this. Unless you're, what, fleeing the country?'

I kept my voice measured. I felt like I was summoning a new and future self, right there in my single room. 'Santiago is the start of everything,' I said.

His expression cleared. 'You're leaving for good. That's your little secret.'

I gave him a grim smile. 'Very good. Now let me guess yours. What was it you said on the way back from the crash site? *I haven't been entirely honest with you?* Questions about Porterfell, voice memos on your phone . . . you're some sort of journalist, right? That's what you were going to confess on the walk down the drive.'

When he spoke next, Jai's voice was measured. 'I would've asked your permission if I'd ever planned on using the audio.' He sat on my bed, leaned forward and examined the backs of his hands. 'I wanted to tell you, Remie, but when it comes to stories like this, it's always better asking for forgiveness than permission.' I held his gaze. He blinked first. 'When I said I was a broadcast technician I was telling the truth. But I've not been completely open. Look, I'm a podcast journalist, OK? I present an investigative documentary series. *A Question of Guilt*.'

Jai's odd quirks that had me on edge; his interest in the prison, his nose for a story and easy confidence with people, the way he got them to open up – they all made sudden sense in the light of this new revelation. 'And you were going to tell me this when?'

He shrugged. 'At first I wasn't going to at all. I get honest reactions and real stories if I record undercover. Anyway, it doesn't matter. Gaines turned up and I had to make a decision, so for better or worse I decided to stay quiet, all right? I knew I'd get better material that way.'

'Jesus, Jai.'

'Forgiveness not permission. Anyway, then Gaines Two – Foley – showed up and complicated matters. After that, I couldn't find the right time. I was going to tell you. I was.'

I quelled my fury. We'd both kept secrets; at least he'd confessed his. I, on the other hand, was in no position to share information about a bag in a storage locker, particularly with an investigative journalist. '*A Question of Guilt*,' I said. 'So it's a documentary about Troy Foley, I presume.'

He nodded. 'We're looking into US–UK gunrunning.

Foley's organisation specifically – a deep dive into the distribution and use of firearms across the country. The British media has this obsession with knife crime but UK firearm offences are up significantly in the last five years and we want to tell the story of why. We're looking at America's attempts to monopolise the global weapons trade; pro-gun Republicans, relaxation of regulations, that sort of thing. Georgia and Florida seem to be the source of recent imports. We've been out to the trade fairs there to see how they operate, and it's a free-for-all. No one's tracking serial numbers. Second-hand guns are swapped like baseball cards out there. American outfits get them through UK customs smuggled in air-conditioning units, old cars, whatever. Then Foley's organisation collects and couriers them out to county lines gangs.'

I thought of the night Cameron and I scrubbed a van clean in a rainstorm somewhere. I knew the answer but I asked the question anyway. 'And your interest in me?'

'Your brother was part of Foley's operation. You're the closest I've had to a first-hand account of what life was like working for him.' Jai ran his hands across his knees. 'And you're a credible witness; Psychology lecturer at Edinburgh University, experience working with troubled adolescents, vigorous campaigner for Cameron's appeal.'

I felt my stomach turn. He'd done his research.

'Look, it's our job to tell the stories the regular media won't. Gun crimes rise nearly thirty per cent in five years – close to ten thousand cases last year alone – and where's the outrage, Remie? Where are the exposés, the proper, old-fashioned reportage? The mainstream media won't touch it but this stuff is in the public interest. People need to know that our borders are porous, our border force underfunded and short-staffed; the NCA's overrun. This is a crucial investigation.' He grimaced. 'It sounds crass to say it, but since it's my job I will. No one else is going to tell this story, so I have to. If it means using underhand methods, I'm prepared to do that. A conversation with you would clear up a lot of questions.'

28

I told Jai, in no uncertain terms, to fuck off.

He flinched at the vehemence in my voice and cleared his throat. 'Look. I came up here to do a job, just like you. Except things have taken quite a turn. Trouble at the prison. Foley starts another riot and – I'm guessing, but we've got a research team working on it – it's his third strike so he's transferred. But he has someone on the inside; the Serco transportation driver Shelley Talbot.'

I didn't know why I was giving him my attention. Jaival Parik was as duplicitous as everybody else around me and his manipulation wasn't justified by the fact that he claimed to be some sort of crusading truth-seeker, though doubtless he saw it that way. I tried to quell a wave of bleak fury with thoughts of Chile. The drive from Santiago north into the Atacama. The skies at night. It was only hours away now but I knew I couldn't do this alone. *Someone* had to be an ally.

Perhaps the investigative reporter with a cause was the only choice I had. 'It did feel like Shelley confessed to me on the radio back there,' I said, remembering her whispered words. 'She talked about making a deal. Sounded like she'd been taking payments in exchange for aiding Foley's escape attempt.'

Jai's expression softened in response to my cooperation. 'Yeah, that fits. He's got a network of sympathisers; inside men and women paid well to supply him with information. At the moment I'm thinking Talbot's one of two accomplices. She helps get him out, Coben prepares Foley's onward journey.'

'The SUV in the garage,' I said, sitting down on the bed next to him.

'Exactly. But there are complications due to the weather. Shelley's meant to pull the van over and free Foley. He's planning to kill the motorcade cops, then her. But the storm means Shelley crashes the van instead and in the chaos . . .'

'He loses control of the scene,' I said, 'and doesn't know who's where. He checks on Shelley – she looks dead, as does Gaines. Foley's under pressure, has to improvise, so he steals Gaines's gun and ID, kills the young officer, changes into his uniform, heads for the hotel.'

'Right. But he has a nightmare in the woods during the descent. Drops his weapon, gets lost. Reaches us late and is forced to play the role of desperate cop.'

I picked up the thread. 'Then Shelley calls on the radio and it's clear she's survived the crash after all.'

Jai looked bleakly at me. 'And we share this information with him.'

The guilt was back, dense and cloying. I placed a tentative hand on Jai's shoulder and felt the rise and fall of his breathing. A moment later he reciprocated, dropping an arm over mine so that we sat together like a pair of teens in adjacent cinema seats. In the silence that followed, I wondered what would have happened if Shelley had never got through on the radio. Could things have worked out differently? Or if I'd kept up with Foley as we'd climbed the hill?

'It's not your fault,' I said.

He stirred, nodded. 'He had us fooled.'

'He did. Poor Shelley.' I patted his back, dipping my shoulder so he lifted his arm. Our moment of closeness was over and I stood, my legs aching. 'But we're still here, Jai.'

'Yeah. You're right.' He blinked, looking around him like a man waking up. 'We're lucky to be alive. If he'd found a gun up at the crash site, he'd have shot us there and then.'

A gun. The pain in my limbs softened and retreated and the calculations seemed to make themselves. I'd need to hunt Coben and Foley and protect myself, which meant some sort of firearm. There was a room full of rifles rendered inaccessible by a mountainside of snow, but a year ago, in the wake of Cameron's death, I'd been frightened enough to steal and conceal my own weapon. My past self had inadvertently given me an advantage. If I could get Jai safely off the hotel grounds, I could deal with the rest alone.

'Before we get out of here,' I said, picking up my hockey stick, 'there's something I have to collect.'

I could read the relief in Jai's slow exhalation. 'OK,'

he said. 'Me too. Notes and recordings I need. Then we leave, right?'

I wanted to let him down gently, so as I began cramming the barest essentials from my two suitcases into a backpack, I just nodded.

Inside Jai's room I locked the door behind us and switched on the vanity light above the desk mirror. It was enough to see by. The place was twice the size of mine; one of the Mackinnon's luxury doubles with en suite. Jai had scattered his personal effects over the walnut desk, opened a suitcase and disgorged its contents across the cream carpet, plugged a signal booster into the TV socket and dumped his used towels in the bath.

The bed was strewn with papers; scribbled notes and diagrams, dates and times, maps of names connected with lines. 'What's this?'

Jai neatened the papers, began to pack them. 'My notes.'

'Let me see.'

He shrugged, handed them over. At the top of the network of connections was the name *Foley*. Underneath, three names, their relative positions suggesting lines of command. *Hendrick* sat in the middle directly beneath Foley – evidently some sort of second-in-charge. I checked the two names either side, expecting to see *Coben*. Neither were. One was *Diaz*, one *Hammer*. Scanned downwards through the broadening chain, surname after surname; *Schalansky, Ford, Petrescu*. 'The team have been piecing this together,' Jai said. 'Scavenged it from newspaper articles, police arrests, persons of interest, Dark Web forums. Looks like Foley's organisation is bigger than anyone suspected.' I nodded, looking for *Yorke* as Jai continued. 'From what we've managed to determine, the operation is still running,' he said. 'See what I mean about being in the public interest? Many of these senior gang members are still at large, so Foley's been superseded and there are other major players now. Names underlined in red are the ones captured in the sting operation that led to your brother's arrest – Foley is here, there are others here and here. But some seemed to have vanished entirely, probably killed in skirmishes we don't even know about. Hendrick – the guy who deputises, whoever he is – has gone AWOL; last mentioned in communications nearly two years ago. Probably dead in a ditch somewhere.' He passed his finger across the paper, pointing. 'Difficulty is, the assumed names. These guys can build a new identity, complete with documentation, in less than a week. Lots of them will have two or three different passports, use different names depending upon particular jobs or adjust identities with different suppliers. And they share IDs too – use them, then pass them along to the next recipient.'

'No sign of Coben,' I noted.

'That won't be her real name. Most of these will be aliases.'

'And what about Cameron?'

Jai shrugged. 'Not managed to track down complete records yet.'

'He must be somewhere.'

'Guess so, yeah. There are a number of names we haven't pinpointed. Maybe the couriers who do the onward smuggling have a different communication system? Maybe gang membership is more fluid at the lower levels? Turnover must be high, roles transient.' Jai folded the papers. 'It's everything we've got so far. Sorry I don't know more.'

My companion hunted in his wardrobe and produced a black shoulder bag, opened it on the mattress and I watched as he shut the screen on a laptop he'd been charging, wound the plug and wire around his fingers and dumped them into his bag, wincing at the pain in his arm, then gathered up a pair of phones and their charging cables to pack. With that done, he crouched and, from beneath the bed, produced a box in battered red metal the size of a thick paperback. It had been tucked under there and covered with a spare blanket. Audio equipment: outputs at the back, dials on the front, a headphone socket and line of switches, a volume control. Then, with its lead wrapped neatly around it, a microphone. This was the guy I'd spent half the night convincing myself had only been accidentally recording me. He was a one-man broadcasting studio.

He tucked his notes safely on top of the equipment then slung the bag over his shoulder, closing his eyes against the pain. 'Done.'

I withdrew my bunch of keys and began searching for the ones that belonged to the gate and boathouse. 'Listen, Jai,' I said, steeling myself. 'Go back up to my room. Use the balcony stairs to leave. Follow the loch to the perimeter fence and wait for me by the boat. You'll be safe.'

'But – I thought you were coming with me.'

'No,' I said patiently. 'I'm going to deal with things here.'

Jai furrowed his brow. 'Remie.' He dropped his voice to a whisper. 'I've been building an investigation into these people and it's pretty fucking horrible. They're ruthless and violent. They've got no qualms – they will kill you. But you know this. You *know this*. Stop stone-walling. What's waiting for you in Chile that's worth risking your life?'

I could see the journalist in him had got the bit between his teeth and I didn't like it. I had my reasons and they were privately mine and mine alone. 'Just go, Jai.'

He straightened. 'I'm not going to do that,' he said with growing certainty. 'Like it or not, you've made yourself part of this story, Remie. If I leave now, I won't be able to tell it all properly.'

I lifted my hockey stick and gave my companion what I hoped was a measured and determined look. 'Suit yourself. There's one more thing we're going to need,' I said. 'And it's downstairs.'

Outside, Jai pulled the door to his room shut, wincing at the click it made, then nodded mutely, his jaw tight. I moved off as silently as I could and we paused at the top of the stairs, loitering, terror-struck, at the landing banisters. Eventually I approached, lifting and placing my feet with trembling care, dipped my head once out over the banister and tried to get a sense of the corridor below. If I was Foley, I thought, all I'd have to do was wait. No need to go hunting when your prey will come to you. I couldn't see anything down there. I thought about the lifts; quickly discarded the possibility. Checked with Jai. He was breathing in and out through pursed lips. I could see the sweat in the creases of his forehead. He gave me a brief nod.

The carpet was thick enough to muffle most movement but the boards beneath creaked so I stuck to the edge of the stairs and descended slowly, pausing as I was due to turn upon myself at the halfway point and quickly checking what was down there. Empty. But disarray. I stooped to broaden my view of the ground-floor corridor, catching a glimpse of the dust sheets and paint cans. No sign of anyone. I checked again, this time making sense of the changes I could see. A can had been levered open. The corridor lights winked on the liquid surface of the paint. Phone-box red. A brush stood in the can. Jai waited at my shoulder and we looked down the stairs at the corridor below.

There was a message painted on the wall.

29

Daubed and running, it said, *we have 2 trade.*

An arrow had been painted beneath the words, pointing down the corridor towards the kitchens and bar and bleeding in extravagant rivulets. The crude slashes, eerily childlike, made my body temperature drop. The four words confirmed the possibility I'd been contemplating since my passport went missing. *Trade.* They had something I wanted, I had something they wanted. Which meant Cameron's bag. So, *what the hell was in it?* I stepped back into Jai, gave him a shove. We retreated a few steps upwards and I leant against the wall, my pulse drumming in my ears. Had to think.

Jai leaned next to me, staring at the carpet between his feet, breathing unsteadily. I watched as he dabbed at his forehead with the sleeve of his jacket. His breathless whisper was as close to silent as he could get. 'What does it mean?' I shrugged and he glared at me. 'What have you got that he wants?'

'He must mean the boat,' I said. I hoped I sounded confident. 'Listen. The door to the basement is just to the left. Remember it?' He nodded, blinking rapidly.

'What I need is down there,' I whispered to him. 'I'll go. This is my mess.'

Jai pursed his lips in concentration. 'No,' he breathed. 'I'm coming with you.'

I nodded, thankful.

We took the stairs down one by one, planting both feet before waiting in coiled anticipation, then going again. Towards the bottom I ducked quickly out to check the corridor, left then right. The space was shrouded in darkness. There was a light off to the left, coming from the bar. Other than that, emptiness. I hovered at the bottom of the stairs, hockey stick up and arms burning. *we have 2 trade*. The painted message, gravity dragged, was elongating downwards. The *e* of *trade* had become a slick, gradually opening mouth.

There were a lot of things I didn't want to do at that moment, but right at the top of the list was the prospect of following that syrupy arrow down the corridor.

Immediately on the left was the basement door. I worked my keys in and, ever so slowly, turned the knob and pulled it open. One last time before we entered the cellar, I studied the ground-floor corridor, following its dark length to the fault line of light emerging from the half-open door to the bar. I was going to have to go there. First, though, the basement. I made sure we were both inside before I let Jai click his torch on and I locked the door safely behind us before turning. A good thing I did; if I'd checked the depth of the water down there before locking us in, my courage might have failed me. Just the two of us and a single torch beam down there in the flooded cellar, the kind of dank and airless darkness that brought back my experience beneath the snow. Jai pointed the light down and its beam danced stars across ink-black fluid. Water had reached the middle of the makeshift staircase. I reversed down. The liquid slipped up my trouser legs and stopped just below my knees. There it gripped like cramp, cold as ironwork in winter. I heard it draw a long hiss from Jai as he joined me.

'That message,' he said. 'It's not about the boat, Remie. What does Foley mean?'

The dark was a babbling chamber of echoes. The walls streamed. Somewhere I could hear a haemorrhaging pipe guttering. Jai was smart, but if I told him everything, I'd lose his trust. The one thing holding us together was the certainty, however dubious, that we understood each other. But just as he'd kept things from me, I was going to have to keep things from him for his own good. 'Listen,' I said. 'Those paths along the edge of the loch are our only way out of here. There are two; an upper and a lower. The upper is treacherous – there are wooden bridges across three deep ravines, a path that contours along the side of the mountain, slippery and steep until it drops to the water's edge. But the lower? That's dangerous too. Alder's all iced over and snow-fall has covered both the ground and the frozen water. Difficult to tell them apart. Both paths end in a high fence and a locked gate – and I'm the only one with a key.' All of this was true. The next bit I was pretty sure wasn't but I said it anyway. 'They need a guide. Coben's got maps, but she doesn't know the route anywhere near as well as I do. And then there's the boat.'

Jai passed me the torch as he listened. His face was swallowed by darkness. I couldn't read his expression any more. 'If that's true,' he said, 'they'll kill you once you lead them to safety.'

'Which is why we're here,' I said, panning the light across the flooded passageway. I got a blue-grey impression of floating flotsam. 'Down here is the one advantage we have.' The corridor guttered around us as we sloshed past the site team's room on the right, then the boiler room. I panned the light across the big boiler. It squatted in the dark, lapped by bobbing debris.

Directing the light at the next door along, I turned to Jai. 'It's in there.'

I had to lean in to shoulder the door open. The water swirled and licked as I made my way inside. The Mackinnon had a number of these old storerooms; paperwork graveyards from the long years pre-dating computer storage. Dust-caked filing cabinets queued up in back-to-back rows, library-like walkways between them. One of them had been upturned by the rising water and listed drunkenly on its back. Looked like a year's worth of old hanging files had exploded; sheets of paper stuck to my legs in clotted layers. The place dripped and popped like a wet cave. I thrashed towards the far corner, where the cabinets had been pushed against a series of wobbly wall-mounted shelves, most now empty. I placed the torch down carefully, ensuring it spotlit my work, dropped an arm behind the filing cabinets and removed the old damp box files I'd carefully arranged back there, throwing them aside. I reached around, hoping what I was searching for wasn't water damaged. It was our only chance of escaping with our lives. Jai watched open-mouthed at first, but his expression changed when I removed the rifle wrapped in an old dust sheet.

'Whoa,' he whispered into the wet darkness. 'How long has that been there?'

I unwrapped the gun, casting aside the sheet and pocketing a palmful of cartridges. Relief flooded through me; it was dry and looked much as it had the last time I'd set eyes on it. Gaines's demonstration of the hunting rifles earlier in the evening was about as close as I'd come to ever using a firearm. In the days following Cameron's death, I'd kept the gun in my room, practised holding it, raising and aiming the thing. But that had been a year ago and now it felt entirely unfamiliar in my hands; unnaturally sleek and weighty. I struggled to break it open and check the chambers. Two bullets already there where I'd left them over a year ago. I flipped the safety catch back and forth. Jai was assessing me carefully. He didn't even need to ask the question.

'I can explain,' I said, my voice echoing. 'After my brother was killed, I got scared. I thought I needed protection. But you might have noticed police don't take women very seriously, particularly frightened ones. I had no concrete evidence of any threat but it kept me awake at night. I thought I was losing my mind – I'd hear noises on shift, thought there was someone in the darkness outside. Paranoid fears.' I hefted the weapon awkwardly. 'So I took this from the gunroom. Kept it safe for a while just in case someone was coming for me.'

'You mean Foley's gang?' Jai was almost speaking to himself. 'Why? Did your brother tell you something? Secrets about how the organisation was run? Because if that's the case, Remie . . .'

'I was helping with Cameron's appeal and I don't think other gang members liked the idea he might get out,' I lied. 'Used to keep this under my bed but then I started stressing about what I'd do if they moved me, or if someone found it. So I ended up hiding it here. Always intended on returning it, but . . .'

'Can you use one?'

I shook my head. 'You?'

Jai shrugged. 'Went shooting once.' He rubbed his palms against his pockets and gnawed at his lower lip. 'This place is horrible,' he said. 'But I don't want to go back up there.'

'You don't have to follow the arrow,' I said. 'I do.'

'We have certain advantages,' I whispered as we reached the stairs again. 'I don't think he knows there's two of us. And he has no idea we're armed.' I handed Jai the gun. He took it reluctantly, examined the thing in his hands as if seeing it for the first time. 'Take the safety off. Follow me down the corridor towards the bar but at a distance. You're not going in, I'll do that. Wait at the door, out of sight. Be ready to shoot.' Jai listened. His gaze had the kind of distance that implied an all-consuming inner dialogue. I don't think he was seeing anything. 'Probably won't come to this. But if it does I'll raise my voice,' I told him. 'Doesn't matter what I say – wait for the raised voice. That's your signal. OK? Can you do this?'

He blinked, turned to me. 'Yeah,' he whispered. His voice cracked. 'I follow. Wait at the door. You raise your voice, that means it's turning bad. I ...' he tried to swallow. 'I attempt to get a shot in.' I watched him wince at the dry lump in his throat. 'This is crazy,' he croaked.

What could I do but nod?

Above ground again the daubed message, sagging slowly open as it bled, appeared increasingly psychopathic. As I looked along the corridor towards the light emerging from the gap in the bar-room doors, I felt fear push at my throat. Jai held the rifle awkwardly and we made our way forwards, our feet squelching, the going painfully slow. Approaching that light from the bar was like descending into some sort of hell.

Closer to, I saw the door to the kitchen was open. Coben could be hiding in there. This could all be a trap. I waited, my skittering pulse thrumming. When pushed back far enough, the swing door jammed open against a section of uneven tiling. Inside, the light was on and I caught a glimpse of the kitchens' interior. It was a chaos of thrown-about drawers, their contents disgorged across worktops. This was the noise we'd heard from the roof; I'd placed it perfectly – the rattle of blades.

There were usually knives everywhere in there, but from a quick scan I saw that the knife blocks had all been emptied. I imagined Foley and Coben sifting through them, deciding which weapons would most effectively dismember their enemies. I took another step forward. The fridges stood open. Food on the floor.

The place looked empty.

I met Jai's gaze, nodded across the corridor to the bar and tried to give him a reassuring look. He crept to his position by the doors, back against the corridor wall, rifle held loosely across his chest.

I checked the time. 4.40 a.m. Walked past Jai, pushed the doors open and went inside.

Troy Foley was sitting at a table, eating chicken one-handed, a foil-wrapped carcass before him amongst cast-about napkins. No longer the upright Gaines Two, he slouched, clawing at the meat with the grubby fingers of his one working hand. His left arm was inside his police jacket, the sleeve hanging loose at the shoulder. He'd leant a hunting rifle against the table top, barrel up, and he'd pulled out the chair across from him. I took a few faltering steps forward, willing my legs to work properly. Foley's face was badly damaged; his left cheek and chin a raw, scraped mess, the blood dry in his ear, the collar of his shirt soaked red. When he blinked, one eyelid didn't work properly.

He gestured, grunting. Unable to sit back because of my backpack, I leaned forward in the chair opposite him. Through his open jacket, I could see Foley's damaged left arm was bandaged against his torso. You couldn't fix dressings like that alone, plus he had a rifle. That meant two people, but I couldn't see Coben. I'd expected to find them together. I thought about Jai and anxiety gnawed.

Foley's eyes followed me as I checked the room. He cleared his mouth and spoke through a feral smile. 'Needn't worry about your missing guest,' he said. His accent was stronger, harsher than before. 'She's with me.'

'You killed my brother,' I said. I'd never said the words aloud before and they came in awkward shapes. It wasn't easy to keep my voice down but I needed to for Jai. 'You killed him a year ago in that riot.'

Foley had a tumbler of whisky before him. He sipped it, watching me over the rim of the glass, closed his eyes briefly as the alcohol burned, then cleared his throat. 'Few years back you took one of my drivers out. Franks, his name was. Smashed his hand to frigging bits, if I recall.' He nodded at my Midbow. 'Lethal in the wrong hands, those things. In the end I had to put the poor kid down.' I hoped that didn't mean what it sounded like. Foley ran his tongue along his upper teeth. His drawl was infuriating. 'Irony is, I actually promoted your brother to replace him. Which I think makes everything else afterwards kind of your fault as much as mine.' The blow landed, driving the air from me. He was lying about all of this, he must be. I thought of Jai at the doorway, back against the corridor wall, rifle ready. I just needed to raise my voice and he'd swing into view. I'd need to duck and cover.

Keep your hands on the hockey stick, I told myself. *Don't let go.*

'So yeah, I had to do something about Danny Franks,' Foley continued, 'and then I had to do something about Cameron Yorke, and the commonality between those two cases,' he said, tugging at the chicken with his good right hand and chewing, 'is you. Maybe if you hadn't been pursuing your brother's appeal so hard, things might have been different. Maybe if you hadn't encouraged him to make plans, things might have been different. His ambition became dangerous.' He gave a one-shouldered what-can-a-guy-do shrug, sipped his whisky and proceeded to talk through his food. 'When you serve notice of appeal, co-defendants' solicitors let their clients know. So I knew you were up to something on your brother's behalf pretty quickly. I couldn't have Cameron getting out on – what, substantial injustice? Fresh evidence? Whatever. I couldn't allow it.'

I found I was leaning forward on my stick, my arms trembling. I'd cleared a path for Cameron's rise through Foley's organisation; created the conditions that meant my brother had to be murdered. It was all my fault. If I'd just kept out of it ... but I never could. I'd committed my teens and twenties to trying to understand Cam. Pitied my parents for their unwillingness to empathise; doubled-down, followed through.

Except, no. This was Foley's manipulation. He was trying to break me. I straightened. Kept my voice down. 'What is it you want?'

He ran a greasy napkin across his mouth. 'You know what I want, Remie.'

I did, but I wasn't going to be the one to say it. 'Enlighten me.'

Foley crumpled the napkin one-handed, then closed the foil neatly over the top of the chicken. I watched as he cleaned up in curiously fastidious sweeps, pushed aside the carcass and placed the palm of his right hand on the table. 'It's been a long and fucked-up night so I'll get right to the point. Cameron stole from us.' He sipped, sucked his teeth. 'Now you have something of mine and I want it back.'

30

I let that sink in. I'd suspected something like this for a year but, until my passport went missing, I'd never been totally sure. I hadn't stolen and hidden a rifle because I was helping with Cameron's appeal – though it might have sounded plausible when I told Jai. I'd done it because I was the only one left alive who knew the whereabouts of a certain bag.

I'd first had the thought in the days that followed my last ever visit to Cameron in Porterfell. His last words on the subject played in my head. *'If anything ever happens, I want you to clear it out. All of it is yours.'* At the time I hadn't thought much of it but after his death the words had new significance. It was like he'd anticipated, expected even, his life being endangered. In the middle of a silent night shift the day after, sitting alone at reception, I'd turned the conversation over in my head. Possibilities had begun to present themselves, and with them came threats.

What if, I'd thought to myself, my brother wasn't talking about the kind of modest savings plan I'd urged? Maybe Cameron hadn't simply put a little away each time he was paid and had instead perpetrated a grander, more dangerous, sort of larceny. Maybe his ambition had, as Foley put it, become dangerous. And, if that was the case, maybe Foley had figured out what my brother was up to. Imagine his fury: discovering his organisation was missing a chunk of money and, coincidentally, a co-defendant launched an appeal against his conviction? Cameron Yorke walking free with Troy Foley's cash? It couldn't be tolerated. And the other thing that couldn't be tolerated: the money being smuggled out to his sister. The sister who was currently planning a long trip to Chile, according to informer Shelley Talbot. Shelley. A woman adept at appearing as though she liked to talk when in fact she was being paid to listen. Shelley had spent a lot of time at the bar drawing out my story. What I hadn't realised until now was how she'd been feeding it all back to Foley.

Clarity at last. There was indeed a reason Troy Foley had chosen this particular February night to escape. There was a reason why the site of the crash had been planned so close to the Mackinnon hotel. And that reason was me.

'I don't know what you mean,' I said. The words sounded hollow and I knew it.

'Let me clarify,' said the man across the table. 'Just before I had your brother killed, a helpful prison guard reported a conversation he'd heard; a conversation in which Cameron Yorke told his sister – a regular visitor to Porterfell – about a savings plan and a storage locker. Naturally I was interested and paid young Cameron a visit. Delivered a threat to him. And during the course of our conversation, it became clear the lad knew exactly what I was after. Soon he realised he was a dead man either way and clammed up. Must've loved his sister, eh?' An unbearable sadness dragged at me. I wiped my eyes. Foley continued. 'So I know you have access to a locker in some facility somewhere, and I know there's a bag that belongs to me. And I also know that you have all the necessary details to access the bag.'

I tried not to dwell on Cameron's final, desperate moments as he'd attempted to shield me. There would be time for mourning later. Right now, I had to hold it together and somehow out-think this man. 'And if you get your money?'

He used his good arm to tap the breast pocket of his coat. 'Well, in return, you get your passport,' he said, 'and you're on your way. So I'm guessing that on your big loop of keys, there's something that opens a locker. Hand it over.'

I tried to swallow. 'Not as simple as that. Electronic keypad with a six-digit code number.' Foley's face tightened. A couple of years behind bars had left him out of touch. 'I'll give you the number,' I said. 'I don't care about the bag. I just need to catch my flight.'

Foley grinned. 'You expect me to trust you?'

'I swear. I'll give you the number. The correct number.'

'No you won't,' Foley said. 'You'll give me a number that doesn't work and by the time I discover my mistake, you'll be long gone. I didn't trust your brother and I don't trust you. Seems we'll have to pay a visit to this storage place together.'

My stomach heaved. *No way.* Very slowly, I slid down in my seat. Made it look like exhaustion. Jai would need a clear shot and there was a chance I might kick the stock of Foley's gun away from his hand; buy my accomplice a valuable second or so. 'Not if I kill you first,' I said.

'Excuse me?' said Foley icily, stiffening.

This was it. I raised my voice and spat, '*You heard, Foley.*'

It came out high and clear. I waited for a shot. Jai's voice at the door, at least.

Nothing happened. Except that Foley stood up, lithe like an animal, leaned across the table and struck me hard in the face. For a man of about my size, he had a vicious hook. My chair went over and I crashed to the floor, rolling off my backpack with my cheek blazing, teeth rattling in a spinning head. He was over me pretty quickly, leaning in with a face contorted beyond recognition. An animal anger, as well as his injuries, had transmuted him from man to monster. His good hand came at me and he crushed my throat. I was disabled by a pain so sudden and intense I felt my pulse drum behind my eyes in nauseous flashes. My windpipe closed inward. Foley stank of sweat and blood and desperation. An unyielding iron band across my thyroid cartilage, closing my airway. I threw my arms up and drove my fingernails into something – the man's face, I hoped – and sucked in a quivering rill of oxygen, drawing frantically through a collapsed throat.

Then he let go and stood.

I managed a shuddering intake of air. It was like breathing broken glass. My front was wet with the monster's spilt whisky, its smell somehow revolting. I pushed myself back with the heel of one boot. My vision was a wet blur.

Foley's shape had taken a step back. He was holding my radio. 'If I didn't need you alive,' he said, 'I'd have very happily strangled the life out of you, bitch.' He pressed the radio against his chest and awkwardly twisted the volume knob then examined the screen. Satisfied, he spoke into it. 'It's me. Where are you up to?'

He drifted beyond the blurred field of my vision and I lay on my back, my throat glowing, trying to regulate my breathing. Somewhere across the room, Foley was talking into the radio but I couldn't make out the words. *Where was Jai? What was I going to do?* Hauling air through my swollen windpipe, I tried to bring the room into focus, to gather together the details. The carpet beneath my head. My hockey stick, the cloth tape peeling from the handle. *Breathe.* An upturned chair beached on its back and, beyond, the familiar shapes of the bar I'd run six nights a week for the last eighteen months. The ceiling roses. Smoked-glass wall lamps set either side of sepia-tinted scenes from Mackinnon history. The photo of the geese Shelley Talbot had professed to like so much; the bar stool where she'd perched as she let me talk, reeled me in, reported back to Foley. Same bar stool Jai had chosen at the start of the night. Coben must have Jai, I thought, breathing in broken parcels. Which meant she had the rifle and any advantage we'd once possessed was gone. Must be her on the radio. I had a vague sense of Foley giving instructions. They'd be taking me with them and there was no way off Farigaig by road, which meant we were heading down to the water, making the journey along Alder's edge to the boathouse.

It was a walk I'd done many times before. In the summer, the lower path, the one that hugged the inlets and beaches, was green and glistening, peaceful at sundown but by day thronged with guests, birdwatchers and walkers. In those warm months, when the rainwater channels feeding the loch were at their lowest, kids hopped across stepping stones where the tributaries of mountain streams joined the main body of water. It was a flat and gently undulating route to the boathouse, lengthened slightly as it wove in and out, matching the shape of the shoreline. The upper path, though, forked left beyond the terraced gardens and cut through the woods. It was more direct but potentially treacherous. I'd told Foley about Barnacle Bridge before. I just had to pray he hadn't remembered.

He was over me. I flinched and cowered.

'You're going to take me to the boat,' he said.

I had to use the hockey stick to get myself upright.

31

He waited while I unlocked the bi-fold doors, and we made our way into the darkness. I led, my Midbow a walking stick as we shuffled between terrace tables and out into the deeper snow of the lawn. My neck throbbed and my vision flexed disturbingly. I leant on the stick, and managed one last look back at the Mackinnon as we crossed the open space. I had a strong feeling I would never return. The building that had been home to me for a year and a half stared implacably back, dishevelled but unmoved, its flanks flooded with slipped snow, its terrace doors open and the lights on within. I imagined for a moment how the place might look to the first officer on the scene, fresh from the station in Inverness, leading a team of police across the threshold sometime tomorrow. The fallen tree and the broken frontage. The lobby empty and the cryptic message painted on the corridor wall. The cellars flooded; the kitchen vandalised; the empty bar open to the night. My bedroom with its abandoned suitcases.

Foley jerked the rifle at me. 'Move.'

The snow beneath our boots was already churned

MARTIN GRIFFIN

up, a confusion of prints drawing a diagonal line across the lawn towards the loch edge. They were fresh. That meant Coben and Jai were ahead of us. Not necessarily together, I told myself; could be one after the other. Perhaps Jai had been disturbed while he waited outside the bar for me and had withdrawn hastily to safety. He knew what he was dealing with, he was a careful man and there was a chance, however small, that he'd made some circumspect escape. All of which meant he could be among the trees on the route down, ready to spring me free.

The path would be splitting in a matter of minutes. As soon as we were down the steps beyond the gardens I'd have a choice to make. Maybe it would even be a life-or-death choice; the route that carried on to the loch then proceeded along the water's edge, or the upper path through the pines. My feet and hands had only just recovered feeling and the prospect of descending to the water and following Alder's inlets through the sub-zero night in clothes still wet from the cellar-flood made me ache. I'd been in earnest spelling out the dangers to Jai; in winter, the little deltas where streams met the loch were often flooded and, with temperatures as they were, I didn't like the idea of hobbling over unstable ice on senseless feet, clothes sticking to my skin, never sure where ground ended and water began.

The other route – the higher one through the woods – was better. I began nurturing a particular prospect; a possibility attached only to this alternative path. This second route struck off to the left, sticking to higher ground as it passed through the trees. Further up Farigaig's sides, the mountain streams were a series of deeply cut torrents, foaming down to the flatter ground below, treacherous, particularly when gorged with winter water. The upper route included wooden bridges crossing deeply carved ravines – the drops beneath the wooden structures were long and sheer – before weaving down to the boathouse beside the perimeter fence.

It would be a good place to launch an attack. I feared it would be my last opportunity.

Just before the junction I misjudged the incline and lost my footing.

My left boot twisted and my Midbow went from under me. I crashed into the snow. The floor thumped the air from me and I lay for a moment on my back-pack, groaning, star-peppered sky above, a quilt of snow below. Foley, stooped himself now as his injuries began to take their toll, regarded me with a black scowl, breathing clouds. I tried to swallow, my neck a burning brand of bruises, and felt, for the first time, defeat worm its way through me. I could just lie here, I thought. Close my eyes and slowly die.

'Get up,' Foley grunted, gesturing with the barrel of the gun.

I raised an arm, shivering violently. 'Give me a hand,' I croaked.

He backed away a step and adjusted his rifle-grip, using the inside of his right elbow to press the stock against his hip. He kept the barrel pointed and the index finger of his right hand tight around the trigger. 'On your feet.'

I planted the hockey stick, rolled on to my side and pushed up until I was swaying upright. We waded on through thick drifts, each step agonising, until we reached the junction. The moon illuminated a single line of snow-churn – straight on, following the hill down. Two people had descended to Alder's edge and worked their way along to the boathouse. Coben and Jai. Was Coben leading Jai against his will? It looked that way, unless the tracks had been made at different times. I clung onto the possibility that Jai was ahead of her; that he might be safe and unharmed, even waiting to help me.

The bridge was off to the left. If I led Foley that way now, following the higher path into the woods, I'd be breaking fresh snow. And that meant Jai wasn't somewhere in front of me and I was on my own. Foley had noticed too. This was it; follow Jai or strike out and head for the bridge. There was only one answer. I turned to Foley. 'The route up there through the woods is quicker,' I said.

Into the trees we went.

Thick cedar, larch and pine grew densely, which meant less snow to fight our way through, but also knitted canopies that blocked the moon, shadows so confusing we had to plant each foot carefully. The woods banked high on our left as the hill climbed, and quickly dropped away from the path to our right.

Tangled overstorey scraped back and forth in the wind; trunks and branches creaked, eddies of snow-mist chased their tails at our feet. I heard owls and the bleak cries of crows. The steep beck-channel chattered in the distance. I could hear geese. I'd often heard them flying over the hotel at all times of the night and there were always plenty around Barnacle Bridge.

Soon, the hill to our left became an ice-rimed boulder the size of a house. The path cut around its base and beyond there was just enough moonlight to pick out a lively torrent of water tumbling into a deep black ravine, where it smashed onto snow-topped rocks below. Crossing the gap was Barnacle Bridge. We approached. Nesting geese shifted in the dark. Close to, the water roared and the air was wet. I pointed with my hockey stick. 'Watch your footing here,' I said, raising my voice over the noise.

Foley examined the crossing. There was a flurry of wings and a trio of geese took to the air. He didn't look comfortable. For a horrible second I thought he might refuse. Then he nodded and we made our way forwards. My calves were cramping with pent-up anticipation as we began our crossing. This was it. Birds lined the steep banks either side of the ravine, some sleeping, others flapping and strutting. We moved out over the foaming hole, only wet wood preventing us from plummeting down to the glistening rocks below. The balustrade had a slick coating of guano and misted water. Halfway across I slipped, thumping hard against the barrier for balance. Geese hammered upwards, a braying drumroll of winged movement. I stooped, arms over my head, turning. Saw Foley, the moonlight silvering his thin shoulders as he slithered, off balance, arm raised over his face as birds exploded and circled.

This was my moment and my body let me know, pulsing with feral panic. With monumental effort I threw myself against him, barging him against the wooden rail, jarring his hip as hard as I could. The rifle swung in his grip. Wingbeats and screeches. I heaved my bodyweight against Foley's damaged arm until he shouted in pain, bent across the bridge rail. He tried to direct the gun barrel but I pushed as hard as I dared, both palms out against his shoulders.

His feet left the ground and he folded backwards across the rail, eyes wide, roaring in shock and fury. The last thing I saw were bared teeth, an arm pedalling against nothingness, the rifle spinning from his grip. Then he went over the rail. Such was the force with which I'd slammed against him, I was close to following him over. I folded across the balustrade at the stomach, nearly pitching forward but somehow managing to steady myself, fingers slithering against wet wood. I saw Foley drop, a brief three-pointed star, legs open, a single arm raised back towards me, eyes wide and a horrible expression of braced-for-impact terror crossing his face before he fell beyond the shafts of moonlight into the darkness of the ravine. Below, the mountain stream foamed and rushed over a tumble of icy boulders. I saw Foley hit, smashing into the rocks, head thrown back. Didn't hear the impact. The noise of the water and the broken cries of settling birds masked the sound, but I heard blood in my ears and my wretched, ragged breathing.

I'd done it. I panted, weeping with relief, looking down into the churning space for a long time, waiting for movement. Geese circled and settled. Spray filmed my face and hair and I had to keep pushing my wet fringe back. My stomach burned against the bridge rail.

Soon I'd lost track of which black shapes were rocks and which were Foley.

32

Once I was recovered, numb with disbelief, I collected my stick and completed my crossing. On the other side I left the path and followed the edge of the ravine down through glistening woods. I had to get my passport back.

I made slippery and exhausting progress, the cold gripping me, bleak and unforgiving until finally access to the churning beck looked easier. Down through the trees was a route between the chaos of snow-capped rocks. I began using my hockey stick to steady me, but such was the drop I ended up descending on all fours until I'd slithered down alongside the shouting torrent. Water roaring all around, I held my breath and waded in, thrashed up the beck's glistening path until I saw the bridge again. I guessed the point at which I'd tipped him over, then drew a vertical line down with my gaze until I'd detected the outline of Foley. The sight of the dark shape made me burn with fear. I picked my way carefully upstream, feet throbbing in the icy water. Using my stick for balance, I grounded myself against the rush and leant in close to the splayed shape.

Troy Foley had been moved by the water. I'd seen him

fall backwards but he lay face down now, slumped over the curved back of a rock, his legs in the torrent, the current plucking at his boots. No sign of the rifle. Must have tumbled clear. I pulled at his shoulder, and, with an effort, turned him on to his side. His eyes were closed, skin wet and pale, his damaged arm flat across his body. His jaw lolled.

An eyelid flickered and, with a shout of alarm drowned by the roar of the river, I let him go.

Foley's broken body slumped back. He was still alive. I stumbled, breaking the ice on a rock pool, and steadied myself, adrenaline charging. Then I raised the hockey stick, gripping it tight in both hands, bringing it up in an arc until it was above my shoulders. All I could think of was the night I'd smashed Danny Franks's hand, the boy's white face and his open mouth; the sound of his howl. If I'd never brought the stick down that night years ago, perhaps everything would have been different. Now here I was, ten years on, having to do it all again. I faltered. Couldn't allow that, so I thought about the flight. *Heathrow. Madrid. Santiago.* Channelling all my energy into my arms, I brought the stick down once, as hard as I could, against the side of Troy Foley's head just behind the ear. My old Midbow sheared in half, breaking into two neat, even pieces. I let the handle drop into the dark churn of the water, pushed the rest in after it.

Foley didn't move again. His head bled over the rock, across a slick plug of ice into the water as I checked his jacket, probing the outside pocket with impossibly clumsy fingers. No passport. Made sense: he'd meant his inside

MARTIN GRIFFIN

pockets when he'd tapped the breast of his jacket back in the bar, of course he had; inside pockets were much safer. I unzipped his police jacket and pulled it open. Two inside pockets. The numb claws of my hands trembled as I rifled both. Empty. Panic was rising now, hot and sharp. Difficult to breathe. I checked the stab vest. Hundreds of stupid little pockets but nothing in them. I pulled the jacket off him, cast it aside and ran my hands across the front of his trousers, digging pockets to retrieve the keys to the gate and boathouse, then hooking his radio clear, pushing it into my coat, and checking again. My fingers found a wet wedge of notes, my bundle of euros. Nothing else. I was swearing, trying to swallow back tears. *Had he thrown it away? Or maybe he'd never had it.* I was forced to run both palms across his buttocks, feeling for the outline of something in his back pockets, crying and counting my breaths so as not to throw up. *Oh God where was it? Where was it?*

The passport wasn't there.

I must be missing something. Down in the darkness and spray and noise, it was impossible to check him properly. Pulling his legs clear, I unlaced his sodden boots. Wouldn't put it past the bastard to hide the passport somewhere strange. Placed the boots on the flat surface of a rock, then worked at his belt, fingers aching, and dragged his trousers clear. I folded them carefully, making sure the pockets didn't spill. The jacket I'd already thrown to one side. I slithered through snow at the beck's edge to collect it, and found the rifle on the way. It looked undamaged. I grabbed the gun and folded the jacket, added it to the pile. I shucked the dead man out of his stab vest then tried unbuttoning the shirt, but such precision was way beyond my lifeless fingers so I tore it open, yanked his arms free. Collected his clothes together, stomach flipping like a fish, cradled the rifle and crawled between rocks up the side of the gully away from the water, swearing rhythmically as I flogged my way into the woods.

Down in the river, the man who'd killed my brother lay dead in his underwear and I felt nothing but revulsion. Up among the trees, thank God, the air was still and comparatively dry. I put the rifle carefully aside and set to work again, tucking the euros into my bag and kneeling over my stash of recovered items. That final check of Foley's clothes was the most miserable moment in my life. Boots, trousers, stab vest, shirt and jacket pockets – a desperate repeat search that yielded nothing. Dumb re-checking, praying I'd missed something. Then abandoning myself to tears; wondering about giving up.

Until I heard the radio in my coat pocket chirrup into life. *I'd forgotten Jai. Maybe Jai could help.* I plunged a hand into my coat pocket and came up with the radio, hope flaring fiercely. *With two of us looking, I could—*

'Hendrick?' the radio said. 'Where the fuck?'

I don't know how long I stared at the little yellow screen. The voice was a woman's. Alex Coben's, to be exact. Asking after someone I didn't know. *Were there more people out here?* I checked the woods around me. *Not possible.* Wiped my face. Tonight was disorientation upon disorientation. Who on earth . . . ?

'Hendrick, have you got her? Come in.'

I stared some more, my breath caught in my throat. *Her* meant me. *So who was Hendrick?* There was something familiar about the name, something on the edge of memory. A rush of connections came at once. Jai's notes; the sketched network of names he'd shown me back in his room; names connected by lines, Foley at the top, and underneath – directly underneath – *Hendrick*, the second-in-command, with two other deputies. But it didn't make sense. What had Jai said? *Hendrick had gone AWOL. Not mentioned in nearly two years; probably dead in a ditch.* So, was this person back? Out of hiding at long last? Then a thought slammed. *Or was Hendrick fresh out of prison?* I remembered Jai's explanation as he packed his audio equipment. *Difficulty is the assumed names. Lots of these guys will have two or three different names depending upon particular jobs . . .* I tried to swallow, remembering the rest of Jai's words. *They share IDs too. Pass them along to the next recipient.*

Squeezing my eyes shut, I tried putting the pieces together. What if the man in the gully was Hendrick? My God, what if, two years ago, the police had arrested a man who claimed to be Troy Foley at trial – but was simply the gang member currently in possession of that name? Foley's right-hand man had made a scapegoat of himself so the real gang leader could continue to run the organisation. And that meant . . .

The radio bleeped. 'Hendrick?' Alex Coben said, impatient. 'Hendrick, it's Foley. We're good to go. Bring her down to the boathouse.'

33

I knelt among reptilian trunks, staring at the dark clot of clothing in the snow, not really seeing anything. Alex Coben was Troy Foley. Which meant she'd travelled here to help break Hendrick, her ally, out of Porterfell. She was here to reclaim the services of a man who'd spent the last two years assuming her identity and doing time on her behalf.

But she'd done it all tonight because she also wanted to recover a cache of missing money.

I could see with sudden clarity how this was going to end. There was no need to vainly search the pockets of the dead man's uniform. My passport wasn't there; it was down at the boathouse because Alex Coben had it. She was going to be the one at my side while I opened the storage locker and handed over the bag. And I wasn't going to get my passport in exchange; I'd end up finished off and dumped, a missing persons case until, in a week's time, maybe longer, the police would find my body in the boot of some hire car abandoned along the Aberdeen dock front. By which time Coben would be long gone – vanished into thin air.

What could I do? Follow the path down to the boat-house and approach carefully from the woods, arms raised? Plead with her, maybe, try and strike some sort of bargain? The prospect brought a terrible bleakness, a bitter thing which dragged all possibility from me. I buried my face in my hands, trying to think, body aching. Nothing had been as it seemed, right from the start.

I wiped my face, dried my freezing fingers against the piled-up uniform. It was then that the possibility – the one that had been screaming for my stupid attention all along – suddenly became clear. The uniform. The rifle.

It must have been minus five out there in the woods that lined the loch's edge. Minus five in the darkness before dawn. But I stripped down to my underwear nevertheless.

Once I'd finished re-dressing I tied my hair back, looped the rifle's sling over my head so the weapon sat diagonally across my stab vest, pulled my backpack on and headed downward through the trees, working my way through knee-deep virgin snow towards the point where the frozen water met the land. The border, as I'd anticipated, was hard to discern. Once the hillside levelled out and the trees thinned, the flat shoreline was made indistinguishable from Loch Alder by a blanket of crisp white. Sure, there were points where the uniformity of the fall was such that it could only be lying on the iced-up surface of the water, and, closer to, the hummocks of emerging rocks told a story of safety, but that space in between? The edge of one territory and the start of another was impossible to distinguish with any precision. Out here, away from the treeline, the wind was up, driving streamers of broken cloud across a milky field of stars and sending fast rills of snow powder weaving across the frozen edge of Alder. The moon was low over the black blade of Bray Crag, almost full, so that further out where the ice became water, I could see its light on the loch's liquid surface. My phone read 5.35 a.m. as I turned back towards the glow of the Mackinnon one last time. The lights of the bar were still visible through the trees.

Ready to head along the loch, steering carefully clear of the edges, I looked up and saw something else. It was higher up the side of Farigaig on the mountain road, perhaps a mile away. These lights were different. Two shimmering points, moving. I was aware I'd taken a deep breath and was holding it as I watched a vehicle travelling slowly along the road in the direction of the hotel. The snow-slip we'd witnessed up there would soon put a stop to its progress, but that wasn't a thought that reassured me. Could be a farmer, checking storm damage. But another possibility gnawed. Surely the only reason anyone would be out in this weather was if they were responding to a distress call. Our distress call. The vehicle was a distant dot, but even from where I stood I felt confident I was looking at a van. As I watched, it drew to a stop. For a moment nothing happened and I wondered hopefully if I'd witness it turn slowly around and lumber back the way it had come, but instead, more lights. The pinpoint fireflies of hand-held torches.

'No, no, no ...' I whispered through my broken throat, watching. The night was quiet, and across the wooded foothills I was sure I heard the pull and slam of a sliding door. Backup from Police Scotland, rustled up at great expense, no doubt; a rag-tag team of officers on overtime fanning out from the van and heading into the woods, moving between the trees, some in the direction of the hotel, others down towards the water. I tried counting; caught maybe ten torches, moving in pairs. Back on the road, more lights – a second vehicle, this one a car. I watched it pull up, turn around and park back-to-back with the van. One light left the car for the woods, joined a pair below. The other officer, I guessed, was staying with the vehicle in the unlikely event they had to turn back early morning traffic.

A tinny voice made me jump. 'Hendrick?' I fumbled for the radio. Ugly gouts of interference. I dialled down the volume. 'Hendrick, are you seeing this?'

If I was lucky, I might have thirty minutes before the police teams reached the boathouse. I couldn't be here when they did. *Heathrow. Madrid. Santiago.* I began to run. My legs burned, my head spun and my numb extremities throbbed, but the worst thing about that endless lope through calf-deep snow on mannequin legs was breathing through a pulped throat. Somehow I persisted, slithering along the shoreline, the rifle banging against my thigh as I went.

*

The boathouse was a low wooden structure; a place in that liminal space between land and water. The landward side faced the woods, where a door was the only ornamentation on its cedar-clad frontage. The building extended two boats' lengths out into the loch, ending in a pair of large doors that opened to allow the Mackinnon's small cruiser in and out. A pitched shingle roof topped stone footings and a wooden walkway extended around its outside edge, beginning on the shore, following the outer wall of the building, supported on struts and protruding out beyond the front gates another fifteen feet into the water. In the summer, hotel guests brought their kids down here, and, if the weather was fine, the children would run the length of the jetty and launch themselves screaming into the loch. Now, as I approached, I saw that the ice extended all the way to the jetty's end and beyond. It was curious to see the struts of the walkway emerging from a hard, snow-topped surface.

To my left, torches still moved in the woods, fanning slowly downwards. And as I drew closer, movement ahead as well. Foley's slim shape was immediately recognisable in the moonlight. She'd emerged from the landward door of the building. Looked like Jai was with her, still in his yellow coat. I slowed, dropped to a crouch. Moved along the shore until I had a brittle tumble of snow between me and her, pushed the rifle on its loop around to my back and watched. She was facing the wooded foothills of the mountain, examining the lights. I could see a rifle in one hand, pressed against the

MARTIN GRIFFIN

small of Jai's back. She was nudging him along the front of the boathouse. I don't know what happened to my emotions then, but they didn't find a way to the surface. I pushed everything down, concentrated on the lights in the trees and the figures of Troy Foley and Jaival Parik until they moved out of sight. They were going to hide against the back wall of the building. Wait for me on the jetty. Time was running out. I hadn't finished off my brother's killer, I still needed my passport, and pretty soon Jai and I would be bodies.

I switched the radio off – didn't want it to give away my position at the wrong moment – found some reserves of energy and made my way forward. At the near edge of the boathouse I paused. Foley was around the other side with Jai. One option was the ice. I crept to the shoreline. Could I round the building from the loch-side and take them by surprise? I wasn't sure where the water began, so I edged forward, arms out for balance, testing each step. Pretty soon I was on the ice, a fact confirmed when I swept the snow aside with my boot and saw something akin to black polished marble under my feet. I made it another step before I felt it move beneath me. A compass of cracks flitted out from beneath my boots. The ice held, but it didn't feel sturdy. Crazy idea. I retreated to the shore. Up in the woods, the police were making progress, a slo-mo net of lights dropping dreamily downward.

I pulled the rifle strap over my head and cradled the gun. Checked the safety, tightened a gloved finger on the trigger. I could hardly feel it in the cold. The police uniform and stab vest bulked me out and the big coat androgenised. All I'd need to do was fool her for as long as it took me to raise the gun. It was the only plan I had left, so I moved before I could change my mind, upright, confident strides across the front of the boathouse. Then I turned the corner.

34

It must have worked pretty well because as I emerged from the shadow cast by the building, she said, 'Hendrick. About fucking time.'

I raised the rifle. She tried the same but I jammed the barrel of mine forwards, prodding the air. 'Don't even think about it, Foley.'

The woman stilled, grinning in surprise. Jai stammered something that never quite made it to words, his face a mask of fear and confusion. Over his shoulder, I had a chance to study Alex Coben. She was smaller than her prisoner but confident and strong; feet planted apart, back straight, her face raw boned, her mouth a thin line.

'Put the rifle down,' I said. My heart was thundering so hard I wondered if she could hear it from where she stood. I was almost surprised when she obeyed; squatting on those wiry runner's legs to place the gun on the wooden boards of the walkway between Jai's boots. The poor man's heels were dancing, I noticed, and as I looked up I saw for the first time a full-body tremble that was bordering on a seizure. I tried giving Jai a reassuring nod but I guess my expression gave me away, because he gritted his teeth against a shake that wouldn't stop. Behind me, I could hear the first suggestions of woodland movement; distant snow-noise as police officers made their way downwards.

'You can't fire that thing,' Troy Foley said coolly. 'You'll bring the cops running. More importantly, half the mountain will come down on us.'

I licked my lips. Tongue too dry to make a difference. Rush of nausea. 'I want you to give my passport to Jai. Then let him go. Make no mistake, Foley, I will shoot.'

'I don't think so,' she said. She smiled wider, her teeth and the stud in her bottom lip gleaming in the moonlight. I got a creeping acid feeling; something telling me this thing standing on the boardwalk wasn't altogether human. I jabbed my gun again, trying to hold myself together but feeling tears begin to sting. She wasn't going to do as I asked. Nothing scared her. She didn't care what I intended. Jai had closed his eyes and his shoulders were jumping.

'What's it to be, Remie Yorke?' said Foley. My name felt ruined in her mouth. Made me want to spit. She glanced up through the woods over my shoulder, then returned her cold gaze. 'I have the two things you need. So are we going to trade?'

'Give Jai my passport.'

'We haven't got time for this.'

I was stuck. She was right about the sound drawing the police, and the possibility of another avalanche further weakened my position. I didn't have the smarts or experience to change the course of the negotiation. I shouldn't have persisted but I was stuck and I was really fucking frightened, so I kept pushing, hoping repeated forceful instruction would get me what I needed. 'Give Jai my passport and hand him over.'

'Last chance, Remie. Be reasonable.'

Birds moved in the trees behind me, the woods a dappled camo-print of moon and shadow. I didn't know what to do. 'Give Jai—'

She moved quickly, a jink of the hips, a thrust of her upper body – the bit I couldn't see because Jai was between us – and his eyes widened. There was a wet noise, then another. Jai folded over, face a picture of slack-jawed shock. He went down quickly, crashing and curling as he hit the floor. I don't know how close I was to passing out but my body was water. Troy Foley had a kitchen knife in her hand. Long and wide, the blade black with blood.

She'd reached around him and cut twice, through his coat and into the soft flesh of his abdomen. Jai's gloved hands had converged on the wound as he fell, and he lay gasping and blinking, a gathering pool of blood seeping between boardwalk planks. Foley was standing before me, arms thrown out as if for balance, blade up, knees bent, narrowed eyes searching my face. Those horrible empty eyes. Something febrile erupted in me. I pulled the trigger. With a huge, echoing crack, the gun recoiled, the barrel went skyward, my arms jarred in their sockets and my trapped index finger twisted.

Troy Foley was blown backwards, a scarecrow in a high wind.

I staggered, the noise making my ears sing. Black residue stank as the gunshot died. Shouts in the woods. Foley's kitchen knife clattering against the jetty. Around me, the bad smell of blood. My head was a stuttering slideshow I couldn't blink clear.

I heard voices, raised and ragged, then the boom of shifting ground; the gathering hiss of a slip somewhere up in the trees. I turned, expecting a wall of foaming white. Instead I saw nothing but falling stars – torches shuddering in the hands of shouting runners. A low, broadening wave of snow ran its fingers through the trees and a cloud of powder rose through the canopy. I turned back to the jetty.

Foley was gone.

For a crazed moment I thought she'd disassembled; blown into dust like a wicked witch. When I took a step forward all became clear. She was lying on her back below the jetty, on the ice. The stuff was thick enough to hold her – she'd fallen backwards and snow-angeled herself, arms and legs out, head thrown back like a stargazer. Her belly was a red hole. She'd begun to clear snow in her struggles, opening a bloody circle around her and drawing a wide red line in her wake as she pushed herself along Loch Alder, away from the safety of the walkway. Even as I looked, I saw the ice beneath her split; sudden jagged lines appearing, summoned by her movement. I won't forget the supernatural noise of that ice, strange reverberating cracks singing as Foley dragged herself, her weakening arms flapping rhythmically. She wanted to go under, to take my passport with her in a final act of spite.

MARTIN GRIFFIN

Falling lights through the moving woods. Jai was curled up and bleeding fast. I tore my jacket off, stooped and balled it up against his side above the belt of his jeans. 'It's OK, Jai,' I whispered. 'You're going to be OK. Hang on.'

I couldn't tell if he was still breathing. I tried feeling for a pulse, but his hands were pressed hard against the wound and his gloves had filled with blood. A barrage of noises assailed me: below, the spitty exhalations of Foley as she pushed herself away from safety towards deeper water, and in the woods, the slow boom of more rolling snow. Then the shouts of alarm, the call-and-response of disorientation as lights drew closer together, finding each other. Soon they'd be descending towards me like a conjunction or constellation. Fox and Goose.

'Hang on, Jai,' I said, and covered him with the police jacket. 'I'll be back in a second.'

And then I left him.

35

The torches were gathering. Teams checking in, then moving downwards, heading for the edge of the woods and the water, following the sound of the shot. I scooped up my rifle, loped to the end of the jetty, lay on my front and lowered myself over the side, one arm clinging to the wooden slats while I tested the ice with my feet. As soon as I put any weight on it, the stuff emitted a keening sound of rupture. Troy Foley was fifteen feet away across the glassy surface at the end of a bloody line turned black by moonlight. She'd stopped moving and was staring at the stars, one foot lifting and falling as she heeled for leverage.

I knew enough about cold-water shock to understand what was going to happen if the surface gave. Even in summer, deeper sections of Alder – and there were some very deep sections – never got above a couple of degrees and the water could kill. We had to keep guests to the edges, use a series of buoys to demarcate safe-swimming areas. I'd need to spread my weight, like they did on quicksand or swampland. I used the butt of the rifle to double-check the surface. It didn't give, so I lowered a boot and tried again. A spiderweb sprung from beneath the ball of my foot.

The woodland lights were drawing closer. Jai hadn't moved. My body ached with cold. Shirtsleeves and a stab vest – laughable. There was no way out of this, so I lowered myself on to the ice, ignoring the sprouting veins shooting away as they followed the lines of least resistance. I lay down on my front, arms and legs out. What a fucking horror those moments were. The surface held. I lay with my cheek against powder-puff snow, feeling the whole plate rock. Then I began to move, arm over arm, pulling with numb claws encased in wet gloves, my rifle looped around my right arm and dragging at my side. I never raised my head. All I saw was the low curve of Troy Foley's left boot draw closer. The ice below me fired off little ricochet noises. Calling voices in the woodland above. Loch Alder's skin was swaying by the time I reached Foley. I pulled myself up her legs until I was across her knees. Cracks pinged as I searched her pockets.

Inside right, I found my passport. As I was withdrawing my hand, she grabbed me by the wrist.

It was a trap-like grip, those climber's fingers iron. She didn't move her head. I yanked backwards but she held on. Our additional movement tipped the plate of ice we occupied and a feather-fine line drew itself, as if by some invisible hand, right beneath my belly, one side to the other, mazing for the shoreline. I stopped struggling and we lay together, me half on top of her like a clumsy lover. I could hear her spitting her mouth clear. Guess she didn't need to go under to die; she was drowning right here on the ice.

'Cops. Are coming,' she whispered.

'Let me go, Foley,' I whispered.

'Never,' she managed. Her grip grew tighter, her fingers pushing hard between the tendons of my wrist. I pulled again. She held on.

'Let me go!' I hissed, yanking hard. The whole lake listed. I heard a break followed by a wet gulp, felt a puddle spread beneath me.

'Fuck. You.' The words were coming slowly, punctuated by gurgling breaths. She worked her feet, trying to push herself backwards, and whispered, 'We're both. Dying. Tonight.'

I reached my other hand forward, tried grabbing my passport with it, but she yanked my left arm clear, still strong. Her fingers drove into my wrist and I dropped the passport. It fell onto her chest. I began prying at her grip, but that hand of hers was a closed vice. Foley pushed herself backwards, slithering further away. The tattoo on her neck was visible. Small dark-winged butterfly. She tried to say something else – her throat worked in and out – but the words didn't come. My passport slithered up to the base of her neck.

Up in the woods, snow was on the move. I heard another slip hiss to a close; saw the mist rise and alarmed voices follow converging torches. I reached with my free hand again, scrabbling against the belt of her jeans, trying to claw my way up her body. A chorus of lace-fine ruptures criss-crossed all around us. Gulping water was splashing and spreading; sections of ice shearing, plates tipping and bobbing. Foley pushed herself further clear.

Then there was a stuttering volley of cracks and her left elbow went through the ice. Black water spumed. I watched aghast as the lake sheared beneath her – beneath me – and, upper body first, backwards like a glistening seal, Foley went into the water. Head went under, boots went up. I pushed away as the glassy surface disintegrated beneath my hands. My left arm went in up to the elbow and the water gripped like death. I pushed with the right, pedalling madly back from the maw. And when I next looked up, Troy Foley was gone. Her previous position was a black, liquid absence. Loch Alder had swallowed her. The space we'd just occupied, me and her, was crazy-paved in wet plates lapping against each other. It could be a long time before anyone found Troy Foley again. Or my passport.

The grief rendered me momentarily mindless. Everything I'd worked for was spinning away – making a slow, one-way descent to the bottom of the loch, leaving me stranded above. That falling passport dragged my insides down with it. I was an empty shell, tears icing against my cheeks, until the call of an officer nearby shook me alive again. Weeping, I manoeuvred the rifle into a glistening gap between ice-sheets; watched the barrel pitch upwards and the gun go under. I began reversing. Backing away, face against the swaying surface of the ice, numb, devastated. Eventually my foot hit a strut and I looked back to see I'd made it to the jetty. I risked everything, pushing upwards with both arms, turning awkwardly on all fours, balanced on a bobbing tabletop, and I dragged myself back up. The ice was disintegrating below me even as I made it on to the walkway.

The thought of Jai fuelled what movement I had left to muster. I staggered back along the jetty, lungs burning, the iron taste of blood thick in my throat, stooped to check him. But before I could be sure of anything, I looked up to see a figure closing the space between the woods and the boathouse, torch strobing wildly. It was the first police officer.

The rescue team had made it down from the mountain road. Closer to, I made out the figure of a male slowing his run as he saw me; a grey-haired man, face sweat-sheened, skin deeply lined like that of an ex-smoker. He pinned me in torchlight and became a silhouette. I squinted into the bright beam, caught, hearing his vigorous breathing as he struggled to regain composure. I had nothing left any more. The relentless throb of vengeance had given me momentum, but with the impostor dead and Troy Foley under the ice, the feeling was quickly evaporating.

I'd killed to get this far, but there was only so much I could push myself through. It was over.

36

I opened my mouth to concede defeat.

But it was the officer who spoke first, a hurried introduction. 'I'm Inspector Mackey,' he said. 'What have we got?'

I don't know what expression I wore. Despair, exhaustion, confusion. Safely back on land, the horror of the loch was hitting me hard. Beneath the jetty I could hear the water's disparate exo-skeleton chattering against itself. 'What?'

'Constable, tell me what we've got here.' He stooped, placed the heavy torch between us and felt for Jai's pulse, then removed the jacket and assessed him while I stared. *'Constable!'* hissed Mackey.

I was so tired, it took another few seconds to make its way through to whatever part of me was still capable of logical thought. My face was wet with tears. 'Followed the sound of the gunshot down here,' I croaked, wiping my eyes. 'No sign of the perpetrator. We have a male victim. Knife wounds to the abdomen. Been trying to stem the bleeding.'

'Where's your partner?'

A head-spinning seasickness overwhelmed me. 'Lost him in the woods, sir,' I managed.

'Calm down, Constable. Get a grip. No sign of the blade?'

'Further up the jetty I think, sir.'

'And the discharged weapon?'

'Think it's up there too. Haven't looked beyond the immediate vicinity, though. Been attending to the victim.'

Mackey turned and beckoned as two more lights appeared. 'Officers!' he called as the torches approached. 'We've got a stab victim here.' Two more figures emerged from the darkness. A pair of young men. 'Is that Warren?' he barked. 'Stay with this man.' Then he addressed the second of the new arrivals. 'Constable? You are?'

'Mendis, sir,' the man said, approaching.

'Mendis, you're coming with me.' Mackey was feeling for further wounds, running his hands up and down Jai's arms and legs. 'We're looking for a discarded knife and a shotgun.'

I held my breath, squirming and dizzy. More torches emerging from the nearby pines. 'Backup,' I managed, my voice a rasp. 'I'll go and apprise them of the situation, sir.'

I turned to go, my heart a stuttering firework. Walking on watery knees, astounded I wasn't being called back, I found myself drying my eyes, floored by this new turn of events. A team drawn from across two divisions? Led by an inspector who didn't know everyone? Scattered by the unstable snow, alarmed by the sound of a rifle discharged, possibly panicky, maybe not familiar with each other ...

'Down here!' shouted Mackey from behind me, calling out to more approaching officers.

I went slogging upwards into the trees, police streaming past me in the other direction. Ten minutes later, climbing through choked woodland, I had to stop to dry heave, sweating and shuddering. Nothing came up. I washed my mouth in snow, got Jai's blood out of my eyebrows. *Jai.* I should have been with him. He was losing blood, dying alone down there. On the other hand, I told myself, I knew about knife wounds and I knew Jai was out of shape. It was possible Foley's blade had punctured subcutaneous fat, and with the right pressure on the wound, it might be a case of blood loss and tissue damage. Even so, I should be the one with him, pressing the coat against the gash, talking him through it, reassuring the poor man. Instead, I'd left him alone. My passport was in the water, fluttering down to the bottom of the loch, a little pilot fish next to the slow swollen shape of Troy Foley. Only the thought of the bag was driving me on now. If Foley had wanted it so badly, there had to be something in there worth the work; the breakout, the planned crash, the seeking out of the hotel and of me. If I could achieve just one thing, it would be to recover that bag.

I climbed, hating myself as I fought the fine, slack powder of the new slips.

Towards the top I rested. It took me a long time to recover. I was damp with sweat and shivering as I approached the road, moving from tree to tree, eyes on the vehicles ahead. There was a final verge to climb, topped with a wall of gravel-spotted breakers, ploughed-aside waves of week-old snow peppered with pine needles. Beyond, what I could see of the police van suggested it was empty. The squad car had disappeared from view, dropping behind a tumble of snow-boulders as I made my way to the base of the verge. There was going to be at least one officer up top with the vehicles; I'd seen the light of a torch left behind as the others moved down through the pines. I readied myself then hacked up to the road.

A single figure with his back to me as I crested the verge and stumbled over the ploughed snow onto the tarmac beyond. A young, straight-backed shape, torch panning the road. I leant against the squad car, behind him, knees knocking and muscles elastic. 'Hey,' I croaked.

He turned, alarmed at first, then quickly concerned, and hurried over. 'You OK?'

'Just need a minute.'

He waited a few feet away, observing me carefully. He was the age Cameron would have been; a young, red-headed officer with an explosion of freckles and an expression caught permanently between concern and polite determination. Blue eyes assessed me from under a short fringe. 'PC Muir,' he told me. 'I heard the shot. What's happening down there?'

Waiting for the dizziness to pass, I took big, slow, deliberate breaths. 'Knife injury. Male victim. Blade recovered plus firearm.'

'Is there a suspect down there? Anyone apprehended?'

I shook my head. 'No. But the ice on the loch is

disturbed. Signs of a struggle, evidence that they've gone through. Likely drowned.'

Muir gave a whistle. 'The water can be a nightmare, all right. Had to rescue my little cousin once. He had a shock reaction to the cold, you know? Only eight at the time, didn't know what was happening to him.' Muir smiled. 'He'd been trying to swim alongside the geese.' He leaned towards me, timid. 'Can I get you a drink, ma'am? I have tea.'

I looked up. 'Anything stronger?'

He shrugged and smiled. 'If only. No, it's tea or nothing. Tea and Tunnock's.' He leant into the squad car, dug through a bag and emerged with a flask and a black jacket. 'You look freezing,' he said. 'Feel free to borrow this. Here.' He'd unscrewed the top of the flask and held the lid as a cup in his other hand, then, when I'd gathered together the strength to put the coat on and zip it, handed it over.

I kept my weight centred, leant hard against the rear wing of the car and managed to take the drink. 'Thanks,' I croaked, and poured. Something about the warmth of the coat and the comfort of the steam made me want to cry again. The tea and this generous, trusting boy, Cameron's age. Heartbreaking. I tried to swallow a sip of the stuff but couldn't drink it, my throat was too bruised. I passed the flask back.

'Something to eat?' Muir asked.

'I'm good,' I managed. He was still assessing me, trusting but careful. 'Mackey sent me back up,' I confessed. 'I lost it a bit. Wasn't helping down there.'

Muir thought about this. 'It must be hard even with your experience.'

I couldn't help but grin at that. 'Been on the force long, Muir?'

'Well, would you believe it,' he said, inflating his cheeks, 'this is just my third day. It's been a lot of hanging around. They wouldn't even let me drive.' He pushed his fringe back. 'Told me to wait with the vehicle.'

I nodded. 'Did a lot of that myself at the start,' I said. 'But listen, your luck's about to change. The inspector was asking for backup down there. Shouting about needing teams to check the loch's edge and head across to the hotel. I've blown it tonight, Muir. Lost my head. But you could take my place.'

Muir hesitated. 'I don't know . . .'

'Chance to impress Mackey,' I said. 'Show some initiative.'

'Is it normal? To do something like this?'

Poor lad wasn't going to get anywhere waiting for permission. 'The force needs young constables like you to be agile,' I said. 'Problem-solvers. Go on, Muir. And if in doubt, just tell Mackey I sent you.'

The young man paddled the snow with his boot, thinking, then played his torch beam through the woods. Then he handed the flask back to me. 'Right. I'll do that. What's your name?'

I was ready for the moment, but I found it hard to speak, even to a rookie who'd believe anything I said. 'PC 4256 Gaines,' I told him.

The young lad zipped his coat under his chin and

made his way to the edge of the road before turning. 'Feel free to finish the tea,' Muir said, smiling. I raised the flask lid in a toast, watching as he moved cautiously into the pines to begin his descent.

It was only right to wait until he was far enough away not to hear the car start. I tried not to think about the bollocking he'd get later today. I tried not to think about Jaival Parik, about Don Gaines and his family, about Shelley Talbot, about my passport. Tried my best not to think of anything except getting to the bag as I turned the key in the ignition and pulled my seat belt on.

The dashboard clock read 6.36 a.m. Trains to Aberdeen ran once an hour. If I was lucky, I'd catch the 7.11.

37

Four miles out of Aberdeen in Bucksburn is an industrial estate; big, featureless hangers with tacked-on reception offices, stranded in vast seas of empty parking lot. Between an accident repair centre and an engineering firm was Safe Storage. The snow in the car park was churned into slack, slate-grey soup. My cab hissed to a stop. I told the driver to wait and splashed over to reception in my jeans and canvas trainers. There was a shopping centre with a bureau de change and food court outside Aberdeen station, and I'd bought new clothes in H+M, then changed in the ladies' toilets and crammed the police uniform into a bin.

It had been a blessed relief to slough off that particular identity. Slithering down into Inverness in a patrol car and police uniform two hours earlier had been a constant psychological battle with the pain of being utterly conspicuous. Even this early I was the vehicle every casual passer-by would notice; profoundly visible to every commuter and hardy dog walker, every newsagent and cyclist. The radio had fizzed with communication as I'd woven through thick snow in Daviot, hoping the dual carriageway ahead was ploughed. I'd passed an ambulance splashing the other way, its sirens blaring, and gathered from the radio-talk that Jai was alive. The relief had been strong and immediate, soon tempered with terror as I'd followed Millburn Road into town. I'd left the vehicle in the car park of Eastgate Shopping Centre, dropped the keys down a drain and sprinted for the station. Dressed as I had been, the two hours from Inverness had been another excruciating trial. The train was a modest two carriages and progress was leisurely. Expecting to be caught at any moment, I'd spent as much time as I could in the toilets, trying to think a way through my predicament. Was there a chance I could fly without a passport? I didn't think so. I could take an internal flight using only a driver's licence, and a quick search confirmed the destinations furthest away were Heathrow, Newquay, Bristol, Southampton. But where from there? Thinking furiously, feeling increasingly hopeless, exhausted and distracted, I'd squirmed with pent-up nerves every time we'd pulled into a station. There were eleven stops all told – I'd allowed myself to breathe a little easier as we'd pulled out of each one – and the early ones, Dalcross and Nairn, were stupidly busy. There was an officer on the platform at Huntly. By the time I was walking through the open concourse with my journey completed, damp with sweat and dizzy with hunger, I'd convinced myself that there would be a delegation of officers waiting to meet me. But I'd emerged, blinking, into the sunlight on Aberdeen's Guild Street at 9.40 a.m., thinking of a flight to Heathrow leaving with an empty seat in just over an hour, and the connecting flights after that, each with an empty seat. A passing bus had soaked me in half-frozen slurry, a timely reminder that I was, in fact, still here and still free. For now.

My taxi driver had quickly realised I wasn't interested in talking. I felt hollow on the drive north through town, my mind working absently on the story I'd tell once I returned to the Mackinnon. Stick mostly to the truth, I thought, as I watched the buildings slide past, tell them I fled, fearing for my life. Leave out the bit about the bag.

The clock in Safe Storage reception read 10.03 as I announced myself. Just like Cameron had promised, they had a locker under my name. I flashed my licence, wishing it could be that simple at the airport, and was shown down a strip-lit corridor. Yellow doors to storage rooms left and right, and a wall of industrial-looking lockers against the back wall. Tables for disgorging your gear. The smell of disinfectant, a chemical attempt at citrus. Once alone, I thumbed in the six-digit date.

I held my breath, strung taut and awkward, sweating into my fresh clothes as I carried the bag back the way I'd come. In reception I paid off the final chunk of rental fee and closed the account, my scalp tight as I imagined swat teams swooping. Outside in the car, the driver was on his phone.

'Back to the station?' he said, looking up to eye me through the rear-view as I climbed in.

I nodded. 'Just need a minute.'

With the bag on my knees tucked up against the back

of the passenger seat, I unzipped carefully. Just enough so that I could lift the flap of the lid and check inside. Dust bloomed. The inside smelt old.

There was money, I could see that much. Piles of paper twenties in rubber bands. I pushed a hand through them. Lots of wads, once arranged neatly, now tumbled against each other, tipped up in the locker. I thumbed a banded stack and tried an estimation. A hundred notes. So, two thousand per wad? I searched, stirring the contents to count, but giving up, guessing at maybe two hundred thousand. A lot of money. But at the same time, I thought with acid anger burning in me, a feeble amount for someone like Foley to kill for. Point of principle, I thought bitterly. The driver cleared his throat and took a call about his next job. I widened the zip open, pushing the money aside. Something underneath the notes; a stiff, cardboard-backed envelope. A4, sealed. I extracted it.

Up front, the driver finished his call. 'So, to the station?'

I tried to think. *How was I going to explain the money to the police? If I banked it, would someone find out? Was it part of an ongoing investigation? Were the bills marked?* I thought about taking it back, right there and then; leaving it safely here until I had time and space to think. There was too much to process, but no, I thought. Better move it somewhere else. 'Yeah,' I said eventually. 'The station. Thanks.'

As we pulled out of the car park and headed into town, I broke the seal on the envelope, peeling it open.

Inside were papers. I pulled them upwards, scanned their tops. Lists of names. These were details of Foley's associates; details that hadn't yet come to light; names and corresponding aliases. I leafed backwards. UK bank accounts, lists of transactions. American bank details, names of suppliers. *My God.* Cameron had smuggled out documents that could bring down the whole organisation. *Now this,* I realised with glowing clarity, *was the kind of thing Troy Foley would kill for.* I needed to get it to the authorities. If I had the lead investigator's details, I could put this in the mail, recorded delivery; an anonymous source providing everything the police needed to dismantle the entire ring.

I could do it from the station. Wipe the pages clear of prints and then—

Further inside the envelope was a small dark shape. I reached in carefully and pulled it out. Cameron had left me his passport; a final keepsake.

I flipped it open, expecting to see him. But the picture was of a young woman, dark-haired, fresh-faced, not exactly conventionally good-looking but possessed of a youthful poise I found appealing. I looked closer. She was maybe mid-twenties, in a hoodie, standing against a white background and looking slightly startled, as if she'd been caught off-guard by the photographer.

The picture was of me.

The night with the camera. Outside some pub I couldn't find now even if I tried, a lifetime ago. Cameron taking snaps of the doorman; shots of me as I waited for him. I checked the name on the passport and, as I did, I remembered something Jai Parik had told me just a few hours ago. *These guys*, he'd said as we'd examined his assembled list of gang members, *can build a new identity, complete with documentation, in less than a week. Lots of them will have two or three different passports . . .* The name on the documentation wasn't mine. It said Cassie Mailer.

I looked up. The car's dashboard clock read 10.22 a.m.

'Actually,' I said to the driver, hardly knowing what I was doing, 'there's been a last-minute change of plan.' I pocketed the passport and pulled a twenty clear of its rubber band. 'This is for you,' I said. 'Could you drop me at the airport?'

38

San Pedro de Atacama was a tiny, marooned town of dust and gravel.

On its outskirts, weathered wooden fences and single-storey huts lined the streets, and the houses were one-room dwellings with tiny windows. Half-buried truck tyres and chicken wire demarcated property and water towers atop rusty cages dominated dustbowl streets. Away from the paved road of the town centre, Route 23 was nothing more than a gravel track, its edges marked by swept-aside stones, and the passing traffic – mostly flatbed trucks with roll-bars and mud-caked paintwork – kicked up hissing clouds of grey sand that stuck to the skin. On the last street in town, opposite an onward sign for Paso Sico in blistered green paint, was the cinderblock bar where I'd parked my hire car.

Inside, the ceiling was suspended with football flags and the walls decorated with branded beer trays and bleached celebrity photos. I chose a table outside, away from the TV and under a makeshift awning, then ordered Coke and pizza. Once I had my drink, I called Jai.

He picked up on the third ring. 'Remie? For real?'

He dropped his voice to a whisper. 'Are you OK? They pulled your passport out of the loch. They think you're dead. Where are you?'

'Atacama,' I said. 'Chile.'

'You made your flight?'

'Yeah. I had a little help from my brother.'

'I can't believe it!' A delighted burst of laughter cut short by a pained intake of breath.

'Take it easy. Are you OK?'

'Yeah. I mean no, but improving,' he whispered. I could hear the swish of doors and the distant drawing back of a hospital curtain. 'They've stitched me back up, but I'm stuck on this ward for a while. Anyway, forget me, what happened to you?'

It was difficult to know where to start. I sipped my Coke and opted for simplicity. 'Well, I got to Aberdeen in time.'

Jai gave a low whistle. 'I heard the cops talking about a missing patrol car. I'm guessing that was you.'

I smiled. 'It was. They think I'm drowned?'

'Yeah. But last I heard, your colleague was going in to make an identification so it won't be long before they figure out they've got someone else on the mortuary slab.' He lowered his voice further. 'So,' he breathed, 'tell me all about it.'

'Which bit?'

'You went through hell to catch that plane. Come on, I'm a journalist, I live for this stuff.'

I cleared my throat, my tongue and teeth – as usual – coated in desert dust, and adjusted my cheap phone. It was going to be one-use-only, but I was still worried about the police tracking the number. 'Listen, Jai. I have to be really careful . . .'

'I'm not going to say anything. You have my word. No one will ever know I took this call.' The words I wanted to hear. 'I promise you,' he added. 'This is between us.'

'Thank you.' I swapped ears and pushed my hair out of my eyes. 'So I flew into Santiago. Yesterday I drove out here. It's summer, but we're high up so it's not so hot in the daytime. I'm here for the stars.' My Edinburgh colleagues, I knew, would have had a field day discussing my behaviour. Guilt aversion would've come up a lot; intrinsic promise-keeping would have got an airing; I'm fairly sure a number would have accused me of target-fixation. I'd be settling for a prosaic old chestnut: closure.

'The stars?'

'It was my brother's thing,' I said. 'He was an amateur astronomer. Atacama's a kind of bucket-list destination for star geeks. Clear skies, no cloud cover. And the bonus for me is it's pretty out-of-the-way. I made a promise to him.'

'He was the one who wanted you to go?'

'Yes. There's something he wanted me to see.' I sipped my drink. 'It's called a conjunction. Venus, Jupiter and Mars all visible at once. He used to tell me all about it every time I went to visit him; wouldn't leave it alone. I kept putting him off, you know, then after he died I was sort of lost until . . . Anyway, these conjunctions don't come around often, and the conditions mean this will be the best in our lifetimes, apparently. Low over the horizon, they tell me, just before dawn in a few days, all in alignment. Cameron lived for this sort of stuff; he'd have been losing his mind out here. After dark the Milky Way's incredible.'

'Stars,' Jai breathed. 'Who'd have thought it?'

'Listen,' I said, getting to the reason I'd called. 'There's something I need you to go and collect.'

He heard I was serious. 'Give me a minute,' he breathed. 'Nurse coming to check on the guy next door.'

I listened to hospital sounds seven thousand miles away; the swish of curtains, the bleep of a machine, bed-wheels squeaking on a polished floor, and studied the roofs of the dwellings across the road, corrugated iron baking under the evening sun. A man wove by on a pedal bike, his handlebars loaded with plastic bags. Here in Chile it was just before 7 p.m.; a TV sports commentator was gabbling in Spanish and inside the bar a tray of beers was being delivered to a cheering table.

On the phone I was in two worlds at once but present in neither, like a ghost.

'Ready?' I asked, then told Jai about the folder of material. 'It's got everything you need,' I said. 'Names and aliases, dates, transactions, even bank accounts. I didn't have time to study it in detail – just had a couple of hours' layover in Madrid – but it looks like it has everything you need to bring down Foley's organisation. So I airmailed it to you, care of the Mackinnon. You want a podcast that's going to change the world, Jai? Everything you need's in that folder.'

'Your brother risked everything to collate the file ...' he whispered hoarsely. He was right. My eyes filled with tears. I was wiping them when my food arrived. Jai continued. 'He got the file to you somehow. And that was what Foley's gang wanted back – *we have 2 trade*. But how did they know you even had the documents?'

'A prison guard overheard a conversation we'd had while I was visiting him. They knew what he was trying to do, and they had Shelley Talbot watching me in case I was planning to vanish. She talked to me at the hotel bar each Friday night. I ended up telling her everything.'

'So they knew you were leaving? Which explains the timing of the prison break.'

'Exactly,' I said. 'Got to go in a minute. Jai, this number will be out of use from tonight, OK?' After the call I'd be opening the back of the phone with my knife and removing the sim card and battery. There'd be time for a walk into town; I'd dump it all in a bin on the plaza by the church, then I'd get a cold drink, listen to a band and watch the sky. It wouldn't be properly dark until just before nine, but the hour before that would see the heavens slow-bloom with immeasurable stars, each a universe of parallel possibilities. 'Don't forget to delete your call history,' I told him. Then I added, 'I'll be in touch again sometime.'

Jai hesitated and I watched the sun descend, listening to him breathe. 'Good luck,' he whispered, then cleared his throat. 'It'd be great to see you again one day,' he said.

'You too,' I told him. It was the truth.

39

Backstage at the Roundhouse in Camden, there's a green room. It's the kind of place I'd only previously caught sight of in documentaries, a white-walled industrial space with a high ceiling and polished concrete floor. Tonight there are long trestle tables of neatly arranged glasses, bottles of white Burgundy sit shoulder-deep in ice buckets and there's a bar serving cocktails on black napkins. The music is ambient and the lighting is low.

It's the British Podcast Awards aftershow party on a warm Saturday evening in July, eighteen months after the events at the Mackinnon. Season Three of *A Question of Guilt* has been greeted with critical acclaim and a huge listenership; in the awards press release they're handing out, a glossy sixteen-pager covering nominees over twenty categories, they describe how it 'gathered prime-time TV and international press coverage as its story unfolded', and praise its 'exhaustive research, intelligent analysis and powerful storytelling'. Around me, waiters weave through crowds carrying canapés on oval dishes. A muscular young guy with circular glasses and a fledgling beard has a clipboard of printed notes and leads a team with branded microphones as they circulate, recording vox pops. Around the edges of the space, there's a lot of good-natured commiseration with short-listees who didn't win, but the focus is on the area against the far wall where a temporary spotlit backdrop, emblazoned with sponsors' logos, has been erected. It's here delighted winners gather to record their interviews and have their photographs taken with the stand-up comedian who's hosting the ceremony. There's the Listener's Choice winner, the hosts of the show that took the Best Culture and Arts Award and the production team behind the Podcast Moment of the Year. And, in the middle of it all, I can see Jaival Parik. Jai doesn't look like he's stopped talking since his win – Podcast of the Year, no less. A lot of the men have opted for black tie but Jai's chosen a checked shirt and a royal blue blazer and he habitually tucks his long hair behind his ears. He's put a glass of red wine down fifteen minutes ago and his body language tells me he's lost track of it. When I last spoke to him, three months earlier when he heard he'd been shortlisted, I insisted that if he were to attend any sort of awards evening he should keep his AirPods in his pocket rather than leave them in. It's nice to see he's done so.

Around me are happy faces, champagne flutes, clutch bags and mobile phones. The air echoes with talk and music and laughter. Nobody notices me. My white shirt, black jeans, charcoal apron and drinks tray render me beneath notice. I've cut my hair short and dyed it, changed my name and moved cities. I've had eighteen months of practice at becoming virtually invisible and I'm getting good at it.

Over at the bar I buy a large glass of red. I pay by card since my passport has made it possible to open a new bank account. I have to clean the cash before depositing it, of course; nowadays I buy foreign currency, spend what I need as I travel and, in the last few days of any visit, exchange a big chunk into sterling before flying home and depositing it. It certainly beats the tiny transactions at supermarket self-service tills I cautiously began with, or – another trick from the early days – swapping twenties for tens at Post Offices ('I'm posting ten pounds to each of my nephews and I need nice new notes if that's OK . . .'). The early days. I suppress the memories with an involuntary shudder; the constant fear of capture in those first few months, the compulsive trawling of news websites, the frantic phone calls with Mum as I assured her I was OK and my plan would work. I deepen my breathing, refocus; position the wine on my tray and weave into the crowd, heading for Jai. He's looking handsome in his blazer and pressed shirt, healthy and a little slimmer, fully recovered but tired around the eyes. He's finishing a conversation with a lady in a cocktail dress and I get right up to him before he turns.

'Malbec, sir?' I offer the tray.

Jai's face is split by a grin. 'Lifesaver!' he says, taking the glass, swirling the contents and sniffing, eyes closed. He doesn't even register me. Like I say, I'm getting good at being invisible. 'Nothing beats a good Malbec,' he says, nose over the glass.

I take a risk and say, 'Congratulations on your win.'

He sips, puckers his lips briefly, then swallows and exhales, gaze distant. 'Thank you,' he says.

And that's it. He's accosted by someone else and I retreat. I'm already smiling at the thought of texting him later, from an unknown number, of course, as I shrug off my persona, place the tray at the end of the bar and blend into the crowd. Weaving away from his line of sight, I reach the doors that take me back to the reception area, and turn one last time before I go. I can tell immediately that Jai's realised who he's just talked to. He's alert, eyes scanning the crowd, expression one of amused wonder.

Outside I turn left onto Haverstock Hill and begin to walk. It's getting dark but despite the conditions there's nothing to see above; the cloudless curve of sky over Camden is a dusty yellow, bleached by city lights that render stars invisible. The air is warm and noisy; there are boisterous queues outside Burger Bites, the smell of meat and spices, kids crowding around a pair of electric scooters at the Quick Stop and delivery bikes weaving.

It's an almost-normal life. No one notices me as I pass under the glazed-tile archway, through the turnstiles and follow the steps down into the underground.

MARTIN GRIFFIN